Wicked Games

BESTSELLING AUTHOR

AIMEE NICOLE WALKER

Dedication

To my father for introducing me to the *Where in the World is Carmen Sandiego?* computer game when I was a kid. It fueled a lifetime of loving adventure, intrigue, and mystery.

Other Books by
AIMEE NICOLE WALKER

Only You

The Fated Hearts Series

Chasing Mr. Wright, Book 1
Rhythm of Us, Book 2
Surrender Your Heart, Book 3
Perfect Fit, Book 4
Return to Me, Book 5
Always You, Book 6
Any Means Necessary, Book 7

Curl Up and Dye Mysteries

Dyeing to be Loved
Something to Dye For
Dyed and Gone to Heaven
I Do, or Dye Trying
A Dye Hard Holiday
Ride or Dye

Prologue

Lucien Clarke

Hôtel Regina Louvre, Paris 2013...

"LUCKY, DO YOU HAVE YOUR HEAD IN THE GAME OR IS IT STILL UP the American conservator's ass?" I hated the nickname but wouldn't give Banks the satisfaction of seeing my irritation. He'd already taken too many things from me. "You were instructed to make a connection with someone employed at the museum so we could gain access to their security systems."

"And I did," I abruptly said before he could say anything more. "You act as if I didn't hand you a flash drive with every access code you needed for the recovery."

"You fell in love with your mark."

I inwardly cringed at the term Banks used but was careful not to let my emotions show. Target. Sucker. I couldn't think of Ryder Jameson in those terms. He was blond, beautiful, and brilliant. When he looked at me, his guileless blue eyes darkened with lust, passion, and love. I thought myself incapable of love again, but Ryder proved me wrong. There was just no way forward for us. I had a job to do which required me to set aside my personal feelings, and if I failed to do so… No. I couldn't let myself get distracted by memories and demons that were better left buried.

Charles Banks, the owner of Old World Antiquities, had me by the balls, and the wicked grin on his face told me he knew it. There was a time when I didn't mind scaling the sides of buildings and evading security systems to recover artifacts and paintings. The adrenaline helped keep the darkness at bay, and it wasn't long before I craved it like a drug. I eagerly answered Banks's calls because there was no mission too dangerous, no challenge I couldn't complete. All that changed when I introduced myself to Ryder. Unfortunately for me, my circumstances were no different from when I met him four weeks prior. I had no choice but to continue my mission and get out of town before it was too late.

"I fucked my mark, Banks. It's nothing new for me. Any means necessary is our motto, is it not?"

"Do you take me for a fool, Lucky? Do you think I've suddenly gone blind?"

I didn't bother hiding the way his words made me bristle, but I needed to take control of the narrative. "Are you implying I've failed to meet the objectives?" I held up a finger. "I found my mark." I held up a second finger. "I obtained all the security details and layout of the museum, including the underground rooms like the labs used for restoring artifacts and the vaults they're kept in during the process." I held up a third finger, but Banks cut me off with a wave of his hand before I could say more. Then he pulled a manila envelope from his briefcase and dropped it on the coffee table in front of me. I recognized what it was immediately.

"Your flight leaves in four hours. You need to pack and leave immediately."

"But the job isn't finished, Banks." I'd never left before a mission was complete. What fuckery was this?

"I'm doing this for your own good, Lucky. Fitz will take over and see the mission through. You're needed elsewhere." He didn't say someplace far away from Ryder Jameson, but he didn't need to, because his expression said it all. "Do not try me, Lucien. I never bluff, and you know it." I did. Without another word, Banks rose from the club chair he'd wedged himself into and left.

The manila envelope on the coffee table might as well have been a ticking bomb. I could pick it up and move onto the next job, or I could stay in Paris with the handsome American man I'd fallen in love with. No, there was no choice for me. I rose from the cream settee and packed my essentials, which consisted of a few changes of clothes, some toiletries, and my laptop. Banks's clean-up crew would dispose of everything else when they erased my presence, well, my Sebastian Deveraux alias, from the luxury suite after I departed.

I went to the balcony one last time. Instead of seeing the Eifel Tower in the distance, I saw the look on Ryder's face when he made love to me the previous night. He'd been so reserved when we first met, but each time we'd been together, Ryder grew bolder in his touches and the places he wanted to make love. Ryder hadn't cared if any of the other guests saw him straddling my hips and riding my cock; he only cared about the way I made him feel. It was the most beautiful gift anyone had ever given me, and I had to walk away from it. Fuck! I wanted to scream the word at the top of my lungs and let it echo off the exterior walls of the majestic hotel but settled for an internal yell that bounced around in my brain instead.

No regrets. It had been my motto since I started working for Banks, and it had never failed me until now. I was consumed with regret until it made me physically ill. I wavered about what to do next until my cell phone buzzed with an incoming text from Banks. He'd sent a photo taken ten years prior of two young members of the British SAS locked in an intimate embrace not unlike the encounter I'd shared with Ryder the previous evening. No words accompanied the photo from Banks, but none were required. I would do as commanded, or Banks would release the photos to the press without regard for the lives it would destroy.

I let out the anguished growl of an injured animal then turned on my heel and went back inside my suite. I kept walking, pausing long enough to grab the manila envelope off the coffee table and slip it inside my laptop bag. I decided not to pack any clothes because delaying one more minute could alter the life of someone I vowed to protect. Rather than leave the keycard inside the room like usual, I decided at the last minute to keep it as a reminder of the nights shared with a man I would never forget.

Chapter One

Ryder Jameson

NERVOUS DIDN'T BEGIN TO DESCRIBE HOW I FELT ON THE NIGHT OF my first gala for the Cincinnati Art Museum. I knew better than most that I owed my job to my mother's social standing and her position as a trustee on the board as well as my father's generous annual donations to the arts. The director of the board, Daniel Perez, had no problem letting me know how much he disliked me and that he wouldn't hesitate to can my ass at the slightest mishap.

"Trouble seems to follow you everywhere you go," he'd said upon our first introduction. "Or should I say priceless artifacts tend to disappear whenever you arrive."

I could've pointed out it had only happened twice, but contrary to what the movies would have you believe, heists from museums were rare. Thefts of priceless artifacts were more likely to occur at the homes of private collectors where the security systems were easier to manipulate and override. Instead of arguing with the dickhead director of the board, I smiled and thanked him profusely for the opportunity. I stopped short of guaranteeing he wouldn't regret it because he very well might.

I didn't attract trouble; I attracted the attention of one troublesome man: Sebastian Deveraux. I'd met the British man in Paris not long after I arrived six years ago, and we had the kind of whirlwind affair you only read about in books or see in movies. Sebastian took me for long drives in the French countryside where we feasted on succulent food he'd packed in a large wicker basket, drank red wine, and made love in fields of lavender. There were weekend trips to Corsica and Nice where we held hands while walking the beaches. I couldn't eat brie, drink cabernet sauvignon, smell lavender, or feel a salty, ocean breeze against my skin without thinking of him and the way he made me feel.

One day, Sebastian was there, and the next, he was gone, and so was *The Card Players* painted by Paul Cézanne and valued at over two hundred and fifty million dollars. It had been loaned to the Louvre by the family who had purchased it at a private auction some years before. The museum was shocked the painting was stolen without triggering any of their alarms, and I was stunned when a picture of the suspect was presented to the staff the day after the heist. A few murmured he looked familiar, but they couldn't remember where they'd seen him.

"You've seen him when he's come to pick Ryder up for lunch. The guy is his boyfriend," Paul Benoit, my lab partner, had blurted out.

Even though the museum couldn't prove for certain Sebastian was the thief, or I was somehow involved, they fired me. After the loss of the man I'd fallen so hard for and my dream job, I went into a downward spiral. I could only get jobs at small museums in Europe that barely paid the bills until a curator in Cairo sought me out because he'd seen examples of my restoration work. Abanoub Shammas either hadn't made the connection to my tenure at the Louvre or was willing to take a risk, because he stuck his neck out for me with the board of directors at the Gayer-Anderson Museum. It was my chance for a second start, and I felt alive for the first time since Sebastian had left. Then history repeated itself. How stupid can one man be? As it turns out, pretty fucking stupid.

"Ryder, fix your face," Celeste Jameson hissed beside me. "You look like you sucked on a fish."

"How exactly does one look after they suck on a fish, Mother?"

"Your mouth is all puckered funny, and you have deep grooves marring your forehead. You're going to need Botox injections before you reach thirty-five."

"Mother, I'm already thirty-five." I gave her a pointed look. "I believe the correct expression is that I look like I've eaten something sour or sucked on a lemon. I'm not sure anyone created a saying about sucking on a fish. Is it a live fish or a dead one?"

"Ryder, you're insufferable," she said with a pained sigh. Was that it? No apology for forgetting my age? I snickered internally. Celeste Jameson didn't apologize; it was beneath her. Or at least the woman she was now, the mother I'd grown up with never would've forgotten a birthday. "Thirty-five?" she asked. I nodded. "What did we buy you for your birthday?" She didn't know because she obviously let her personal assistant handle all the details.

"A week in Fiji."

"I was generous this year. Did you have fun?"

"Define fun?" I asked wryly with a quirked brow, making her blush. I was sure she meant snorkeling and scuba diving, and I did those things, but I mostly spent my time in the arms of beautiful men.

"I don't really want to know, do I?" Mother asked.

"No, you don't, but I got a lot of satisfaction from your gift."

"At least pointing out my shortcomings as a mother has wiped the sour look off your face," she quipped. "Ryder, please don't blow this opportunity. Especially not on a night when we celebrate the local LGBT artists. I would think you would use tonight to meet..." Her words died in her throat. "Is that Archie White? Do my eyes deceive me?"

3

Archie was someone I once loved back when my life was so much simpler. Two guys met during their college days, felt the spark, and acted on it without games and subterfuge. Hell, it seemed like a different lifetime. My mother had never approved of our relationship because she said we were two very different people and wouldn't last. I'd made an ass of myself when I returned to Cincinnati eight years after our breakup to take my new position at the museum. My encounters with Sebastian had left me bitter and jaded, and I thought reconnecting with Archie, a person who had truly loved me, would help me find my way back to the person I used to be. I discovered Archie had moved on and fallen in love with someone else. I hadn't taken it very well, and I owed both him and his boyfriend a huge apology.

"He's here with Ollie," I informed her. Archie's boyfriend was an out and proud pastor who also happened to be a wickedly skilled artist. His drawing of the Roebling Bridge had created quite a stir, and I suspected it would sell for a nice sum during the auction.

"Oh, he's taken then," Mother said, not bothering to disguise her relief. "Ryder, you need to plaster a smile on your face and circulate amongst the artists and guests. If you're lucky, I might have a surprise for you later." Surprises on gala nights for me usually equaled a heist.

"Thank you, Mother, but I'll pass."

"Ryder, you don't—"

I raised my hand to cut her off, and a waiter thought I was calling him over. He was fine as fuck in his black tuxedo, and he cast appraising eyes over my body. I discreetly winked, letting him know I was interested in finding a quiet corner later in the evening. After he was gone, I looked at my mother once more. Most would describe Celeste Jameson as a classically beautiful woman with her blonde hair, fair skin, light blue eyes, and dainty features. You only had to look into those blue eyes for a few seconds to discover there was no warmth inside the woman. She was my mother, and I loved her, but I didn't like her very much. I used to adore the very air she breathed, and I wondered, not for the first time, where things had gone so wrong between us.

"You were going to introduce me to a man who you believe is worthy of sharing my life. Let me guess," I said then took a quick sip as I pretended to ponder my next words. "He's tall, dark, and handsome." My words conjured up the image of Sebastian, which made my chest hurt from the pain and humiliation of his betrayal. "He's well-connected with a big…" I let my words trail off for effect, earning a hoity glower from her. "…balance in his checkbook."

"You'd be wrong," my mother said in a singsong voice. "You've had terrible luck with brunettes, dear." She had no idea how true her words were. "I have a particular blond in mind." Poor soul, whomever he may be.

"Mother, leave Ryder alone. He's only been home for two months, and you're already trying to marry him off."

"Iris, how good of you to—" Mother's words died in her throat when she saw what my younger sister was wearing. "What the devil are you wearing?"

"It's the Chanel gown you bought for me, Mother," Iris said, turning a slow circle to show off the full effect.

"Which you've taken scissors to," she said, pointing to the jagged, uneven layers of soft pink fabric ending several inches above Iris's knees, "and paired with black fishnet stockings and biker boots." Each word was spoken in a higher octave until I worried our mother was seconds away from rupturing an artery in her brain. God, I loved my sister. I had loved her since the moment they brought her home red-faced and squalling. She was still every bit of the hellraiser she was then, and I never wanted to see her brilliance diminished.

Iris raised her right foot, showing off the red, signature heel of Christian Louboutin. I had no idea a person could buy designer biker boots. Mother made a hissing sound of disapproval.

"Mother, why don't you find the ladies' room and compose yourself," I said calmly into her ear. "Your face has turned an unnatural shade of red that matches the heels on the Louboutin boots. People are starting to stare."

"They're not looking at me," Mother hissed before she spun as elegantly as she could in her floor-length formal gown made of aqua blue silk. It reminded me of the water off the coast of Fiji.

"Atta girl, Iris," I said, clinking my champagne flute to hers.

My twenty-eight-year-old sister looped her arm through mine and smiled impishly. "Thank you." Iris then cleared her throat and said, "'Where have we gone wrong with our children, Edmond?'" She clutched her imaginary pearls and schooled her stunning features into the appalled expression we'd seen on Mother's face when she said those words to our father. "I'm suffocating more and more every day in their home, Ry."

It didn't slip my notice that she hadn't referred to the mansion in Indian Hill as her home; it was *their* home. I knew exactly how she felt. Where had the warmth and laughter gone? I hardly recognized it as the same house we grew up in. Hell, for that matter, I hardly recognized my parents. Edmond and Celeste seemed like strangers to me and to each other. While I would never categorize them as Ozzy and Harriet, they had at least liked one another.

Just because I was a bitter, angry person didn't mean my precocious sister needed to be. "I have a spare bedroom in my apartment. Move in with me, Iris. It'll be like old times."

"You and me versus the world?" Iris asked.

"Exactly. You have an engineering degree from Vanderbilt, so use it. Live your life for you and no one else. You also have access to your trust—"

"Don't," she said abruptly. "You didn't use the money our grandparents set aside, so neither will I."

"I haven't used it yet because I haven't found a suitable purpose. If it came down to being miserable with my circumstances, you better believe I'd access the funds I needed to improve my life."

"You mean like the time you lived in squalor while licking your wounds after getting fired from a prestigious museum?"

"I wasn't desperate enough," I told her.

"No, you thought it was a well-deserved punishment." I wanted to tell her she was wrong but couldn't. "Then there was Cairo."

After the second heist, I kept my mouth shut when they presented photos of the man they believed had breached the security system to steal a small statue of Anubis valued at six million dollars. Sebastian looked different in the photo, but I recognized the square jaw I'd nibbled on every day for a week leading up to the theft.

"You sure know how to sour a good mood."

"You don't need my help in that regard, Big Brother. Did you see Archie is here?"

"Yes, and I also saw he brought his boyfriend with him." Unlike our parents, Iris had loved Archie. He was the only guy I ever brought home who didn't ignore my precocious, teenage sister. She was fifteen at the time and loved when Archie invited her along on some of our dates. "He's happy, Iris." Speaking of Archie, I had an apology to make. I leaned over and kissed Iris's temple. "I think you look stunning." Mother had an absolute conniption when Iris had cut her long hair for a short, asymmetrical look, but I thought it made her elegant bone structure look even more striking. "Think about my offer. I meant it."

"I know, and I love you, Ry." Iris kissed my cheek then flagged down a waiter for a flute of champagne before walking away.

I spotted Archie and Ollie standing by the drawing of the Roebling Bridge that had captured everyone's attention. When I walked up on them, they were discussing the origins of the bridge. They were understandably skeptical at first but graciously accepted my apology. I was ready to put the chapter behind me and move on, but to where, I had no idea.

Throughout the time I spoke with Archie and Ollie, I became aware of a buzz in my central nervous system. I wasn't dizzy or knocked off-balance, but something was off. I'd only tossed back one flute of champagne, and I'd taken care to eat dinner before the event because a man could not live on finger foods and snacks alone. I wasn't tipsy. I was…alive. Every single one of my senses was on high alert as they only had been in the presence of one man. Sebastian Deveraux.

After I parted with Archie and Ollie, I decided to seek refuge in my office to try and center myself once more. Sebastian wasn't in Cincinnati; it was just my overactive imagination getting the best of me. My nervous system was always out of whack at gala events thanks to the backstabbing son of a bitch who broke my heart… twice. I couldn't say I was waiting for the other shoe to drop because it already had. Fate couldn't possibly be so cruel as to place Sebastian in my orbit again. I flopped in my chair and reached for the bottle of expensive Scotch I kept in my bottom drawer. Things didn't seem so bad after a few drinks of Scotch. I froze when someone firmly knocked on my office door, and my heart raced at the possibilities. Yes, it could be one of the board members, a trustee, or someone from the museum's senior staff coming to lecture me on my absence, but I doubted they noticed I left. It could be the fuckable waiter coming to claim the silent offer I'd given him, or it could be… No.

I rose to my feet and crossed to my office door. Leaning against the frame was the smiling face of my oldest friend. "Well, hello there, Dr. Love," I said, unwilling to pass up the opportunity to tease Trent about his name. "I didn't know you were coming tonight."

"It was a last-minute decision. Starting the party without me, eh?" He nodded toward the bottle of Scotch and half-empty tumbler beside it. "Do you have another tumbler stashed somewhere in your massive desk? If not, I'll drink it straight from the bottle."

"How gauche," I teased.

"Sometimes a man just has zero fucks left to give."

I tilted my head back and laughed at the misery etched on his handsome face. His normally immaculate blond hair looked like he'd recently run both hands through it, or maybe he'd had help. I stepped aside and gestured for Trent to enter. "I have an extra tumbler even if I never have anyone to drink with."

Trent accepted the glass and knocked the Scotch back with one drink. "Please, sir, can I have three fingers this time?"

I quirked a brow and aimed a dirty grin his way then poured him three fingers' worth of Scotch. "There's only one thing I know that drives a man to drink like that," I said as Trent devoured the second glass. "My mother is in a mood tonight too. I wonder what got into them."

"It wouldn't be my father," Trent said. "He's too busy screwing his secretary to worry about thawing out my mother's—"

"Whoa," I said, holding up my hand. "This isn't the direction I wanted to take the conversation, but extra points for trying to distract me. I merely wondered the reason for their mood. Is your mother trying to set you up with someone too?"

The smile Trent gave me was pure wickedness. "Oh yes," he agreed.

"Who is the poor sap?" I asked then took a drink of my Scotch.

"You."

I choked and coughed for a few seconds, and Trent came around to pound on my back. "Is this what they taught you to do in med school when someone is choking?" I asked in an anguished whisper. My throat and lungs burned as I attempted to laugh. "You're an evil bastard."

"I could be *your* evil bastard if you play your cards right," Trent leered jokingly. There was no way in hell anything romantic, or physical for that matter, would develop between us. We had a good laugh at our mothers' meddling ways and how terrible they were at picking dates for us.

We both stilled when there was a knock on the door. Trent lifted a brow as if to ask if I was expecting company, and I answered with a shrug. Trent crossed the room and opened the door. "Well, hello there, handsome." Trent stood to the side, allowing me to see my visitor. It was the gorgeous waiter. "I'll just be off," Trent said. "Three's a crowd."

"It doesn't have to be," the waiter said, looking Trent up and down like he was an ice cream cone he was dying to lick.

Trent glanced over his shoulder at me and said, "Call me for lunch soon. I want to catch up with you."

"Will do," I said, returning my attention to the young guy who sauntered into my office. "Close the door and lock it," I instructed once we were alone.

"Yes, sir."

Perhaps the night was looking up after all.

Chapter Two

Lucien

I'D ARRIVED IN CINCINNATI AT NOON AND CHECKED IN AT THE 21C Museum Hotel under the alias of Christian Somersby. I had hoped to catch a quick nap after almost twenty-four hours of nonstop travel, but my room wasn't ready yet. The once historic Metropole Hotel had been reimagined as a contemporary art museum in the heart of Cincinnati, known as the Queen City. Instead of sleeping, I toured the impressive collections on display before enjoying lunch at the Metropole restaurant. One nice thing I could say about Banks, he always put us up in lovely hotels, made sure we had access to the finest foods available, and provided sexy wheels that would give any car enthusiast wet dreams. I was very fond of the Aston Martin waiting for me in the parking garage at CVG international airport. My burner phone rang before I finished my glass of Pinot Grigio. I was tempted to ignore the phone in case it was Banks calling to go over the details of the artifact recovery one-more-fucking-time but didn't want to miss a call from the hotel clerk if my room was ready early. It must've been my lucky day because the adorable Ms. Crusoe informed me my room was indeed ready.

I'd made it as far as stripping down to my boxers and climbing between the soft sheets before my phone rang again. I knew it would be Banks, and ignoring his calls would only ensure he kept calling until I answered.

"Banks," I groused into the phone. "I need to sleep so I can be at my best tonight."

"Rough getting old, isn't it?" my boss countered.

Rough would be my fist smashing his porcelain-veneers once I finally got out from under his control. It would fucking happen, but until then, I'd play the part of his submissive servant well. "Something like that," I murmured.

"Lucky, are you sure you're up to this job? We can't afford any distractions." It wasn't the first time he expressed concern about my capability to pull off a job, but all the other times involved the presence of a certain blond-haired, blue-eyed man I couldn't forget no matter how hard I tried. Banks hadn't said anything about Ryder working at the target museum, but something was clearly up. I decided to familiarize myself with the staff even though Deverish obtained all the details we needed to recover the fanyi ritual wine vessel before he broke his leg in a freak accident. Banks had made it clear to me I wasn't his first choice for the mission, but Diggs was entrenched too deep in his current assignment to take over for Deverish.

Ryder. My heart raced with the possibility of seeing him again, but my gut painfully clenched because there was no way it would be a happy reunion. "I got this, Banks. Unless there's something you haven't told me."

"I wouldn't keep pertinent information from you, Lucky. Get in, get out, and get home."

Home. I didn't know the meaning of the word anymore. There were grand structures with immaculately designed rooms where I could lay my head at night, but I'd never call them home. The only time I'd ever felt at home was in Paris with Ryder. It wasn't the gorgeous city, Ryder's tiny flat, or even the luxurious hotel room that had made me feel like I could finally let down my guard and breathe; it was Ryder. His heart was the only home I had ever known and ever wanted.

"Will do, boss. Now, if you don't mind…"

"Yeah, I know. You want your beauty rest. Be sure to set the alarm," Banks said like I was an unruly child who couldn't be trusted to get out of bed and dress himself.

"On it." I hung up without so much as a goodbye.

Moments before, my eyes had been hooded and heavy with pending sleep, but I now found myself wide awake, wondering if it were possible. Was Ryder in Cincinnati? There was no hope for me going to sleep without knowing one way or the other. I pulled up the website for the Cincinnati Art Museum and looked through the pages lauding the staff's qualifications and passion for the arts. I couldn't find a picture of Ryder anywhere, but maybe this museum didn't include information about their conservators. I began looking online at recently published articles on conserving and restoring art in the local papers and found a few with his name listed as the author. I googled his name and the museum together and found a brief article announcing that the Queen City's very own Ryder Jameson had returned home to work as a director of art conservation at the museum where at least one of his family members had presided as a trustee dating back to its inception. I learned the current family member on the board was his mother, Celeste. The article detailed some of Ryder's education and extensive training, but most of it was about his mother and her role as a trustee. I noticed the article wasn't printed in the arts section of the paper; it was part of the society pages.

"How odd," I said out loud. "Ryder isn't listed on the museum's site with other directors and the museum has never formally announced his employment. Were they ashamed of him?" I knew the answer to the question just as I knew the reason behind their decision. Shame washed over me. *I'm sorry, Ryder.* My apology didn't seem like much of a consolation considering I destroyed his faith in humanity and possibly ruined his life.

Exhaustion finally overpowered my remorse, and I drifted to sleep for a few hours. I felt the opposite of refreshed when I woke up and as ravenous as if I hadn't eaten a few hours earlier. I knew going to the gala event at the museum wasn't a good idea, and it wasn't part of my game plan, because Deverish had already obtained everything the team needed to recover the vessel after the gala ended. All I had to do was sit and wait, but I couldn't. Included in the portfolios Dev had left for me in the glove box of the car was a ticket for the black-tie affair. I hadn't packed a suit and either had to go with a more casual look or charge one to the credit card that came with my latest identity. If I did, Banks would likely be alerted, and he'd know why I was buying the suit.

I looked at the few things I'd packed and decided the black, V-neck sweater and charcoal gray pants would need to suffice. I knew fully well clothes didn't make the man. I could walk into the gala wearing the fluffy bathrobe hanging in my hotel bathroom and make the attendees believe I belonged. It was all in the way a man carried himself.

I treated myself to barrel-cut filet with a cognac peppercorn sauce and lobster tail at Jeff Ruby's Steakhouse on Walnut Street before heading to the museum for the gala. The stately building with its grand staircase and tall columns was illuminated by large floodlights reminiscent of something you would've seen at an old Hollywood movie premiere. Hell, the museum had even rolled out a red carpet for the attendees to walk, lending importance and sophistication to the evening.

I was careful to avoid photographers who were on hand to commemorate the evening for the rich and the connected. I handed my invitation to an attendant then snatched a glass of champagne off the tray of a passing waiter whose smile indicated I could have whatever I might like. I ignored his offer and kept walking until I found the perfect spot to keep an eye on the door as well as the activity on the first floor and the beautiful double staircase leading up to the second story.

I watched in awe as a young woman wearing a butchered couture gown, black stockings, and biker boots mingled through the crowds with her head held high. She dared anyone to sneer at her and smiled smugly when no one took the challenge. I didn't know the young lady, but I had behaved in a similarly brash way when I was younger, and it nearly cost me everything. She must have sensed my regard because she turned her head in my direction once she reached the bottom of the steps. Her light blue eyes twinkled with mirth when I raised my glass in a silent salute. It wasn't smart of me to engage with anyone in the crowd, but I couldn't resist. Rather than head in my direction, she pivoted and headed up the grand staircase.

I watched the people milling around, hoping for a chance to see Ryder without him noticing my presence. It turned out to be an easy thing to do with so many people checking out the displays set up to showcase the local art talent. I knew by the way my hair stood up on the back of my neck Ryder was near before I even saw him. I hardly recognized the distant, unapproachable man standing on the second floor observing the crowd below him. Tucked away in a quiet corner, I observed his mother approaching him and noticed he didn't look pleased about whatever they discussed. It wasn't long before the lady with the jagged pink dress joined them, and I realized her twinkling blue eyes were nearly identical to Ryder's. She had to be his sister. They spoke for a few minutes before the lady accepted a drink and disappeared from my sight, leaving me to catalog the myriad of changes I saw in Ryder.

The man I fell in love with always wore a carefree, charming smile on his handsome face; the man I still loved scowled at everyone except the young lady in the pink dress. His posture was stiff and unyielding instead of warm and inviting. Guilt burned in my gut like cheap booze because I was the reason for his misery.

In Paris, we'd been too busy having sex to do much talking. At the time, I was fine with it because my cover story only went so deep, and if Ryder had gone digging, he could've discovered Sebastian Deveraux wasn't real. In Cairo, well… It wasn't much different from Paris except our time together was shorter. I regretted knowing nothing about Ryder as I watched him speak to his mother and sister.

After a few minutes of solitude, Ryder made his way down the stairs and walked over to a couple who were so lost in conversation they hadn't heard him approach. The trio's exchange was brief and somewhat awkward before Ryder excused himself with a polite but cool smile and headed away from the crowd. Rather than follow him, I decided to hang out and see if he returned. Surely, he wasn't leaving so early in the evening? I continued people watching until I realized at least forty minutes had passed without Ryder returning. He'd seemed upset, and the urge to assure myself he was okay was stronger than the voice inside my head screaming for me to leave the museum and come back when it was time to recover the wine vessel. I didn't listen, but I never did when it came to Ryder Jameson.

On the way up the ornate steps, I literally ran into the two men I saw Ryder speaking to earlier. They both looked disheveled and aroused, which explained the hastiness of their steps. The guys were nearly the same height, and both had dark hair, but that was where the similarities ended. One had an olive-toned complexion and dark eyes and the other was fair with pale green eyes. They made a striking couple.

"Pardon me," I said. "I'm looking for someone. I saw him speaking to you earlier. Tall, blond hair, and blue eyes. His name is Ryder Jameson."

"We haven't seen him since we spoke to him down in the Great Hall," replied the guy with dark eyes.

"Damn," I said, noting I sounded irritated. "Thank you, anyway."

Deverish had left behind detailed blueprints and notes, so I knew where to find the offices of the various directors unless they'd hidden Ryder's desk in an unmarked broom closet someplace. Even then, Dev was so thorough he would've memorized and marked the locations of the broom closets in case he needed to duck inside one to avoid detection. I found the office for the director of art conservation, but I didn't need the sign on the door to tell me where Ryder was. I heard his voice and recognized the sounds he made when he was enjoying a hard fuck. My heart fell to my stomach, but I deserved nothing less. From the corner of my eye, I saw a tall, svelte woman with long, curly black hair quickly exiting an office at the far end of the hall from Ryder's. She wore a floor-length, scarlet dress which clung to her legs and hips, leaving nothing to the imagination. I'd recognize her confident, sexy walk anywhere. The woman stopped when she reached the corner of the hallway and glanced over her shoulder. I fucking knew it. The cocky smile on her crimson-painted lips meant a big headache for me and even bigger trouble for Old World Antiquities.

Ignoring my instinct to confront Ryder, I went in pursuit of the woman in scarlet, knowing it was futile. Sure enough, the hallway was empty by the time I turned the corner she had rounded less than a minute before me. *Fuck me.*

Chapter Three

Ryder

THE BALCONY OF MY HIGH-RISE APARTMENT AFFORDED A SPLENDID nighttime view of the bridges Cincinnati was best known for, but I'd stared at the lights so long everything had gone out of focus for me. All I saw were blurred dots against an inky, dark sky. I heard life all around me, from the cars honking on the streets below to the laughter of two of my favorite people coming from my apartment, but I felt far removed from all of it. Isolated. Alone.

The sliding glass doors opened behind me then came the hesitant steps of someone who wasn't sure if they should intrude upon my solitude. A spicy, rich-smelling cologne mingled with the rich tobacco scent of the celebratory cigar I held firmly between my index and middle fingers.

"I wasn't aware you smoked cigars," Trent said, stepping up beside me. He turned and leaned his back against the rail and looked at me. I could feel him searching my closed expression for clues. "It's a bit nippy out here, isn't it?"

I welcomed the numbness from the cold. "I only smoke cigars on special occasions."

"Such as successful galas."

"Absolutely," I said, trying to inject enthusiasm into my voice. *More like ones that a certain sexy thief didn't ruin with his presence.* I felt my mouth tilt up at the corner in a sneer. Then why was I so fucking miserable?

"Did things not go well with the sexy-as-fuck waiter?" Trent asked.

"What is this? High school?"

Trent snorted. "I wasn't asking for a blow-by-blow recounting of your office sexcapades."

I quirked a brow. "Blow-by-blow?"

"All I meant is you don't look or sound like a man who just got laid. So, either it didn't happen, it was horrible, or you regret it."

"None of the above," I replied. "An orgasm is an orgasm. Makes no difference if it's with a bendy waiter or achieved with my fist."

Trent let out a long whistle. "Wow. The situation is worse than I thought."

"The situation?"

"You're much too young to be as jaded as our parents."

"Age has nothing to do with it," I told Trent.

"Man, I'm not sure what to say other than I'm sorry. At first glance, you look like the guy I grew up with, but it didn't take me long to see the changes. What happened to harden your heart and wipe away your boyish smile, Ry?"

I thought about unburdening my soul to Trent. Only my family knew the truth, and they didn't know everything. I'd kept my interactions with Sebastian in Cairo to myself. Maybe talking to someone would relieve the pressure in my chest. I might've acted on my instinct if the sliding door hadn't opened.

Iris stepped onto the balcony and gasped. "You have cigars and didn't offer me one?" She had discovered a fondness for cigars and bourbon when she was still in high school. "I'm definitely going to take you up on your offer to move in now. Where are you hiding them?"

"In the humidor in my study." I'd made no attempt to hide them.

She tilted her head back and sniffed the air appreciatively. "Smells like fine Cuban tobacco."

I lifted the cigar to my lips, inhaled deeply, and held it until my throat burned before slowly exhaling the smoke. "Only the best in all things for a Jameson. Help yourself."

"Don't mind if I do," Trent and Iris said at the same time, making me laugh.

"Dr. Love," Iris said with a dramatic gasp. "You're going to ignore the American Medical Association's warning about the negative effects of tobacco use?"

"Miss Jameson," Trent said primly. "Are you going to ignore the etiquette lessons you learned at boarding school?"

"Fuck yeah," she said, turning to go back inside.

"That goes double for me," Trent said when we were alone again. "I haven't smoked in five years. I'm due for a good Cuban."

"Are we still talking about tobacco products?" I teased.

"Ah, Havana," Trent said wistfully. "Swarthy men with beautiful dark eyes, and… Well, let's say it's become my favorite vacation spot."

Iris returned wearing my tuxedo jacket as protection against the chilly, early November breeze. She carried a crystal decanter of bourbon in her left hand and two Cuban cigars in her right.

"I'll grab us some tumblers," I said, moving toward the door.

"Don't bother," Trent said. "We'll pass it around like old times."

"So gauche," Iris teased, unaware I'd used the same term earlier in the evening.

"That's me," Trent said with a careless shrug. "Just ask my parents."

I knew they were pissed when he'd decided to become a small-town pediatrician, but I had to say the choice looked good on him.

"Aren't we past the age where we live for our parents?" Iris asked.

"Fuck yeah." I took the decanter from Iris and raised it for a toast. Iris and Trent lifted their cigars. "To living our own lives."

"Cheers to that," Trent said.

"Woohoo," Iris added.

From there, things got a little foggy.

A shrill sound pierced my peaceful slumber, making me realize my pounding head felt three times its normal size. "Fuck," I groaned. My mouth felt as dry as the Sahara desert and tasted like I licked the bottom of an ashtray.

"Answer the phone or fucking shoot me. You'll put me out of my misery either way."

My whole body tensed as I recognized the voice from the pillow beside mine. "What did we do?" I whispered hoarsely as the phone blessedly stopped ringing.

"Not a damn thing," Trent said.

I took a chance and opened my eyes and immediately regretted it. We hadn't pulled the curtains closed before we fell asleep and even the gloomy light from a rainy morning burned my retinas. "My head," I whined. "There's someone inside my skull stabbing my brain."

My phone started ringing again, sounding louder and shriller than the ringtone normally was.

"Please, Ry. If you ever cared about me as a friend, you'd shut your phone up. I'm so fucking hungover right now."

"Me too." I reached for my phone, but it wasn't on my nightstand where I normally kept it. "Damn it. Where is the stupid thing?" I sat up too fast, and a wave of dizziness washed over me; my stomach pitched. I sat still for a minute to get my bearings and sighed in relief when the phone stopped ringing and the urge to vomit subsided.

"They'll call back," Trent said, sounding muffled. "It's the fourth call in a row. You sleep like the dead."

I carefully turned and saw Trent had buried his head beneath the pillows. I was relieved to see he was wearing a t-shirt and vaguely remembered pulling a shirt and sweats out of a drawer for him. I looked down at myself and saw I wore similar clothes.

"We didn't fuck."

Trent lifted the pillow from his head and glared at me. "You don't have to sound so damn relieved. You're horrible for my ego."

"I'm sorry, Trent. I don't want anything to ruin our friendship. I feel like you and Iris are all I have in the world."

He placed a warm hand between my shoulder blades and rubbed. "I have an idea how you can make it up to me."

"Didn't you just hear what I said?"

"Not that, idiot," Trent said. "Lie back down here and look disheveled with me. I'll snap a photo and send it to our mothers. It'll make their day. Hell, it might make their entire year."

I chuckled and gingerly stood up to find my phone. "And then our mothers will start nagging us to meet with their wedding planner."

"True," Trent agreed. "Okay, so it wasn't my best idea."

"I'm amazed you can think at all, buddy."

I found my phone in the tuxedo pants I'd haphazardly thrown on the floor sometime in the early morning. It started ringing almost as soon as I had it in my hand. Seeing the caller ID, I groaned out loud.

"She must have an informant in the building." I wasn't in the mood for her shit, so I silenced the call.

"What?" Trent asked.

"It's my mother. Someone probably told her you didn't leave last night."

"No one in your building knows me."

"Wrong. I'm pretty sure I added you to the list of approved visitors when we arrived last night. I bet Robert called her."

"The older gentleman working the concierge desk?" Trent asked in disbelief. "You think he's on Celeste Jameson's payroll?"

"Stranger things have happened."

My bedroom door suddenly flew open and bounced against the wall. "Sorry," Iris said from the doorway. She was shielding her eyes like she expected to find us in a compromising situation.

"Nothing happened," I told Iris. "You can look."

Iris smiled sheepishly. "I hate to sound like our mother, but I'm disappointed in you, Ry. You had a beautiful, compassionate man in your bed and didn't—"

"Ris," I said in a warning tone.

"You need to call Mother." My sister's worried expression sent a foreboding shiver down my spine. "There's an emergency at the museum."

Not again. Same story, different museum.

My heart was in my throat when I called her. "Mother, I did not... I would not—"

"I know you didn't do anything wrong, Ryder," Mother said, interrupting me. "Unfortunately, Daniel Perez isn't convinced. You need to go to the federal building to speak with the FBI immediately. Let me know when you're on the way, and I'll make sure Richard meets you there." Richard Kensington was our family attorney, and I was relieved to know he would be with me. "Do you want Dad and me to come too for moral support?" Her offer stunned me. This was the same woman who'd forgotten I turned another year older. She sounded like the woman I called after my first accident. I had missed her more than I realized.

"Just the lawyer is fine. I'll shower and head to the federal building. I won't be long. Do you know the names of the agents I should ask for?"

"I don't, Son. I only met them briefly this morning and was too stunned to remember their names."

"What was stolen?"

"I'm going to wait and let you find that out from the FBI so they can see your genuine reaction and know you couldn't possibly be involved." I appreciated her confidence more than I could express, but three museums and three heists with me as the common denominator spelled big trouble. "Are you sure you'll be okay? I know things have been strained between us for some time, but I believe we can be better."

"I'll be okay, Mother. Sadly, I'm a pro at this by now. I want better for us too. I'll call you afterward." I disconnected the call and blew out a frustrated breath. "I can't believe this has happened to me again."

Iris walked over and hugged me tight. "It's going to be okay, Ry."

I wanted to believe her, but I knew better. "Thanks, Ris."

"Is there anything I can do?" Trent asked from the bed. He looked sleep-tousled and gorgeous. Why the hell couldn't I have fallen for him instead of a man who was determined to destroy my life one pound of flesh at a time?

"No. I need to shower and get going. You guys can stick around as long as you want. There's plenty of food in the refrigerator." I sounded like I was just going to the office for a routine meeting instead of an interrogation that was likely to last hours.

"Don't worry about us, Ry," Iris said.

"Iris, I'll treat you to brunch before I head back home," Trent told her. "Ryder, I want you to call me as soon as you can."

"I will," I assured him and offered some semblance of a smile before I disappeared into my bathroom to take a quick shower. My walk-in closet had an entrance from the bathroom and the bedroom, so I was fully dressed by the time I stepped back into my empty room.

I looked at my reflection in the mirror as I put on the emerald cuff links shaped like shamrocks given to me by my grandfather. "I could certainly use a little luck of the Irish today, Pops," I said, noting the somber, black suit and muted navy tie I'd chosen to wear.

I had dressed for a funeral, but it was fitting since I was staring down the death of my career and every professional dream I'd ever had.

Chapter Four

Lucien

I SHOULD'VE CALLED BANKS AS SOON AS I CAME UP EMPTY AT THE MUSEUM. By not calling him, he had assumed my mission to recover the fanyi wine vessel was successful. I knew delaying the conversation would only make his reaction worse, but I needed time to think. I hadn't alerted him that Carmen Santiago was on the scene either. It wasn't the first time Old World Antiquities had gone head-to-head with Carmen, but it was the first time she'd beat me to the punch. How?

A nagging suspicion about the job had started forming in my brain the minute I realized Banks was keeping facts from me. He hadn't wanted me to know Ryder worked at the museum, but I could easily shove my doubts aside in that regard. Banks wouldn't want to risk me getting distracted by a "piece of ass" because, according to him, they were a dime a dozen. Not knowing Carmen was on the case though? To my knowledge, it was a new development. At face value, it could be explained away by Dev's freakish accident landing him in the hospital. He'd required surgery to pin his bones together, so it was possible for Carmen to move in without anyone noticing while our setup crew transitioned from one agent to the other. But the job still felt off.

I glanced at the clock and noticed it was nine o'clock in the morning. Fuck! Banks was going to be so damn pissed off. I dreaded the confrontation but couldn't delay the inevitable any longer. The news had already broken about the heist at the museum, and his smug arse would think I was in possession of the vessel. I bit the bullet and dialed his number.

"Good afternoon, Lucky," Banks said when he answered the phone on the first ring. "Did you have an indulgent lie-in to celebrate a successful mission?"

"It's nine o'clock in the morning here," I said dryly. Nothing I ever did would be good enough for the man, regardless of how quickly and efficiently I completed my missions.

"Still a late start, is it not? What time should I send Reeves over?" Reeves was our transportation expert. I never knew how he got the recovered items safely away once I handed them over to him, and I didn't care. I focused solely on my job and expected the others on the team to do the same.

"Send Reeves on to the next job, Banks. There's nothing for him to transport."

"What?" Banks asked tersely. "Is this a sick joke? I'm not laughing one tiny bit. The *heist* has already made the world news, Lucky. What are you playing at?"

"Carmen struck again."

I heard muttering from the other side of our connection, but I couldn't make out the exact curses he'd chosen to mutter. Banks didn't mind blackmailing a man to do the dirty work for him, but he seldom spewed profanity. It was beneath his station in life. "You've got to be fucking kidding me. How is it I didn't even know she was on the hunt for the vessel? She's a bold minx and loves to challenge us. Why is this time different?"

"I've been asking myself the same thing since I discovered the vessel was already gone when I arrived. Something about this entire mission feels off to me, Banks."

Banks was silent as he considered my words. "Lucky, everything about this mission has gone wrong from the very start. There were variables we didn't account for."

Like the reappearance of Ryder Jameson? I wisely didn't ask it, because without some extra digging, I wouldn't have known Ryder was in Cincinnati. Then again, Banks made it his job to know the ins and outs of every job which often included the most vulnerable museum employee. He sent his advanced scouts to get the lay of the land and get a feel for the pulse before we moved in. Banks assessed risk and reward better than anyone I'd ever known, including my father, who amassed his fortune by advising others on how to invest their money and navigate volatile markets.

"It's possible Carmen moved in during the transition time, but it doesn't feel right. As you said, she's the kind of woman who gets in your face and dares you to beat her." The more I thought about Carmen's sly smile from the previous night, the more certain I became. Some serious fuckery was stirring.

"True," Banks admitted after a brief pause. "Lucky, what exactly are you trying to tell me?"

"Banks, we're thinking the same thing. She's working with someone on our team."

"No fucking way," he said adamantly. "Cleary the mission failed, but it wasn't the first time, and it won't be the last."

"It was my first failed mission," I pointed out. "Carmen's never bested me."

"Lucky, is that what's going on here? Your male pride is wounded because a girl beat you."

"A woman," I corrected, "and not at all. I've admired her skill for a long time, and I've felt it was only a matter of time before she claimed the upper hand. That isn't what happened last night."

"How can you be so sure? Deverish's injury *was* the upper hand she needed. You only arrived twelve hours before the recovery was set to occur. I knew there was a big chance for things to go wrong. It's why I'm not screaming and carrying on." He wasn't screaming and carrying on because it wasn't dignified. Banks didn't need to act uncouth to get his way; he only needed to trot out the information he had on us to ensure our cooperation.

I narrowed my eyes as I stared out the hotel window. *I knew there was a big chance for things to go wrong.* Such as? Someone stealing the vessel before I could recover it? My capture and arrest? How wrong was he willing to allow before admitting something sinister was at work?

"I suppose you think Deverish threw himself down the flight of steps to set this all up? Do you think he's fallen victim to Carmen's charms?" Banks could sneer all he wanted, but it was only because the man was devoid of all emotion except greed.

"I didn't blame any of this on Dev, so don't put words in my mouth, Banks."

"Who then? Percy?"

"Is Percy the one who scouted this job and set up all the arrangements?" I countered.

"Yes."

"No wonder you're not as upset as I thought you'd be." I snorted. "You were already mentally prepared for a certain level of collateral damage."

"What are you blathering on about now?"

Was it possible he didn't know the men were former lovers who'd had a very nasty breakup after Dev caught Percy in bed with another man? If so, I had to revise my belief about the man. Maybe Banks *wasn't* on top of everything and everyone who worked for him.

"Huh-uh," I said, shaking my head even though he couldn't see me. "I'm not a snitch, but I advise you to pay a little better attention. Maybe you don't randomly pop in on the others as you do with me,

Banks. You're getting a little sloppy, and it just cost you a cool million dollars."

"Well, since you seem to know everything that's going on, you get to stay behind and investigate the circumstances for me, Lucky."

God, how I wished he would quit calling me by that stupid nickname. "You want me to stay behind and look into what went wrong?"

"Deverish and Percy are still in Cincinnati, are they not?" Banks asked snidely. "You claim to have inside information about the two of them, so it's now up to you to figure out who fucked up, when they did, how they did, and whether one of them, or both, deliberately sabotaged the recovery efforts. I want daily reports." It was a rare thing for Banks to drop the F-bomb, so I knew he was pissed off.

"I'm not your bitch, Banks."

"You are for as long as I say you are, Lucky," he snarled into the phone before disconnecting.

I continued to stare out the window for a long time after I set my phone on the coffee table until the voice of the news broadcaster finally penetrated my fog.

"We're outside the federal building where sources say the FBI has already begun interviewing museum staff about the heist. Jessica Peabody is on site with more information. What do we know, Jessica?"

"Hello, Carl. I wish I had breaking news for you, but the feds are keeping things quiet. What we do know is someone overrode the cameras and security system at the museum in the middle of the night and stole a priceless artifact dating clear back to the Shang Dynasty. The item is valued at…"

I stopped hearing a word the reporter said because I saw the only man I'd ever truly loved walking up the steps to the federal building. *Ryder.* Shame washed over me once more, and I realized there was more unfinished business to settle in Cincinnati than finding out how Carmen was able to steal the vessel out from underneath me.

Chapter Five

Ryder

I ARRIVED AT THE FEDERAL BUILDING BEFORE MY ATTORNEY. RATHER than wait for him on the street in the pouring rain, I went inside and asked to speak to the agents in charge of the art heist at the museum. I was familiar enough with the procedure to know they'd show me to a room where they could observe my habits and behavior. Did I sweat, fidget, or twitch? Did I bite my lips and cower in the corner? I had nothing to hide, so I calmly sat in the room and waited for Richard to arrive.

It was close to eleven o'clock by the time he appeared. "Ryder," he said, extending his hand. "I apologize for arriving so late, but I expected your mother to call and inform me when you were on the way."

"The lack of communication was my fault, Richard. I'd told Mother I was taking a quick shower and leaving to come here, but I realize our idea of a quick shower varies," I said wryly. "I should have called her when I was on my way."

"I'm glad to see you're in good humor."

"I have nothing to hide, Richard. I know you'll want me to say as little as possible, and I will follow your advice, but it's my experience this goes better when I'm as upfront with information as possible. Wasting their time is only going to piss them off, and they need to find whoever stole the item. I'd rather cooperate than hinder the investigation."

"I understand and appreciate your candor. I'm sure the agents in charge will too."

The door to the interview room opened five minutes later, and two agents entered the room. They wore somber suits and expressions to match.

"I'm Agent Kiphart," the male agent said then gestured to his female partner, "and this is Agent Marshall."

Neither agent extended their hand to us in greeting. They sat down in the chairs across from Richard and me. Kiphart set down a folder on the desk in front of him, pulled a pen from his shirt pocket, and removed a legal pad from the file. Agent Marshall folded her arms on the table and studied me. He was the note-taker, and she was the observer.

"I assume you know why we asked you to come down for an interview?" Marshall asked.

"To be clear, you didn't ask me to come down for an interview. My mother called me and said there was an emergency at the museum. She was the one who advised me to come down to speak to the agents in charge."

"Your mother didn't tell you what occurred?" Marshall asked while Kiphart began making his notes.

"No, ma'am."

"Let me inform you then," Kiphart said, looking up from the legal pad and eyeing me like I was public enemy number one. "Sometime during the night, a person, or persons, broke into the vault located inside the lab that is under your supervision and stole"—he opened the folder on the desk—"a fanyi ritual wine vessel dating back to the

Shang Dynasty."

"Damn," I said, sitting back in the chair. "It's a gorgeous piece."

"How long has the artifact been in your care, custody, and control?" Marshall asked.

"I just started working at the museum in September, and the wine vessel was already there. The restoration was nearly halfway completed at the time. I can't honestly say when the museum acquired it. The information is documented in the files, of course, but it isn't something I need to have memorized to do my job."

"You're the director of conservation, and you don't know how long an object has been sitting in your vault?" Kiphart countered, never looking up from his legal pad.

"Agent, my client isn't going to answer the same question twice. You asked how long it was at the museum, and he told you he couldn't say because it was there before they hired him. He can't answer for events occurring before his arrival."

"I can tell you the deadline for completing the restoration," I offered. "Would that help?"

"Sure," Marshall said.

"We planned to feature the wine vessel in an exhibition from December first to January fifteenth. We were to return the fanyi to its owner by the end of January."

"Who knew the museum had the fanyi in the vault? Is the information ever released to the public?" Kiphart asked. "Does the museum post updates on their social media accounts or website? Are there live feeds allowing people to watch the restoration process?"

"Some museums will do those types of things to build up excitement. It's good marketing. Our videos or photos don't go viral like the feeds for watching live giraffe or hippo births at zoos. We haven't posted anything about the fanyi vessel since I arrived. Again, I can't say what occurred before they hired me as director."

"This is the third time a heist has occurred at a museum where you worked." *Worked? As in past tense.* "Do you believe in coincidence?"

They either worked fast on running my background, or Daniel Perez started pointing the finger in my direction the minute he was notified about the heist.

"Don't answer the question, Ryder," Richard said. "We're not here to discuss fate versus circumstance."

"Agents, no evidence was ever linked directly to me the first two times, and you won't find it this time around either. I didn't steal the vessel, nor did I help someone else do it. Give me a polygraph. I promise I'll pass." The only reaction from Agents Kiphart and Marshall was a brief glance exchanged between them. Had they expected me to offer? Then Kiphart wrote something down in his notes.

"We'll keep it in mind," Marshall said. "Let's talk about the gala. Can you walk us through a timeline of events?"

They listened without interruption as I walked them through my evening. Marshall watched while Kiphart scribbled. We paused for a few seconds until he finished.

"Thank you," Kiphart said. "Now maybe you can account for the time you disappeared during the gala. Several staff members mentioned you were missing for around an hour, maybe more."

Several staff members? I snorted. Richard bumped his knee against mine in a warning.

"Something funny, Mr. Jameson?" Marshall asked.

"Funny? No. There are maybe two or three people on the entire staff who speak to me. Most of them look through me and pretend I'm not in the room. They don't like or trust me, and I feel the same about them."

"Interesting," Kiphart said, finally looking up to meet my steady gaze. "Do you mind telling us where you disappeared to, sir?"

"I retreated to my office."

"Because?" Marshall prompted.

"It's where I hide my Scotch."

"Is there anyone who can corroborate your story?" Kiphart questioned.

"I think you already know the answer to the question," I replied, earning an irritated glance from him. "There are security cameras everywhere in the building, especially in the hall outside my office and lab."

"Cameras in the area were hacked. The actual footage was replaced with the feed from the previous night," Marshall said. "So, why don't you enlighten us?"

"My childhood friend, Trent Love, joined me for a while. He would give you a statement if you required one."

"He was with you the entire time you were absent from the party?" Kiphart asked.

"No."

"Is there anyone else who stopped by your office for a *drink*?" I didn't like his snide tone.

"No," I said. "I did, however, have a visitor stop by, but he wasn't there for my...Scotch."

My answer got Kiphart's attention. He lifted his head and searched my face to see if I meant what my pause had applied. I knew what he was thinking when his gaze lingered on my lips for a few heartbeats before rising to meet my eyes once more.

"Who was your *visitor*?" Kiphart asked, eyes still locked on mine.

"I didn't catch his name, but he was a waiter who worked for the caterer the museum hired for the event."

"Is it possible the waiter used this *encounter* to gain access to the vault?" Kiphart asked.

"No orgasm is that good, Agent. The waiter didn't fuck the access codes to the lab or the vault combinations out of me." Richard nudged me a little harder the second time. I knew I was pushing things but couldn't seem to help myself.

"Are we through here?" Richard asked.

"Not quite," Marshall said holding up her manicured finger for my attorney to hold on. "Mr. Jameson, where were you between the hours of midnight and six o'clock this morning?"

"I had overnight guests who can vouch for my whereabouts. My sister, Iris, and Trent Love both came back to my apartment after the gala. We arrived at eleven, and none of us left until it was time for me to come here. And before you ask, it wasn't possible for me to sneak off without them knowing. Trent's a light sleeper, and I would've woken him by getting out of bed."

"Bed?" Kiphart asked, raising a brow. "Busy night."

"That's enough out of you, Agent," Richard said.

"I hate to spoil the image you have of my slutty behavior, but Trent is just a friend. We both had too much to drink and passed out." I held up my hand when Kiphart started to comment. "Don't believe me? You can talk to the manager of my building and ask to see the footage from the security cameras."

"We're done here," Richard said tersely. He pulled out a card and slid it across the table. "Requests to speak to him again will go through me. We're leaving, Ryder."

"One last thing," Marshall said just before we reached the door. I paused and turned to face her. "Does the name Lucien Clarke mean anything to you?"

"No, I don't recall meeting anyone who goes by that name."

"Let's see if you recognize his face? I don't have a dick pic in the file, unfortunately," Kiphart said snidely. I seethed and started to walk toward him, but Richard put his arm out to bar me from making the biggest mistake of my life. Kiphart sneered as he pulled out a picture from the file and held it up for me to see. *Déjà vu.* "I can tell by your reaction you do recognize this man. Why don't you please take a seat so we can chat a little longer?"

I returned to the chair I'd just vacated and flopped down on it. All of the fight had left me. "I knew the man as Sebastian Deveraux. In your photo, he's speaking to my ex-boyfriend and the guy he's dating now. Their names are Archie White and Oliver Knight." Interesting how some cameras were tampered with but not others.

"You have a history with this man, don't you?"

I nodded in disbelief then spent another hour baring my shame and humiliation to them. After I finished, the two agents left the room presumably to discuss what they wanted to do with me next. They must've decided there wasn't enough evidence to hold me because they turned me loose. I was numb by the time we exited the federal building. I left my car in a parking garage two blocks away and was glad to see the rain had let up a little while I was inside getting interrogated. I knew I should call my parents, Iris, and Trent right away, but I wasn't ready to talk to them. I needed time to process what I learned.

Lucien Clarke. The name somehow suited the man better than the alias he presented to me. The agents weren't willing to share any details about him, so I knew nothing more than I did when he left me in Cairo.

I paused at the corner and waited for the crosswalk signal to change. The traffic light turned yellow, and the approaching traffic slowed down. Suddenly, a black Aston Martin came to an abrupt halt in the crosswalk in front of me. Startled, I took a step back. The passenger window rolled down, and I was stunned to be looking into the dark eyes of my tormentor.

"Get in the car," Lucien Clarke said in his clipped British accent.

Chapter Six

Lucien

RYDER'S EYES WIDENED IN ASTONISHMENT, AND HIS MOUTH FELL open in a silent gasp. Maybe his gasp was audible, but it was hard to know when the asshole in the Honda behind me repeatedly laid on his horn. Ryder's shock turned to rage, and he took another step back. *Honk. Honk.*

"Get in before you cause a big scene that neither of us can afford right now." *Honk. Honk. Honk.*

I knew Ryder was going to refuse me when he glanced up and down the sidewalk looking for someone to call out to, but the police had already focused their energy and resources on blockades at the museum and directing traffic near the football stadium where an NFL game was taking place. *Honk. Honk. Honnnk.*

I decided to go with another tactic. "I know you have questions, and I'll answer every single one of them. Get. In. The. Car." *Honnnnnnnnnk.* "That's it," I said, reaching for my seat belt. "I've had it with rude Americans."

Ryder opened the passenger door and got in before I could

unbuckle and get out to deal with the prick behind me. "Go!"

"Put on your safety belt," I teased, putting the car in drive and hitting the gas. "I really wish you would've let me pound the piss out of the guy."

"I thought you didn't want to create a big scene, *Lucien*?" I tried not to show my reaction to hearing Ryder say my real name. How long had I wanted to hear him say it? During sex, afterward while holding him in my arms, or through the phone telling me how much he missed me when we were apart? "Are you surprised I know your name? You'll be happy to know the FBI knows it too. It seems like your crimes have finally caught up to you. Good luck getting away with it this time, you duplicitous bastard. I should call 9-1-1 right now."

"You can call the authorities, but it won't do you or them any good. I didn't take the wine vessel, and they can't prove I did. Besides, I won't answer your questions if you turn me in."

Ryder wanted to counter me but couldn't. If he wanted to turn me in, he would've done so immediately. "You sure picked a flashy car to drive for a man wishing to remain undetected."

"It's very fast," I countered wryly. Ryder wasn't in the mood for small talk and didn't reply. "Where are we going?"

"I'm not the one behind the wheel. All I know is we're not going back to my apartment. It's never worked out well for me."

"Ry—"

"Save it," Ryder snarled. "I don't know why I didn't scream loud enough to raise the dead when I saw it was you in the car. Maybe it's morbid curiosity, or maybe I want the fucking closure your previous disappearance acts never gave me. Regardless, whatever we've had between us is over after today."

"We can go back to my hotel room." I could feel the scathing look Ryder gave me.

"Like that's ever worked out better for me. You must think I'm a fool."

"No, I don't," I said quickly. "We just need someplace private we can talk."

"Since when did we start talking?"

"Ryder, I—"

"Do not say my name in a patronizing tone of voice, you smug, son of a thieving whore."

"You don't need to insult my mother, Ryder. I assure you she isn't involved." I quelled the smile trying to spread across my face. Beneath Ryder's fury simmered an emotion much stronger and so profound it vibrated off him. I recognized the emotion, and my dick began hardening in response. Lust.

"Fine," he snarled. "Take me back to your hotel room. Let's get this over with."

Ryder said nothing else until we arrived at the hotel. "Really? You're staying inside a museum? Talk about irony. Do you steal the towels and robes from the luxury hotels before you scurry out of town? Is your urbane polish nothing but a veneer?"

Ryder knew fully well the ways my inner beast and baser needs could make a person forget all about the polish that had initially caught their attention. I'd never felt bad about using my looks, charisma, or my body to get what I wanted until I met Ryder. Then each day became one regret after the other until my life was nothing more than a cold existence. I recognized the same loneliness when I looked into Ryder's stunning blue eyes. I couldn't remember a time when I hated myself more.

"Come on," Ryder said irritably. "I have things I need to do this evening."

Rage and lust were such a heady combination, and it was all I could do to keep from pushing Ryder up against the lift wall and giving him the reunion we both so badly wanted. I didn't speak to him, and I kept my hands in my pockets to prevent myself from reaching for him until we arrived at my hotel room. *Don't cross the line again. You've caused him enough pain.*

"Are we doing this or not?" Ryder challenged when my hesitance became obvious.

I made the mistake of looking at him. Ryder's rage and lust had the same effect as an explosive orgasm. His face was flushed pink and his blue eyes looked hot enough to scorch me. His bottom lip looked swollen like he'd been chewing on it during our drive. As I stared at Ryder, the tip of his tongue darted out to soothe the offended flesh. Knowing I could be making the biggest mistake of my life, I unlocked the door and gestured for him to precede me into the room.

I locked the door and followed him inside. Ryder stopped when he reached the center of the suite then looked around the room. What did he hope to find? The vessel? Then he turned to face me, and with his eyes locked on mine, Ryder began unbuttoning his suit jacket. He tossed it on the sofa and quirked a brow like he wanted me to do the same.

I took off my black leather jacket and laid it over a piece of modern metal art doubling as a bar stool. I could still convince myself we were only going to talk until Ryder deftly removed his cuff links and carefully placed them on the stained-glass coffee table.

"I'd appreciate it if you don't steal my cuff links when my back is turned. They were a gift from my grandfather."

"I didn't bring you here to fuck you," I said, walking toward him. "I wanted to—"

Moving faster than I knew he could, Ryder reared back and punched me in the face. I automatically reached for my nose and was shocked when I saw there wasn't any blood on my hand. My lips throbbed and felt like they would split in two if I so much as twitched them, but it didn't stop me from roaring, "Fuck!"

The second punch was just as fast and landed in my solar plexus, knocking the wind right out of me. I doubled over, right hand bracing myself on my knee while I wrapped my left arm protectively over my stomach to prevent him from landing another blow. I tilted my head and watched him from beneath my eyelashes. I'd let Ryder have those two shots, but I wouldn't allow a third to land.

"I would've kicked you in the balls, but I have plans for them. I want my pound of flesh, and I want it right-fucking-now, Lucien."

Chapter Seven

Ryder

SEB…LUCIEN LOOKED AT ME THROUGH NARROWED EYES LIKE HE couldn't believe what he was hearing. It should've shamed me how good my throbbing knuckles felt and how disappointed I was I hadn't bloodied his nose. What kind of animal must I be to get turned on by a liar, a cheater, and a thief? How was it that feeling my hand connect with his flesh in a fit of rage was more intimate than having the waiter's tight ass clenching my cock the previous night?

I stalked toward Lucien and towered over where he'd remained doubled over to catch his breath. "Stand up," I ordered. "I haven't even started with you yet."

Lucien did as I demanded. There wasn't an ounce of apprehension on his face when he licked his lips hungrily. He stood his ground when I lunged forward, gripped his shirt, and yanked it, rending the fabric and sending buttons scattering across the floor. The green and blue scales on the dragon tattoo covering his chest were as vibrant as I recalled. The art stretched from one delicious pectoral to the other with the dragon's long, forked tongue curling around one nipple, and its barbed tail curled around the other. I'd traced every inch of Lucien's tattoo with my tongue many times; of course I hadn't imagined its detail and vibrancy.

Leaning forward, I sank my teeth into the dragon's head, eliciting a grunt and a hiss of pain which turned into a lusty moan when I bit down harder. I relaxed my jaw and released his flesh then stood up straight. Lucien's skin was a purplish-red where blood had risen to the surface, but I hadn't broken the skin. I ran my thumb over the angry grooves my teeth left behind. It would leave a mark for several days, and knowing that made my dick harder.

Looking into Lucien's eyes, the guilt and remorse from before were gone; I only saw lust. "You want to punish me?" he asked. "Then do it. Take what you need." I could tell he wanted to say more but wisely kept his mouth shut. Did he think we could move on from here and be what? Friends? Lovers? Friends who are sometimes lovers?

"Fuck you, *Lucien*."

"I wish you would," he quipped. Damn, his uppity British tone had always been such a turn-on, but I found no semblance of the cocky man I'd first met. "Or are you going to punish me by giving me the biggest pair of blue balls mankind has ever seen?"

Taking Lucien by force wasn't part of my game plan, but I hadn't expected him to challenge me. Lucien's raised, proud chin and glittery dark gaze said, "Do your worst."

I shoved him, and he fell back on the sofa. Lucien looked up at me with hungry eyes as I slowly loosened my tie and removed it. I looked at the expensive silk in my hand then back at him as an idea occurred to me. I placed one knee between Lucien's spread legs and the other on the outside of his right thigh. A cocky grin slowly spread across his face when I held the tie in front of him. I slid the silk between his lips then tied it firmly at the back of his head while trying to ignore the way Lucien rubbed his erection against my leg.

"Oh, how the tables have turned. I used to be the one begging for you like a bitch in heat," I whispered in his ear. "I gagged you so we wouldn't disturb the neighbors." While true, it wasn't the only reason. I needed the barrier so I couldn't kiss his full, lush mouth. I had every intention of burying my cock deep inside his willing ass, but kissing was different. My days of long, intimate kisses with this man were over.

Lucien lifted his hands to touch me, but I knocked them away. "You lost the right to touch me." He blinked a few times as if my words packed a harder punch than my actual fists. "This isn't about two halves of a soul reconnecting, Lucien. This is me fucking you out of my system. When I'm done; I'm walking away. I never want to see you again. Am I clear?" Lucien nodded, but in his eyes, I saw how much he wanted to argue the last point.

I stood up from the sofa and slowly began undressing. I shouldn't have liked the hungry way his eyes roamed over every new inch I uncovered, but I reveled in it. Did he notice the changes in my body and recognize I spent far too much of my free time in the gym? I wasn't the only one because his body looked harder and leaner too. My dick was leaking by the time I kicked off my shoes and stepped out of my pants and briefs. Lucien moaned when I fisted my hard-on and started stroking it.

"I'm not sure you want me as badly as your eyes indicate. I am so fucking angry right now, and I can't promise I'll be able to contain it. I hate you, Lucien, but I'm not the kind of man who brutalizes others. Are you sure this is what you want?" *Stroke up, rotate wrist, and stroke down. Repeat.* Lucien nodded eagerly. "I won't be easy, and you will feel me for days."

Lucien briefly closed his eyes and whimpered then he crooked two fingers as if to say, "Bring it on."

"Wave your hand or slap my thigh if you want me to stop at any time, okay?" Lucien nodded. "Get on your knees and get your ass up in the air." I didn't trust myself to touch him more than was required, so I fished a condom and a packet of lube out of my wallet rather than allow my eyes to linger too long on his body. As for Lucien, I felt his intense gaze on me, beseeching me to look in his eyes instead of watching my hand roll on the condom.

"Ass in the air," I reminded Lucien when I saw from my periphery he hadn't moved. I heard his frustrated groan but didn't face him again until I heard him reposition himself on the sofa. It was my turn to groan at the beauty spread before me.

Lucien had chosen to kneel on the center sofa cushion and grip the back of the couch, so his beautiful ass was on full display and at the perfect height for me to fuck. Lucien arched his back and spread his knees wider, presenting his perfect pucker to me. I saw goose bumps pebble his flesh as I approached and felt a tremor of anticipation ripple through him when I placed my right hand on his hip.

"This is new," I said, looking at the bold, black strokes of the Chinese symbol for regret tattooed between his shoulder blades. I swallowed hard. For the first time since I got in the car, I second-guessed my intentions. What would I gain from having sex with him one last time? What kind of closure could it possibly be? It was misery, wrapped up in regret, and stuffed inside heartache. Did the Chinese have a symbol for dumbass?

I almost changed my mind, and had even taken a step backward, until Lucien reached behind him and started circling the rim of his ass with his middle finger. I stepped forward and knocked his hand away before I ripped the lube packet open and squeezed half of it on my middle finger. My goal was to prepare Lucien's tight ass for my cock as efficiently as possible while trying to avoid intimacy. Lucien's moans of pleasure killed the idea, and I fingered his ass longer than I needed to because I liked watching Lucien fuck himself on my three fingers. I waited until he almost came then pulled my fingers out, leaving his pucker to twitch with desperate need while I smeared the rest of the lube on my cock.

I slammed balls-deep inside him on the first thrust. The tie muffled Lucien's shout, but it was still loud enough to get my attention and that of anyone in the rooms on either side of us. I fisted his hair and pulled his head back while I lowered my mouth to his hear.

"Do you need me to stop?"

Lucien shook his head vigorously, so I pulled all the way out and slammed back in. I kept his neck arched as I continued to fuck him at a punishing pace. We'd fucked hard before, and I remembered how much he'd liked it. I wouldn't last long, but I didn't need long to get my point across.

"I hate what you've done to my life, and I hate you. I'm going to treat you like you treated me, then I'm going to walk away." Lucien released a broken moan, but it was impossible to know if it was from anguish or pleasure. He did not attempt to stop me, so I gripped his hip and his hair harder. "I'm going to fuck you, use you, and humiliate you, Lucien. See how much you like it. I'm going to be kinder than you were to me." I felt the telltale signs in both our bodies that we were approaching climax, but I didn't stop fucking him. "I won't tell you I'm in love with you then disappear. I won't reappear in your life and whisper words of regret in your ear and say how much I missed you or try to convince you I never wanted to be apart from you. After today, I will never see you again."

Under me, Lucien stiffened, and his ass strangled my cock. He grunted and groaned, and I knew he was splattering his load all over the fancy hotel sofa. I released his hair to slide my hand under his jaw and lift his chin. In the past, I would've kissed him hungrily as I filled his ass, so the gesture was familiar and automatic. Instead of kissing him, I said, "Never again."

Then I released his face and gripped his hips with both hands, fucking him hard and deep. Fireworks exploded behind my closed eyelids as pleasure flooded my system and his ass milked every last drop from me. There were no post-coital cuddles. I pulled out of Lucien without a word and disposed of the condom in the small trash can that looked like it was made from melted plastic products. Lucien said nothing as I got dressed and slid my jacket on.

I didn't even look in his direction, but I heard him reposition himself on the couch as I walked toward the door. "Wait," he exclaimed when I'd almost reached freedom.

I knew I should keep going, but he sounded broken. The orgasm hadn't wiped away my fury, but it weakened my resolve. "What?" I asked without turning around.

"You forgot your cuff links." Lucien rose from the couch and walked toward me. "I would've found a way to return them to you."

I slowly turned around and looked at him. Tears swam in his dark eyes, and I could feel my fury rising again. What right did he have to be hurt? Who did this fucker think he was? I held out my hand, and Lucien dropped the cuff links in my palm then wrapped my fingers over them. My skin burned where he touched me.

"I don't have the right to ask you for anything, Ryder, but I will never forgive myself if I don't ask."

"What?"

"One last kiss. Please."

I wanted to say no out of spite, but I couldn't. I wanted it too. I wrapped my hand around Lucien's neck and leaned toward him. He met me halfway, and our mouths crashed together in a gnashing of teeth, tongues, and lips. I tasted rage, anguish, longing, and so many other things I was afraid to name. We gasped and cried into one another's mouths, and I might've kissed him for hours if not for tasting the salty tears both of us cried. I wrenched my mouth away and left before I could make a bigger fool of myself.

"Not another damn tear over him," I vowed.

Chapter Eight

Lucien

AFTER RYDER LEFT, I STAYED IN MY HOTEL ROOM AND MOPED FOR the rest of the night and far into the next morning. It wasn't the outcome I had wanted when I pulled up alongside him on the street, but it was what I deserved. A busted lip, sore abdomen, tender ass, and a bruising bite mark in my flesh was getting off easy for my crimes against Ryder. I was already dreading when the aches and marks faded because they were the last things I would ever receive from him. Did that make me a twisted, sick son of a bitch or what? No matter how much I regretted the way things ended with Ryder, I had to admit we were finally through, and I still had a job to do.

Around eleven o'clock, I roused myself from my pity party for one and drove to the Millennium Hotel where Deverish would continue to stay until he could fly back to London. As far as I knew, Dev didn't know the fanyi was stolen out from under me or that I had remained in town. I wanted to keep it that way so I could gauge his reaction. I knocked firmly on his door, expecting to wait several minutes while he hobbled to the door on his crutches, but instead, it flew open after only a few seconds.

"Fancy seeing you here," Percy said, leaning indulgently against the doorframe wearing a loosely belted hotel robe. He was disheveled, reeked of sex, and looked as surprised to find me outside the door as I was to see him inside Dev's room.

"Is Deverish here?" I asked.

"Of course, he's here. Why else would I be here?" Percy asked, rolling his eyes. Then he turned around and sauntered back into the room. "What are *you* still doing in town?"

"Get Dev, and I'll tell you."

"Be right there, dear," Dev said from somewhere inside the bedroom. It was the first time I smiled in days. Old World Antiquities didn't host annual picnics or Christmas parties, so it was rare I got to spend much time with the other crew members. There were a few recovery jobs where Dev and I masqueraded as a married couple, and I had enjoyed his wit immensely.

"All is forgiven, huh?" I asked Percy, who'd sat on a gold velvet Queen Anne settee that looked too dainty to support my weight. Dev's lover was shorter and much thinner than either of us and looked like he belonged in the elegant setting.

Percy gracefully crossed his right leg over his left, causing the robe to ride up in places and exposing the length of his toned thigh. "I didn't pull a Sharon Stone just now did I?" he asked, repositioning the robe to cover himself more discreetly. His attempt at modesty didn't fool me, and the wicked grin on his face said he knew I'd read him correctly. "All isn't forgiven, but we're working on it."

I opened my mouth to inform him that trust wasn't earned on his back, but who the hell was I to judge or lecture him? "I hope it works out," I finally said. "At least the two of you have a chance at happiness."

Percy tilted his head to the side and studied me. "And you don't?"

"Not a chance in hell," I admitted. *Ryder.* God, his goodbye kiss would haunt me forever.

Not for the first time, I wondered what Banks was holding over Deverish's and Percy's heads. Or, had they chosen this life willingly? Could they walk away without a backward glance or would Banks squeeze their balls and pull them back? I suddenly regretted the comment I made to Banks the previous day. I shouldn't have said anything that could cause either of them grief. Even though I didn't know Deverish well enough to trust him implicitly, I knew enough to know he wouldn't undercut Banks. As for Percy, the only thing I knew about him was how much Deverish cared for the man. I knew lust and love clouded a person's judgment and made them overlook the obvious. Hell, hadn't I counted on it with Ryder in Paris and Cairo? I was willing to put my faith in Dev up to a point, but the jury was still out with Percy.

"To what do I owe the honor of your presence," Deverish asked as he hobbled into the room on crutches. It was startling to see someone so smooth and graceful looking so clumsy. His hair was as disheveled as Percy's, and he'd made no attempt to tidy the mess eager hands had made. "And why the devil do you look so glum? You look like someone just stole your—" His green eyes widened suddenly. "The hell you say."

"I haven't *said* anything, Dev."

"Not so much with words," he said, awkwardly lowering himself beside Percy and exposing his dick and balls at the same time.

Percy tsked, then said, "Darling, we're not on those kinds of terms with Lucien." He covered Deverish's groin then placed his hand possessively over Dev's hairy thigh.

"Why are those robes so damn short?" I asked, changing the subject. "Percy nearly flashed me, and you did."

"Babe," Deverish admonished lightly. "You shouldn't taunt someone as hard up as Lucien. He gets the wrong idea every time." Dev looked at me, and the smile slid from his face. "Has Carmen Sandiego struck again?" Beside him, Percy snorted, but he'd never seen the

50

woman to know how closely Carmen resembled the fictional character, both in looks and in name.

"She has," I said, nodding. "I saw her slinking around in the hallway where the directors' offices and restoration labs are and knew I had my hands full, especially since I hadn't known she was on the hunt here."

Deverish threw up his hands. "Don't look at me, Lucky. I had no fucking clue. She hadn't presented herself to me before my accident, so she must've moved in while I was recuperating after surgery. The woman loves to boast about the time she beat me to the Picasso painting in Italy, and she never misses an opportunity to taunt me. She either assumed I was gone or knew I wasn't going to be a challenge."

"But she would've expected Banks to send backup. There was something different about her the night of the gala too."

"Different how?" Percy asked while Dev continued to study me intently.

"There's something different about you too," Dev said before I could answer Percy. Dev's eyes zeroed in on my busted lip. I expected him to mention it, but he didn't.

"He looks sad," Percy said like I wasn't in the same room with them.

"I'm used to him looking like a sad sap, pet. This is different, more intense." He glanced at my lip again then returned his gaze back to my eyes. Dev's green eyes sparkled with mirth.

"Let's focus on what I came to discuss," I said, trying to get them back on topic.

"Do you mean your friendly little interrogation to see if Percy or I were involved in helping Carmen steal the vessel out from under you?" Neither of them looked offended I'd momentarily entertained the idea they were behind it, but then again, they would've had similar thoughts if the situation were reversed. "Why would either of us risk Banks's wrath?"

Banks *was* holding something over their heads too. "I know you weren't involved, Dev, and no offense intended to you, Percy, but you don't know enough about the operations to give much away to Carmen beyond where we're staying and what we're driving. You don't set the times for the recoveries or arrange transportation for the items."

"None taken," Percy said simply. "Especially when it's true. Banks may be a deviant, but he's a brilliant one. He only tells us what we need to know to complete our individual jobs. It's why we click so well together. I hate his fucking guts but still admire the well-oiled machine he runs."

"Why don't you tell me what's really bothering you about the job?" Dev said. "I can see there's more going on than Carmen finally getting the best of you."

"Mmm-hmm," Percy said, cuddling into Dev's side. "You might not believe it now, but you can trust us, Lucien."

I needed to talk to someone because I had carried it inside me for too long. The question was: how much did I reveal? All of it, including my history with Ryder? Wasn't discovering Ryder's presence in Cincinnati the first time I felt the wiggling worm of doubt burrow inside my brain? It was, so telling Dev the partial truth wasn't going to do any of us good. For the next thirty or so minutes, neither Dev nor Percy said a word or moved from their positions. They were a rapt audience hanging onto my every word. I started with meeting Ryder in Paris and worked my way to the events at the gala and my reunion with Ryder the prior day. When I finished, I was both drained and relieved to have spoken my sordid history out loud. I wasn't looking for absolution, and I didn't need mollycoddling. I needed answers—at least when it came to the Cincinnati job.

"Wow," Dev said, looking stunned. "I guess your busted lip makes sense now." Percy nodded beside him. "We don't know a damn thing about one another, do we? I had no idea you were carrying that inside you. I knew you were distant and cold at times, but not the reasons why."

"We're not permitted the opportunity to get to know one another," Percy said. He looked up at Dev and offered a smile. "You and I wouldn't have fallen in love if not for the blizzard popping up out of nowhere and stranding us together for days."

Dev placed a gentle kiss on his forehead. "They were the best four days of my life, even if I pushed you away a time or two."

"All of it is behind us now, Dev. We're forging a new future with trust and honesty."

I was pretty sure they'd forgotten about my existence until I cleared my throat, pulling their attention back to me. "I'm truly happy for both of you, but I need to figure out what's going on here."

"Why do you care so much?" Dev asked. "What's really at stake here?"

"If I can find out who is fucking Banks over, maybe I can use it to my advantage to get out from under him once and for all."

"And get your man back," Percy added. Winning Ryder's trust, respect, and love was a pipe dream I couldn't allow myself to believe.

"We want in," Dev said, leaning forward and extending his hand. "I'm stuck here for at least another month."

"Me too," Percy said. "I convinced Banks someone had to stay behind and look after Deverish. We might as well use whatever time we have to brainstorm and start nailing arseholes to the wall."

"Let's do it," I said, bumping Dev's fist then Percy's.

Chapter Nine

Ryder

THE DAY BEFORE THANKSGIVING, I SAT AT A TABLE IN MY FAVORITE coffee shop shredding a blueberry muffin instead of eating it. The *closure* with Lucien hadn't left me in a better place; it made me feel like a miserable monster I didn't recognize. I didn't hit people. I didn't take my anger into the bedroom and use sex as a weapon. I hated the man I'd become, and I felt lost and afraid I would never recover the person I used to be before I met Lucien Clarke. My professional life was caught up in a cyclone of fuckery that wanted to rip, tear, and destroy everything in its path. The fanyi vessel was still missing, and I was still at the top of the suspect list, even though my alibis, both during the gala and after, were validated by Rhys, the sexy waiter, Iris, and Trent. Nothing my mother said could sway Daniel Perez from putting me on leave, but she did ensure I still received my salary during my suspension.

From the smoldering ashes of my life came one bright spot: my mother. She was trying her damnedest to undo years of indifference and return to the loving mother Iris and I once knew. I don't know if it was the heist or Iris moving out that caused the abrupt changes, but we were grateful, if not a little concerned the pendulum was swinging too far in the other direction. Indifferent to suffocating was a huge adjustment for us to make.

I glanced up from destroying my muffin when the bell over the door chimed. I stiffened when I saw Ollie walk in. I hadn't seen him around since the night of the gala when I apologized for my behavior. Our eyes met, and he looked as if he wanted to talk to me but wasn't sure he should. After a brief hesitation, Ollie walked over to my table.

"Ryder, are you okay? You look…"

"Like hell?" I suggested, feeling my mouth tipping up at the corner. "It's because I feel like hell. I've felt this way ever since the night of the gala." It was the biggest understatement I'd ever made. My world was a dumpster fire with me trying to put it out by pissing on it. I ran both hands through my hair, not caring how it looked afterward.

Ollie pulled out a chair and sat down without waiting for me to invite him. "Did they fire you?" he asked hesitantly.

"Put on paid leave until they can be sure I wasn't the one who helped Lucien Clarke steal the wine vessel." I looked at Ollie with earnest, pleading eyes. "It wasn't me, Ollie. I don't know why I care what you think, but I'm telling the truth."

"I believe you, Ryder." And I could tell he did, even though I'd given him no reason to believe him. "Do you have a past with Lucien?"

"You could say that again," I sneered. For reasons unknown to me, I opened up and told Ollie about Paris. He listened quietly and without judgment, which I appreciated more than I could express. "Art is my life. What will I do if I lose my job?"

"Fight for your job, Ryder. Don't roll over and play dead." He tipped his head to the side for a second like he had something he wanted to ask but wasn't sure it was a good idea. "Was he the one you got into the car with after you left the police station?"

My eyes widened in alarm because I hadn't seen Ollie when I searched the sidewalk before I got in Lucien's car. I thought about denying it, but instead, I said, "It was him."

"What did he want?"

"To convince me he was innocent," I replied. It wasn't exactly what Lucien had said, but then again, I didn't give him a chance to talk.

"Which time?" Ollie asked. "Priceless artifacts were stolen both times he appeared in your life." I groaned. "Wait. Did this happen more than twice?"

I nodded. Knowing it would kill what little respect Ollie might have for me, I told him the rest of the sordid story. Surprisingly, instead of condemning my stupidity, he looked confounded.

"I don't mean to sound cruel, but if the museum knew you were working at both museums at the time the items were stolen, why did they risk hiring you? Wouldn't you be too big of a risk? I'm sure an art conservator is an important job, but aren't there ones with less... baggage?"

I was about to remind him I was hired as a director when the truth of his words hit me. I sat up straighter and felt more alert than I had in weeks. "Ollie! I think you're onto something. Why the hell would they hire me?" My mother didn't flex enough muscle for them to overlook my history. "Unless..."

"They wanted a scapegoat."

"There's no other explanation," I said. "Regardless of what Lucien says, he must be involved with someone on the museum board. How else could he have gained access to the event?"

"You need to talk to Agents Kiphart and Marshall."

"I already have," I said. "I'm not convinced they care."

"They care about the truth, Ryder. You just have to make them see you're not guilty. Offer to take a polygraph. Wait," Ollie said abruptly. "Surely, there's an insurance adjuster assigned to investigate the theft." I nodded. I'd already met with Pierre Simpriani twice. I'd offered to take a polygraph for him too, but neither the feds nor the insurance adjuster seemed eager to accept my offer. "There's the person you need to get on your side and make them hear you."

I got to my feet so fast I nearly knocked my chair over. "Thanks, Ollie. You've helped me sort things in my brain and stop moping. Congratulations, by the way."

"For what?" I asked.

"I heard your Roebling Bridge drawing sold for five thousand dollars. It's the largest amount any piece of art has sold for since the museum started the event. It really is a stunning piece."

"Thank you."

"See you around, Ollie."

When I reached the sidewalk, I pulled out my phone and called my mother. "Hello, darling," she said cheerfully. "Are you ready for the feast Betty is making for us tomorrow?"

"I am," I said honestly, "but I wondered if I could come over and speak with you. There's something bothering me about the heist at the museum."

"Ryder, you don't need permission to come home or to speak to me, but I'm wondering if maybe we should do our best to put the heist behind us. I don't think rehashing everything is in your best interest."

"I'm determined to prove I'm innocent, Mother, and I'll go to any lengths to do it."

She let out a long sigh then said, "Well, your timing is impeccable because I have an appointment to speak with an agent in half an hour."

"Perfect," I said. "Where? At the federal building or the museum?"

"He's coming here."

"Agent Kiphart is coming there to speak with you?" I asked.

"It isn't Agent Kiphart this time. It's Inspector Somers or something from Interpol." Mother lowered her voice and said, "I'm ashamed to admit how excited I am to see what a real Interpol inspector looks like. He has the most delicious British accent I've ever heard."

My blood chilled, but I managed to keep my voice calm. "Mother, I want to be there when you meet this Inspector Somers," I said firmly.

"Okay, if you think this inspector can help clear your name, then I'm happy to have you join us."

"Oh, I think this Inspector Somers will be able to shed some light on many things." Fury raced through my veins, and the urge to hit something or someone was stronger than I'd ever felt, including the afternoon I went with Lucien to his hotel room. This rage threatened to consume me, and I feared what I would do if I couldn't get a handle on it. "I'm coming over right now."

"Wonderful. I'll put on a pot of coffee and serve the cookies Betty made yesterday afternoon."

I wanted to tell my mother not to bother with niceties because they wouldn't be appreciated. I nearly instructed her to guard the fine china and silverware from the fraud who would be walking into our home, but instead, I said, "That sounds lovely, Mother. I'll see you soon."

Half an hour was more than enough time to make it to my parents' home in Indian Hill if there were no accidents on the interstate. Initially, I had worried about my mother's safety when she told me about her meeting with an Interpol inspector, because no such thing existed, but then she mentioned his British accent. Interpol had agents not inspectors, but that wasn't my issue. Gun-toting, badge-waving Interpol agents were an example of Hollywood hype that had become a mainstream belief. Interpol is an international organization which acted as a network for law enforcement agencies around the world. While their work is valid and important, they wouldn't send a British agent to investigate the heist. I knew who had balls big enough to meet with my mother while masquerading as an international law enforcement agent.

Lucien Clarke hadn't left town after all. The question was: what was I going to do about it?

Chapter Ten

Lucien

I HAD TO BE OUT OF MY FUCKING MIND. THERE WAS NO OTHER REASON TO explain me choosing an Interpol inspector as an alias to gain access to Ryder's mother. The woman had sounded so intrigued and eager to help, and I felt like the horrible human being I was. I just couldn't see any way around it, because there had to be an insider on the museum staff, the board of directors, or one of the prominent trustees. Celeste Jameson was a trustee, *and* I'd learned through the interviews I'd discreetly conducted, she was the sole reason the director had agreed to hire Ryder. While I doubted the woman had the kind of clout to convince Daniel Perez to hire a conservation director with Ryder's history, he had squarely laid the blame on the Jameson family. The pompous windbag was convinced the Jamesons pulled off the heist together. He'd leaned forward and confessed he'd pointed the FBI in their direction, but without proof, there was nothing the agents could do.

Deverish's inside person was Mae Yung, the Asian art director. Dev hadn't wined and dined her; he'd approached her about lending a Neolithic piece of pottery to the museum for a future exhibition. Banks was genuinely an antique collector, and there were many occasions we used pieces of his collection to gain access to a museum. May Yung had invited Dev into her offices where she inspected the piece and gave him a tour of the lab where she could conduct a few tests to ensure the pottery was authentic and not a replica. Sometimes we deliberately used fakes because it garnered the same access as the authentic pieces did.

Mae Yung was naturally the first person I wanted to speak to since she was the Asian arts director and the one responsible for the fanyi vessel. Had she suspected her interaction with Dev, and if not, were there any other potential clients that stuck out in her mind as suspicious? The answer was no and no. Neither Deverish nor anyone else she met caused alarm bells to go off in her head. I noticed she was one of the few that didn't throw Ryder under the bus. The only thing she'd mentioned about Ryder was his passion for his job and his friendly smile. To her, those things made him innocent. I left the interview convinced the extent of Mae Yung's involvement were her interactions with Deverish.

I'd discreetly worked my way through the board of directors and museum staff. No one other than Daniel Perez had tripped my alarms, but I couldn't trust myself to be objective in his case. He had the most scathing things to say about Ryder and Celeste, and it potentially clouded my judgment when it came to him. I hoped the trustees could shed new light on dealings at the museum, but I wasn't going to hold my breath. Banks was starting to lose his patience because the longer I stayed in Cincinnati, the longer he was short another man in the field.

The Jameson home was north of Cincinnati in a wealthy neighborhood called Indian Hill. According to my research the community was a mix of old and new money, which showed in the styles of homes. I saw graceful, old homes built around the turn of the nineteenth century as well as newer mansions built in the last decade. Some homes sat on smaller lots while others were surrounded by sprawling estates.

The Jamesons' family home sat on a large estate surrounded by a stone wall that was built more for looks than protection. I drove up to the ornate, wrought iron gate and rang the buzzer on the intercom system. After identifying myself, the gates slowly opened and I drove down the long winding driveway which circled in front of a massive stone and cedar structure. The main part of the home was stone and looked like it was built more than a hundred years ago. Since then, wings were added on to the east and west sides of the original structure. Rather than trying to match up stone colors, the architect chose materials which complemented the original stone. Tall, narrow windows lined the east and west wings while stained-glass windows graced the original structure. As grand and regal as the house was, the amber-colored cedar siding made it look warm and inviting.

Behind the home sat two massive outbuildings and a paddock where horses ran and frolicked. The home was lovely and picturesque, and I could picture Ryder growing up here. I should've known by the way Ryder's hips moved when he rode me he was an accomplished horseman. My heart throbbed painfully in my chest when I remembered the way we parted three weeks ago. Someone else would be on the receiving end of his skill from now on. Maybe I could find a way to clear his name while obtaining the answers I needed to close my investigation. Hell, I was even starting to think like a law enforcement officer thanks to Percy's merciless coaching. He loved mystery books and movies and watched detective dramas all the time. While admitting most things were probably dramatized for television, he did offer some handy advice and coached me on technique. I'd spent my adult life evading law enforcement, not imitating them.

I parked the boring sedan in front of the home and killed the engine. I missed the Aston Martin so fucking much, but Inspector Christian Somersby would hardly drive something so extravagant. The doorbell was answered immediately by a pleasant woman who looked to be in her mid-fifties. I assumed by her uniform she was part of the household staff.

"Hello, ma'am. I'm Inspector Christian Somersby with Interpol. I have an appointment with Mrs. Jameson."

"Yes, she's expecting you." She stepped aside and allowed me to enter the breathtaking foyer. The home could rival the finest I'd seen in England. Marble floors and columns, a winding staircase with a gleaming wooden banister, and dark wood everywhere the eye could see. The windows adorning the front of the home afforded plenty of sunlight to prevent the space from feeling gloomy and oppressive. "I'm afraid she's taking an important call in her office. She asked me to show you to the library if you arrived before she finished."

I smiled cordially and said, "That's no problem at all. I don't mind waiting." I did, but what the hell was I going to say? "I can't linger in case her son happens to show up." No, I very well couldn't tell her the truth. The hairs on the back of my neck stood up, and I wondered if it was a result from thinking about him or—

"I'll take it from here, Betty," Ryder said firmly, approaching from the hall to the east wing. "Inspector Somers is it?" he asked when he stopped just to the right of me.

I turned and faced Ryder, knowing the disguise I wore wouldn't fool him for a second. The corner of his mouth briefly twitched like he wanted to smile, but his anger won the battle, and he continued to scowl at me. His eyes didn't widen in surprise, so was he expecting me? I knew I'd find out once we were alone in the library. "It's Somersby," I corrected. "Christian Somersby." I extended my hand because it's what the housekeeper would expect.

Ryder squeezed my hand in a bruising grip, giving away how angry he was. I should've worried the FBI agents were in the library waiting to pounce, but I somehow knew better. Ryder was going to allow me to carry out this farce, but why? Curiosity? Did he hope I had information he could use to exonerate him? "Follow me," Ryder said, dropping my hand and walking back toward the east wing.

I followed a pace or two behind his casual stride, noticing his posture was rigid with tension. Ryder didn't utter a word until we were alone in the library with the door shut, then he spun around and charged toward me. He fisted my jacket in both hands and jerked me forward until our mouths were mere inches apart.

"What fucking game are you playing now, Lucien?"

"How'd you know it was me?"

Ryder shoved me away, turned his back toward me, and ran his hands through his hair. "Are you fucking kidding me? You think a stupid fake mustache and a wig are a decent disguise? You have to know the feds would've shown your picture to everyone they interviewed, including my mother."

"No one has made the connection so far," I countered.

"Well, that's because they don't know you as well as I do. You didn't think I'd recognize your chin dimple or your square jaw?"

I was too flattered to form a response right away other than to grin broadly at him. "I didn't expect you to be here when I interviewed your mother. Are you worried about me, love?"

"Wipe the smug smirk off your fucking face right now before I knock out a few of your teeth. And do not call me your love. This isn't funny, Lucien. Even if the disguise had worked, I still would've recognized my blue tie." I could've reiterated that I hadn't expected to run into him but didn't.

I looked down at the blue silk tie I couldn't seem to stop touching after Ryder left. If I looked close enough, I could still see the slight impression left by my teeth. "Well, it's a very lovely tie, and you so carelessly left it behind." *Left me behind*, I wanted to add but wouldn't. I had no right to be hurt over his behavior. "Finders keepers."

"You can keep the tie as a keepsake. You can wrap it around your cock and—"

The library doors opened suddenly, cutting off Ryder's words. We both jerked apart like we were up to no good then stared at each other for a few heartbeats before we both turned our attention to the beautiful woman who joined us.

"I'm so sorry to keep you waiting, Inspector," Celeste Jameson said, offering me a brisk handshake. "I see you've met my son, Ryder. We're hoping we can help each other out."

"How's that, ma'am?" I asked.

"We all want the same thing, Inspector, which is to find out who connected with the museum is responsible for the heist. You'll find your thief, and we'll restore my son's good name," she said confidently, wearing the look of a determined mother. "I'm convinced someone has decided to pin this crime on him, and I will not stand for it."

"I think we can help each other then."

"Good. Let's get comfortable." Celeste led us over to a lovely sitting area with a velvet settee and leather club chairs. She and Ryder sat beside each other on the settee while I took a chair across from them. The furniture was modern but crafted in the old English style with great care put into the finishing touches. The bronze nailhead trim around both the velvet and leather pieces were hammered into place by hand instead of a machine. My mother would love the richness of the burgundy velvet used for the sofa and the buttery, ivory leather used for the chairs.

I noticed a sterling silver tray in the center of the ivory and gold marble table. Celeste gestured to it and said, "Betty put together a tray of coffee and cookies for us to enjoy. Please help yourself."

"Mother, I'm sure *Inspector* Somerby isn't in the mood for coffee and cookies. I bet he wants to get straight to the interview so he can get on with the next interview. Isn't that right, Inspector?"

I could feel Celeste looking between her son and me. I knew the right thing to do was to agree with Ryder and get on with the interview and stop antagonizing him, but the daredevil look in his eyes made me think naughty things and made me want to do even naughtier things to him.

"Ryder has a blue silk tie just like the one you're wearing," Celeste said abruptly.

I ran my hand over the cool silk while maintaining eye contact with Ryder. "He has very good taste."

Chapter Eleven

Ryder

"WELL, IN THIS CASE, *I* HAVE GOOD TASTE," MOTHER SAID, completely unaware she was seeking help from the same man who ruined my career. The irony was big enough to choke a man, but I had other things I'd like for Lucien to gag on. "I bought it for him when he graduated with his master's degree. It's his lucky tie."

"You don't say," Lucien said, stroking the tie as intimately as he would a lover. "This is my lucky tie also. It was a gift from someone after a very memorable occasion as well."

"Oh, a lovely lady?" Mother inquired. I wanted to demand she stop making nice talk with Lucien and get down to business, but it would only make her suspicious. I received my first manners and etiquette lesson before I cut my teeth.

"A lovely man," Lucien told my mother.

"Forgive me," Mother said, placing a dainty hand over her chest. "The mother of a gay man should know better than to make assumptions."

"It's quite all right, Mrs. Jameson. Shall we get started? I'm sure you have better things to do the night before a holiday than talk to me. I hope I'm not interrupting your baking." I snorted.

"Oh, hush, you," Celeste said, making a shushing noise at me. She turned to Lucien and said, "Please, won't you at least join me for a cup of coffee?"

I seethed inside while I wanted to shout at the universe to stop throwing this man in my path. We weren't star-crossed lovers destined to keep finding one another. I realized my mother was right about one thing though. Lucien, under the stupid guise of Inspector Somersby, might help us gain access to the information I need to clear myself since I had no real friends at the museum. I had committed myself to doing whatever it took to restore my good name, and if it meant working side by side with the man who caused me the trouble, then so be it.

I tuned out the small talk Mother and Lucien engaged in to do some thinking. Lucien wouldn't be here if he stole the vessel, which meant someone else had, and he wanted to find out who and how. Lucien was interviewing museum staff, directors, and board members to find out who the leak was so he could trace it back to the person who stole the artifact. Why? What would he gain? Was his life in danger because someone else got to the vessel before he did, or was this all part of his show? Was this an act of pride?

My gut told me it wasn't a ruse, but I couldn't trust myself when it came to him. Lucien had blinded me with lust when we first met, took advantage of my loneliness on our second encounter, and three weeks ago... I couldn't let my mind go there. I'd done everything possible to ignore the memories of hitting him then fucking him in his hotel room. I wasn't proud of my behavior that day. I couldn't let myself think about our tear-stained faces and salty kisses either.

"Mmmm. These shortbread biscuits are delicious," Lucien said, breaking into my thoughts. "I didn't expect to find them this good outside the United Kingdom."

"Betty's grandmother is British, and she taught her the traditional ways of baking and cooking. My family reaps the benefit of her knowledge." Mother patted the sofa like an idea just occurred to her. "Why don't you join us for dinner, Inspector. Beef Wellington and Yorkshire puddings are on the menu."

I stared intently at Lucien, willing him to look my way so I could silently communicate what a bad idea it was for him to stay for dinner. He ignored me and washed down his cookie with a drink of coffee. "I really shouldn't."

"Oh, but you should," Mother countered.

"Let's see how you feel about it after we've finished the interview."

"We have nothing to hide, Inspector," Mother said, patting my knee.

Lucien finally looked at me. The cookie crumbs in his fake mustache ruined his austere expression. I lifted my hand and brushed my finger over my upper lip, and he quickly wiped his mouth with the linen cloth Mother had handed to him with a plate of cookies. I wanted to find humor in the ridiculous situation, but too much was at stake for me. It was clear my reinstatement wasn't happening anytime soon, and no other museum would hire me after this third strike.

Then the solution came to me. I would use Lucien like he'd used me. I would find what I needed to restore my reputation then turn him over to the FBI.

"Isn't that right, dear?" Mother asked me.

"I'm sorry, Mother. I tuned out for a brief second and didn't hear what you said."

She narrowed her eyes in concern. "I was telling Inspector Somersby that Daniel Perez was the most likely suspect."

"I'm sure Perez has said the same about us, Mother." I looked at Lucien and played along with his game. "Let me guess, when you interviewed the esteemed director, Perez claimed my mother was the only reason he hired me. He stated he knew it was a bad idea because of my history but did it anyway." I put my finger over my lips and pretended to think. "He said it was either because he had so much respect for my mother or she pressured him to do it. Perhaps he worried about losing the huge amount of money my family donates to the museum each year."

"Something like that," Lucien said with a smirk. "You've been giving this some thought."

"I have too much time on my hands and very little to do since my suspension."

"You went out on a date with a lovely young man this weekend," Mother said. Oh boy. Lucien's eyes darkened, and his nostrils flared. He didn't like the notion of me dating someone else, eh? Too bad.

I nodded my head. "True, and I plan to see him again this weekend," I lied.

"Really?" Mother asked hopefully. "You didn't tell me."

"We haven't finalized our plans." I should feel ashamed for getting my mother's hopes up, but seeing the possessive gleam in Lucien's eyes temporarily made me forget my sanity.

"I'm so happy to hear it, Ryder. After I found out you were staying for dinner, I acted hastily and invited Ezra and his parents to join us."

"Um, what?" I asked, whipping my head around to stare at my mother. Was that a soft chuckle I heard coming from Lucien's direction? I didn't dare look at him. "You invited them, and now you're inviting Inspector Somersby. Is Betty prepared for these extra guests?"

"Of course," Mother said, rolling her eyes. "I'd already discussed it with her before the Inspector arrived. Simone's call was the important one I took before joining you."

Simone was Ezra's mother. She and my mother went back a long way but hadn't seen each other in twenty years. Simone and Paul moved back to Cincinnati recently because Ezra had accepted a teaching job at the University of Cincinnati the previous year. My parents hosted a dinner party the previous week to welcome them back, and

I liked Ezra right away. He was handsome, funny, and uncomplicated. I asked him on a date without my mother's prodding, which she took as a good sign. We went to dinner then a movie and had a great time, but neither of us felt a spark between us. We both agreed we could always use another friend and exchanged numbers.

"I don't want to impose," Lucien said, looking uncomfortable. "In fact, why don't we continue with the interview, so I can let you nice folks get back to your evening."

"Sounds good," I said, even though I liked the idea of making him jealous.

"It doesn't sound good at all. I'd love for you to join us, and I promise you won't be intruding," Mother said.

"We'll see how the interview goes," Lucien said noncommittally. "Back to Perez…"

"The board of trustees hired Daniel Perez two years ago," Mother said. "It wasn't a unanimous vote. Personally, I didn't care for the man while everyone else thought he could walk on water because of his tenure at the Smithsonian."

"The Smithsonian?" Lucien asked, sitting up taller.

"You mean you didn't know?" Mother asked. "How is that possible? It's usually the first thing he tells you upon introduction. He's the most pompous man I've ever met, and believe me, I've known many in my lifetime."

"Why would he give up a spot at the Smithsonian to work at the Cincinnati Art Museum?" Lucien asked.

"You don't have to sound like Cincinnati is one of Dante's circles of hell," Mother chided gently.

"I'm not a religious man, Mrs. Jameson, so I don't give much thought to heaven or hell. I apologize if I offended you. I assure you it wasn't my intention. I've enjoyed my time in the city, and I've found the people to be warm and friendly." Not all of them, I thought, remembering the bite mark and bruises I'd left on him.

"You've never heard of Dante's Inferno?" I found myself asking.

"Excuse me?" Lucien asked.

I knew from our brief time in Paris that Lucien was a highly educated man. He was extremely knowledgeable about art, food, books, and wine. I knew for a fact he was fluent in at least four languages. During our trips, he'd always tell me the history of the areas we visited and show me landmarks and the stories behind them. I'd imagined Lucien came from a privileged life like mine and attended one of the finest boarding schools in Europe, but maybe his urbane polish was nothing more than a disguise too.

"It comes from *The Divine Comedy* by Dante Alighieri. The first part is titled 'Inferno' and details Dante's journey through the nine circles of hell. 'Inferno' is followed by 'Purgatorio' and 'Paradiso.' It's the depiction of a man's journey toward God and rejecting sin."

"I've heard of it, yes, but I haven't read it," Lucien said, staring into my eyes as I wondered which level of hell he'd land in. He was treacherous and a betrayer, so according to Dante, it would land him in the ninth circle along with Satan and Judas. Then again, if I put faith in an Italian poet's words, I'd land in the seventh circle just for lying with other men. I wasn't a bit sorry either. Well, I was sorry for lying with this particular man, but I didn't see homosexuality as a one-way ticket to hell.

"Forgive Ryder," Mother said nervously, "he takes art and literature very seriously."

"Too seriously," I said with a self-deprecating smile. I needed to get the man on my side, not alienate him. "I apologize for taking us way off track. Dante's Inferno has absolutely zero to do with our discussion."

"I find it fascinating though," Lucien said, looking and sounding sincere. "Perhaps we can discuss it after dinner." He was looking for an excuse to get me alone. Fine. I could be alone with him and not tear his clothes off.

"Absolutely," I said jovially.

"Wonderful," Mother said, rubbing her hands together.

"As for Perez," Lucien said, "you make a valid point, Celeste." My mother practically preened when he used her first name. "I'll see what I can dig up."

"You'll share with us, won't you?" she asked, leaning forward.

"I'm afraid I won't be able to tell you much while I'm investigating, but I promise to share information with you as soon as I can."

"Fair enough," Mother said smugly.

Lucien continued to ask us both questions about our dealings with the directors, staff, and trustees. From there, he moved on to the night of the gala. Was anyone acting nervous or suspicious? Did anyone disappear for an extended period of time? The FBI knew about my office romp with the waiter, but I had hoped to keep that tidbit from my mother. I told Lucien I wasn't aware of anyone disappearing. He stiffened and entered another note in his phone. When he looked up, our gazes collided. Once again, Lucien's eyes had darkened with possessiveness and anger. What was the source? Had he found out where I'd gone and whom I was with? A childish part of me wanted to rub it in his face, but I wouldn't with my mother sitting beside me.

Someone knocked softly on the door, so Mother rose gracefully and went to see who it was. "I'll be right back, gentlemen."

"Don't you want your mother to know about your extra activities on the night of the gala?" Lucien asked softly.

"Would you want your mother to know?" I countered. Lucien tipped his head to the side to acknowledge the point. "How did you know?" Had the agents shared the information with anyone?

Lucien set down his phone on the table and leaned forward. "Do you think by now I don't recognize the sounds you make when you're fucking?"

He heard me in my office with Rhys? It felt like the temperature in the library had suddenly risen twenty degrees. I fought the urge to pull my shirt away from my skin to cool off. I would not give him the satisfaction.

"Did it make you hard, Lucien?" That wasn't the question I

should've asked, but when had I asked the right things or made the correct moves when it came to this man?

"You were only going through the motions with the guy. Who was he?"

"An adorable waiter," I replied, searching for words to dispute his claims about how good it was. I wanted to call bullshit, but it would be an outright lie. "Before you ask, the FBI has already investigated him. It's doubtful he was involved, but then again, I have a horrible track record with men."

"Touché."

"Ryder," Mother said from the doorway, "Ezra and his parents have arrived for dinner. I can't believe we've been in here talking for two hours. Will you please show Inspector Somersby to the powder room so he can wash up for dinner?"

"Sure, Mother."

"Thank you, Celeste. Please call me Christian."

"Christian it is then. I'm going to greet our guests. I'll see you guys in the dining room in a few minutes."

Once she left, I faced Lucien once more. The urge to deck him was still strong, but the will to clear my name was stronger. I needed his intel to make it happen, which was the only reason I didn't act on my simmering rage.

"Follow me," I said.

I led Lucien down the hallway toward the guest bathroom then stopped at the door and gestured for him to go inside. Instead, he shoved me inside and shut the door behind him.

"I want to rip that stupid mustache off your face."

"Come home with me after this, and you'll get your chance."

"No fucking way. I told you—"

Lucien fisted my shirt, dragged me forward, and planted his lips against mine.

Chapter Twelve

Lucien

RYDER'S RESISTANCE WAS TOKEN AND DIDN'T LAST MORE THAN A heartbeat. I didn't force my tongue between his lips; he was the aggressor. I parted mine easily and hungrily though, desperate to taste him and feel the arousal vibrating through his body. My dick was hard and aching, pleading for more of his rough treatment. I pressed myself tighter against him, reveling in his hardness pressed against mine.

It felt like second nature to grind against him while sucking his tongue into my mouth. I was seconds away from dropping to my knees and blowing him, uncaring we were in his parents' home or that nothing was resolved between us. I wanted to take, to please, and to fuse the connection I thought lost to me forever.

Ryder came to his wits before I did, wrenching his mouth free of mine and stepping away from me. "Why are you really here, Lucien? What game are you playing now?"

"It's not a game, Ry. Come home with me after dinner, and I will tell you everything."

Ryder ran his hands through his hair and took another step back, looking as if he were fighting the biggest internal battle of his life. "It's not a good idea. It won't change anything. You can't undo our past, and you can't give me back the things you took from me." He wasn't talking about priceless artifacts, and we both knew it.

"Ryder, I know you may never trust me again, but I owe you the truth. I want to give it to you now."

"I felt what you want to give me," he said snidely, looking at the erection straining against my pants. His blue eyes were clouded with lust, hurt, and disillusionment. "God, I hate you."

"You don't hate me, Ryder." Even though he should. "Part of you knows the real me would never choose to hurt you, and it's the same part that's keeping you from turning me over to the FBI. Your cynicism is preventing you from seeing the bigger picture."

"What? That I'm the museum's patsy? I already figured it out, but why do you care?" Ryder closed the gap between us and got up in my face. "Are you outraged someone else dared to use me? Do you think you're the only one worthy of destroying my life? You're the reason I'm in this mess to begin with, so why the hell should I trust you?"

"We want the same thing here, Ry." He bristled with rage, and I longed to sooth the beast inside him. "We'll find out who is behind this and clear your name. By doing so, it might shed new light on the prior recoveries in Paris and Cairo."

"Recoveries?" Ryder asked incredulously.

Fuck, I hadn't meant to say that, but maybe I had to give him a little upfront before I asked him to accept a lot later on. "Look, we don't have time to get into this right now with your family and their guests waiting for us to join them in the dining room."

"We're not leaving this bathroom until you explain why you said 'recoveries' instead of thefts." Ryder's adorable use of air quotes made me want to smile, but I didn't dare with so much at stake. I'd never seen him use them before and wanted to know when the habit started, but it wasn't the time to ask.

"I'm not a thief, Ryder. I'm a recovery specialist."

He snorted. "Pull the other leg."

I reached between his legs and cupped his erection, and because it was as natural to him as breathing, he pushed against my hand. Unfortunately, he came to his senses and batted my hand away.

"It's a saying, not a request, Lucien."

"I'm familiar with the saying, but it doesn't specify which leg. If given a choice, I'll always grab the one in the middle."

"Do you want me to take you seriously and hear you out?" Ryder asked.

"More than anything."

"Then tell me what a recovery specialist does. You can give me the Cliff Notes version for now."

"Okay, fine," I agreed. "It's not stealing if I recover items that didn't belong to the museums in the first place."

Ryder's brow furrowed. "Neither museum claimed to own the painting or the statue you *recovered*." I was pleased he at least believed I wasn't responsible for the missing fanyi vessel. "They were on..." His words trailed off.

"Loan from private collectors," I supplied.

"You're saying the private collectors didn't own the items they loaned to the museums, and someone hired you to take them back and return them to their rightful owners?" His words rose in pitch as he neared the end of his question. "You expect me to believe that?"

"It's the truth, Ry."

"Don't! I'm not your Ry, and I'm not your love." He was both those things, but it was an argument best saved for another day. "You're telling me the Cincinnati Art Museum obtained the fanyi through illegal channels?"

"No, that's not what I'm saying, or at least I have no evidence of it yet. The illegal activity goes back to the owners, either past or present. Sometimes the current owners aren't aware the provenance documents they received with their purchase were falsified."

"How do they get it past their insurers?" Ryder asked.

"Listen, we need to get out there before your mother comes looking for us. I gave you the Cliff Notes answer to your question. Can we finish the discussion later?"

"In your hotel room?" Ryder asked suspiciously.

"Anywhere you choose."

"We could go to my place," Ryder said. "My sister moved in with me a few weeks ago, but she's in Colorado with friends for the holiday." I thought it was odd his sister chose to spend it away from her family, but I knew nothing about their family dynamics. I'd seen with my own eyes at the gala how rebellious she could be when it suited her.

"We'll decide after dinner. You owe me a conversation about Dante," I reminded him. I placed my hand on the doorknob behind me but didn't turn it. "Your expression said you were trying to decide which circle of hell would be my future home."

"Maybe," Ryder said, looking at me suspiciously. "You're already familiar with *The Divine Comedy*, aren't you? And you let me blather on about it."

"You know how I adore the inner geek hidden by your outer Adonis."

"If we're going to do this, we both need to agree to keep this a professional relationship," Ryder said.

I laughed even though I knew it would only make him angrier. Who did he think he was trying to fool? We couldn't keep our hands off each other for five minutes, let alone for the duration of an investigation. "We can try."

"We will succeed," he said resolutely. I saluted Ryder with two fingers, and he shoved me out of the way to open the door. "You stay here for a minute. Pull yourself together and make sure your wig and mustache are glued on properly. I need to take my mother off to the side and request she doesn't introduce you as an inspector from Interpol. The last thing we need is for someone to point out they do not exist in the way you're implying they do."

"What will you ask her to say?" I asked.

"We can tell our guests that you and I were acquaintances from when I worked in Paris." His words conjured so many images in my mind, each of them stealing my breath away. I could tell he was reliving them too due to the sad expression on his handsome face.

"That will work. I'll give you a head start."

"See you out there, Inspector Gadget."

Betty's tribute to a proper English dinner was delicious, and the only bright spot of the evening once Ryder and I left the privacy of the bathroom. Celeste and Simone spent most of the dinner laughing and reliving old times, while Paul and Edmond Jameson talked about investments, politics, and the state of the world, leaving Ezra, Ryder, and me to fend for ourselves. Of course, Celeste took Ryder seriously when he implied he and Ezra were more than friends and sat them beside each other across from me. Ezra Meyer was smart, funny, and a sexy silver fox with dark eyes. He couldn't have been much older than Ryder, so he was one of the guys who went gray early or purposely dyed his hair. Either way, it looked really good on him. I hated him on sight until I realized nothing was sparking between him and Ryder.

It didn't prevent Ryder from trying to provoke my possessiveness. Every time he caught me watching them, Ryder put his arm on the back of Ezra's chair and whispered something in the silver fox's ear to make him laugh. The little minx thought he could make me jealous with his offhanded comment in the library, but it backfired because his mother would push the match until Ryder came clean or I swept him away to distant shores.

"There's a thought," I said under my breath then forked the last bite of my banoffee pie into my mouth. Ryder was annoying the fuck out of me, but nothing kept me from eating my favorite dessert.

"Pardon me?" Ryder asked from across the table. I couldn't wait to wipe the smug grin off his face. Did he think to play such wicked games with me?

"I remarked on the time," I lied. "I need to report into the office with an update."

"You can use the library, dear," Celeste offered. I wasn't aware she was paying attention to our end of the table, but I should've known better.

"That's very gracious of you, but it goes against protocol."

"Protocol?" Edmond Jameson asked, quirking a dark brow. "That sounds serious."

"I didn't mean to imply my work was exotic and exciting. We're just required to use secure phones when discussing our client's private information. The British accent makes people think of James Bond," I teased. "Thank you for a lovely dinner, Celeste." I told everyone else at the table it was a pleasure to meet them and wished them a happy holiday.

"I'll walk you out," Celeste said, sliding back her chair.

"I'll do it, Mother," Ryder said, smiling at his mother.

Simone said something, pulling Celeste's attention back to her. I smiled at Ezra. "I'll only borrow Ryder for a minute."

"Um, okay," Ezra said, looking puzzled.

Neither Ryder nor I spoke until we reached the front door. "I don't know what time I'll get home tonight," Ryder told me, earning a snort. "What?"

"Stop trying to make me jealous. The only action you're going to have is with your fist while you think about how close I came to dropping to my knees to suck your cock in the bathroom."

"Shut the fuck up before someone overhears you," Ryder said angrily. "I wasn't implying that I was going to spend the night fucking Ezra. I meant I wasn't sure how long before I could get away without causing a fuss. I need to be back here early tomorrow afternoon for Thanksgiving dinner, so maybe tonight isn't the best idea. Do you have a way for me to contact you?"

I slipped a business card from my wallet and handed it to him. Ryder ran his thumb over the name printed on the card, and I swear I felt it in my groin. He looked up at me with a crooked grin reminiscent of the ones he'd given me in Paris. It was too much to hope we could have a future together after one brief conversation in his parents' bathroom, but it was a start. "What's a guy have to do to see your fake Interpol badge?"

"Are you flirting?"

"No, I'm just curious."

"Give me an hour to explain, and I'll show you whatever you want," I pleaded. Ryder inhaled deep, held his breath, and released it slowly. He didn't speak or nod, but I saw the answer in his expressive eyes. "Text me so I'll have your number too."

I left him standing in the doorway watching me leave. I kept glancing in the rearview mirror until the front of the house was no longer in sight. My phone chimed with an incoming text when I reached the end of the driveway.

I want my lucky tie back, preferably without cum stains on it.

Chapter Thirteen

Ryder

I DIDN'T CALL LUCIEN WHEN I GOT HOME FROM MY PARENTS THAT NIGHT, nor did I call him the next day or even the one after. I thought about calling him on Saturday but decided to go clubbing with Ezra instead. I needed time to think without my hormones getting me in trouble. How could I even think about trusting Lucien again? Was it even his real name? I could demand to see his birth certificate, but how would I know if it was real?

"I need another drink," I shouted over the music to Ezra.

"Are you sure you haven't had too many already?" he yelled back.

I rolled my eyes and regretted it because the world started to tilt. "I'm fine," I said, unsure which one of us I was trying to convince. Maybe a glass of water this round, I thought to myself. I wasn't fine. I was angry. I was hurt. I was lonely. I was so fucking horny. Damn Lucien.

The line for the bar was long, so I pulled out my phone to kill time. I posted a selfie I'd taken with Ezra on Instagram with the caption that read: Feeling the "vibe" with this cutie. My Instagram account was connected to my Facebook and Twitter accounts so the status would post to all of them. I was too buzzed to care who might see them or the conclusions they might jump to. Had I been sober, I would've worried about damaging Ezra's reputation. By the time I reached the bar, I had to wait another ten minutes to get the hottie bartender's attention. I had to hand it to the owner of Vibe; they hired the best-looking bar staff. I ordered a glass of water and a drink since it would be a thirty-minute wait, or longer, before I got another chance.

"Hey there, sexy," said a familiar voice in my ear. "Long time no see."

My hands tightened on the glasses, and I turned from the bar to face Rhys, the cute waiter from the gala event. "Hey," I said casually. "How's it going?"

"I'd be better if I had a drink," he said, looking pointedly at the alcoholic beverage in my hand.

I looked longingly at it too. The least I could do was buy the man a drink after he gave a formal statement to the FBI admitting I bent him over my desk during the gala. I mean, I wasn't sure what he'd told them, but he did confirm my alibi. I extended the glass toward him and said, "Care for a Suck, Bang, Blow?"

Rhys smiled devilishly. "I thought you'd never ask."

"Want to find a table?" I asked.

"I could think of something else I'd rather do, but I'll settle for yelling at each other over the thumping techno music."

"Come on," I said, tipping my head for Rhys to follow me then instantly regretted it when the world threatened to turn on its axis.

Rhys looped his arm through mine. "I think I should be the one leading the way," he teased.

We were lucky enough to find a booth toward the back. I sent Ezra a text to let him know where I was so he wouldn't think I abandoned him. I wasn't so buzzed I couldn't think straight, even if my motor skills were a little sketchy.

"Who was the guy?" Rhys asked.

"What guy?" My mind immediately went to Lucien, and I wondered how Rhys had found out about him. Had Lucien tracked him down?

"You've already forgotten about the guy you came here with?" Rhys smiled crookedly then took a drink. "I see you have a pattern."

"His name is Ezra, and we're just friends."

"Same type of friends as us?" Rhys gestured back and forth between us.

"You and I were friendly, but I wouldn't say we're friends."

Rhys tipped his head to the side and licked his lips. "I really like your kind of friendly. Do you think—"

I shook my head to cut him off. "I'm emotionally unavailable. You could do a lot better." If I were honest, I would also admit, at least to myself, I'd become physically unavailable since Lucien returned to town. Sex with Lucien was like eating a perfectly seared filet mignon while sex with everyone else was closer to eating ground chuck. I wisely didn't say it out loud.

"Keep your emotions, sexy. I'm not looking for anything serious. What do you say?"

"There you are," Ezra said, saving the day without realizing it.

"I sent you a text," I told him.

"I know, but you said you were tucked away in the right corner. This is the left."

"I've had too much to drink, and you've apparently not had enough if you can tell left from right."

"I danced my buzz off," Ezra said with a cute pout.

"Let's fix that," Rhys said, sliding over so Ezra could sit down. "We'll flag the first waiter we see. I'm Rhys, and who are you."

"Ezra Meyer."

"Hello, Ezra," Rhys said in a flirty tone.

I expected Rhys to take advantage of our closeness and continue suggesting we hook up, but it seemed he only had eyes for Ezra. I wasn't mad about it, but I did feel a little lonely once the guys abandoned me for the dance floor after a few rounds of drinks. I might've even pouted as I watched them bump, grind, and fuck each other with their clothes on. Fuck! I was so horny. *Damn you, Lucien.*

Not caring about the time or my state of inebriation, I decided to send Lucien a text. I thought it would be cute to ask him if he was taking care of my tie. "Whoa. Two phones," I said, jabbing my fingers at them and hoping to land on the right letters.

I hit send, or at least thought I did, then leaned my head against the back of the booth so the world would stop spinning, and I wouldn't see two of everything. My phone chimed just as I started to drift off. I had to blink several times before I could read the text.

I'm coming to get you.

A wicked grin spread across my face, or maybe it was partial paralysis from alcohol poisoning. Wait. That was a stroke, wasn't it? My face did feel numb, and I was pretty sure I'd started to drool on myself. I squinted my eyes so the two phones became one long enough to tap out a quick reply. *Yeah, baby. Come and get me.*

I set my phone back down and decided to close my eyes while I waited for Lucien. The next thing I knew, I heard his clipped British accent barking out commands. I lifted my head, or tried to, but it was too heavy. I made out words like "hospital," "drugged," and "wanker." The last one made me giggle.

"Fuck, he's out of it," I heard Ezra say. "He wasn't like this when we hit the dance floor."

"Do you think he was drugged?" Rhys asked, sounding panicked.

"Not drugged," I said, still unable to lift my head from the padded back of the booth. "Shit-faced. Need to sleep." I started to slide lower in the booth so I could curl up for a nap, but firm hands gripped my biceps and pulled me in the opposite direction.

"Help me get him out to my car," Lucien said.

"Why don't you carry me like you did the time in Nice. Remember how you pinned me up against the glass wall and fucked me while the ocean roared beneath us? I came so hard. You did too, Lucien. Pretty sure I wore your bite marks in my shoulder for a week."

"Lucien?" Ezra asked. "I thought your name was Christian." *Uh oh.*

I pried open my eyes to see if Lucien was pissed Ezra recognized him without his stupid disguise or because I used his real name, but all I saw was concern. His brows formed angry slashes over his beautiful dark eyes. "It's the chin dimple, love," I said, lifting my hand and touching the groove. "Cum catcher." I thought I whispered the last bit, but I heard Ezra and Rhys giggle like girls while Lucien groaned.

"Come on," Lucien said in a steely voice. "That's our cue to get out of here." Lucien positioned his shoulder beneath mine, inviting me to lean against his strong body. My arm circled his neck and his went to my waist to anchor me against him.

"I could walk right out of here if I wanted to," I proclaimed.

"Of course."

"Do I detect sarcasm, Lucien?"

"Would you expect anything less from a British man?"

It seemed like we had to travel through all nine circles of hell before we exited the club. I felt a lot better as soon as the cool air hit me. "I'm much better now."

"Doubt it," Lucien replied. "Will you two stay with him while I pull the car around?"

"Sure," Ezra and Rhys said at the same time.

I missed the smell of Lucien's cologne and his body heat the instant he passed me off to Ezra and Rhys.

"I'm sorry, Ryder," Ezra said. "I had no idea you drank so much. I shouldn't have left you alone."

"S'kay."

"No, it isn't," Rhys added. "We didn't act like friends."

I started to tell them I was fine, but my stomach chose that exact moment to revolt. I had just enough time to lurch away from Ezra and Rhys before I got sick all over the sidewalk.

"Hey!" a lady shouted. "Watch it."

I didn't just throw up once. I kept retching until my stomach was empty. Shame and humiliation rose up swift and hard; I wanted the ground to open up and swallow me.

"There's Christian or Lucien or whomever," Ezra said. "Let's go, Ryder."

Ezra and Rhys were considerably shorter than I was, but with one on either side of me, they easily helped get me to the curb where the Aston Martin purred. Getting down into the low-slung seat was a different story altogether, but they got me in, and Ezra buckled my seatbelt before he hovered in the open door.

"I'm sorry I ruined our night out," I told him. "I don't know what came over me tonight. I never drink this much."

"You didn't ruin anything. I should've paid closer attention. Will you call me later to let me know how you're doing?"

"Sure," I said, reaching for his hand. "I'm going to be just fine."

"I'll take good care of him," Lucien assured Ezra, but there was zero warmth in his voice. "He'll call you as soon as he sleeps some of this off and has a chance to eat."

"Fair enough," Ezra agreed then shut the door.

Lucien aggressively shifted the car in drive and hit the gas. I closed my eyes because the city lights flashing by made me feel queasy.

"I live at—"

"Shut up," Lucien snarled, cutting me off before I could give him my address. "How could you be so foolish, Ryder? What the hell were you thinking?"

"I wasn't thinking because that stirs feelings and no good ever comes from wallowing around in my emotions. I prefer not to feel anything."

"Be honest with me right now. Do you need to go to a hospital?"

"No," I said. "I'm already feeling tons better since I threw up. I want you to take me home so I can sleep."

"I'm not leaving you alone tonight."

"Lucien, I appreciate your concern, but I'll be fine."

"Forgive me if I don't believe you right now, Ryder. You can either come back to my hotel room with me, or I can take you to the hospital. What's it going to be?"

"Your place is fine."

I was too tired to argue, and I knew he was right. I was still pretty far gone even if my body expelled the booze. The next thing I remembered, Lucien was rousing me from sleep so we could go inside the hotel. Like in the club, he slid his shoulder beneath mine and balanced me against his body to get through the lobby. I was pretty sure I dozed against him during the elevator ride up, and I don't remember much about him getting me ready for bed.

I do distinctly remember seeking out his warmth when he climbed beneath the sheets. "No funny business," I said, resting my hand on his abdomen and snuggling closer against his side. "I don't think we've ever just slept in a bed together."

"They say there's a first time for everything," Lucien whispered.

"Do you ever wonder who 'they' are? Who are these smart people who know so much?"

"Ryder, close your eyes and go to sleep."

"Yes, dear."

Lucien's chuckle vibrated in his chest beneath my cheek, and his hand slid through my hair, massaging my scalp until sleep claimed me.

Chapter Fourteen

Lucien

IF I'D SLEPT ON THE SOFA, I PROBABLY WOULD'VE GOTTEN SOME SLEEP, but I wouldn't have held Ryder in my arms while he snored and drooled all over my chest. I also wouldn't have his hand stroking my cock through my briefs while he dreamed. *Professional relationship. Professional relationship. Professional relationship.* It's what he said he wanted, and even though I knew he didn't mean it, I needed to earn his trust before we had sex again. My cock wept in misery over the thought of not taking this further, or was it leaking with delight from the brief touch? Perhaps both?

I carefully untangled myself from Ryder's long limbs and eager hand before I did something stupid like let him jack me off when he wasn't conscious of what he was doing. I stood by the bed and watched him sleep for a few seconds, fighting the urge to run my fingers through his silky strands of blond hair. Ryder needed sleep, and I needed to think, so I quietly went into the bathroom and started the shower. I brushed my teeth and rolled my options around in my brain while waiting for the water to heat up.

I promised Ryder answers, and I would deliver, but I had to decide how much I should, or rather could, tell him. I tried ignoring the raging hard-on Ryder gave me by coming up with a game plan, but it was too persistent, and his warm hand stroking me was all I could think about right then. I regretted not staying long enough for him to ease his hand beneath my underwear to touch my bare skin, so I stroked myself while pretending it was Ryder's hand touching me instead. I had lain in bed stiff, aching, and wanting for hours. My release built inside me as I thought about the dirty things Ryder used to whisper in my ear. It felt so fucking good.

The bathroom door opened, and I felt the electric charge in the air announcing Ryder's presence without me turning to look. Knowing he could see me through the glass doors only made me hotter, and it only took a few more strokes before I grunted and came hard. I stood silently beneath the spray for a few seconds as the orgasm and hot water eased the tension that had taken my body hostage while waiting for Ryder to reach out to me.

"There's a spare toothbrush in the drawer," I said, breaking the silence. I turned to look at Ryder then. He stood in the doorway unabashedly staring at my body. The thick head of his dick had escaped its cotton prison, proudly pushing beyond the elastic waistband. I loved the smell of his arousal and his salty essence, and it took more strength than I knew I possessed to stay right where I was instead of going to him.

"Have many guests, do you?" Ryder asked, his voice thick with sleep and lust.

I ignored his taunt and started washing my hair, feeling his eyes on my every move. Nothing I said would appease Ryder, and I didn't want to argue with him, at least not before breakfast. He released a frustrated sigh, then I heard him opening drawers until he found the one with the spare toothbrush.

"You have a lot of stuff for someone who lives on the run," Ryder remarked as he tore the toothbrush from the package. "Do you pack it all back up or leave it behind when you bolt?"

Maybe I had overthought things the past few days. Perhaps the best way to share information with Ryder was to answer his questions as best I could and build trust rather than toss up a lot of roadblocks to steer him in the direction I wanted him to take. If he asked something I couldn't answer, then I'd tell him so and explain why the best I could. I'd hoped to eat breakfast first, but it would only look like an evasive maneuver.

"I pack the essential things and leave the rest for our cleanup crew to dispose of," I said, meeting his gaze in the mirror. "I'm not normally in a city long enough to accrue as much stuff as you see in there."

"Cleanup crew?"

I rinsed the shampoo from my hair then reached for my body wash. "We have an advance scout who sets up our arrangements, we have a transportation team who moves the recovered items, and we have a cleanup crew who erases our existence. Then there are the techie people at headquarters who are responsible for manipulating cameras and overriding security systems." I knew it was risky to share this with him, but it was the only way he'd trust me again.

"Holy fuck," Ryder said, pulling my attention toward him. He held the toothbrush suspended in the air, and a ring of toothpaste foam circled his parted lips. His expression was a mixture of astonishment and awe with a little bit of horror thrown in. He put his toothbrush back in his mouth and vigorously scrubbed his teeth, signaling our conversation was over, at least for the moment. I continued washing my body while waiting for the proverbial other shoe to drop.

Ryder didn't say anything else until I had rinsed off and reached for the faucet. "Might as well leave the shower running since I'm get-ting in next." I hoped we would be sharing showers before too much longer.

I opened the door, reached for the towel, and stepped on the rug outside the shower as I wrapped it around my waist. Unable to resist punishing me, Ryder slid his boxers down his long legs so I could see what I was missing out on.

"Are you going to stick around for the show?" he asked. I quirked a brow, but I knew what he meant. Fuck yes, I wanted to stick around and watch him fuck his fist, but I wouldn't.

"It would only be fair since you barged in on me, but I think I'll allow you the privacy you denied me. I'll order breakfast from room service."

"I like my bacon crisp and scrambled eggs—"

"Dry," I said, cutting him off. "I haven't forgotten." I couldn't read Ryder's expression, so I decided to press on. "I'll lay out some clothes for you to wear so you don't have to put your smelly clubbing clothes back on."

"Thank you," Ryder said after an awkward pause.

"Okay, then. I'll just…um…" I headed for the door, but Ryder stepped in front of me, blocking my path.

"Thank you for last night, and this morning."

"This morning?" I asked.

"Technically, both your acts of kindness occurred this morning." When it was obvious I wasn't following, Ryder said, "Picking me up at the club was one, and getting out of bed before I could do something I would regret was the other."

"Oh," I replied, sounding like I'd had the wind knocked out of me. Ryder's words had packed a punch, and it dawned on me just how much work lay ahead. I was resolved that someday he wouldn't use my name and the word regret in the same sentence. "You're welcome."

Ryder stepped aside, and I exited the bathroom in search of clothes for both of us to wear. It was only when I heard the bathroom door shut behind me that I realized I was holding my breath. Why? Was I waiting for him to call me back and tell me he'd changed his mind about us only being professional allies? It wouldn't be that easy, nor should it be.

I quickly dressed in a pair of sweats and a comfortable tee then left similar items for Ryder to wear on the bed. I'd ordered the food, retrieved my laptop, and read halfway through a scathing email Banks had sent regarding the length of my investigation by the time Ryder appeared in the sitting area of the suite. I had to bite my lip from saying something stupid like "I love seeing you in my clothes."

Ryder looked at my shirt, and his eyes widened in surprise. "You're wearing my shirt," he said in a voice that was half accusatory and half awe. "It was my favorite shirt."

I looked down at the faded "Versailles" in navy blue print on the light blue cotton. "I bought it for you during one of our weekend trips."

"I thought I'd left it behind in Cairo, but you stole it." Somehow he almost sounded angrier than when he thought I was an art thief. "Take it off right now. I want it back."

"Come and get it then," I said, prepared to fight to the finish. This shirt was the one thing I refused to leave behind because it had belonged to Ryder. I could remember every time he wore it, and the way his scent clung to it for weeks after I took it with me. I would admit to no one the tears I shed when I was forced to wash the shirt.

"You think I won't?" Ryder asked, advancing.

"I think you're mad about something else and blaming it on the fact I reclaimed the shirt I bought for you in France."

"Reclaimed?" he asked scathingly. "Is that the same as 'recovering' priceless artifacts?"

"There you go with those cute air quotes, Ry. I don't know when you started using them, but I find it irresistible."

"How can anyone think air quotes are cute? They're supposed to be condescending. You have problems."

"I have ninety-nine problems, but your use of air quotes isn't one of them. You're making it very difficult for me to behave, so stop distracting me."

"Me?"

"Yes, you," I said. "What were we discussing before you flaunted your air quotes at me?" I tipped my head to the side like I was rewinding our conversation in my brain. "Oh yes. You mentioned priceless arti-facts. You and I both know there's no such thing as priceless when it comes to material things. There's always a value placed on art."

"What did you mean when you said I was mad about something else?"

"You're pissed off because you want me even though you can't trust me. You're angry because I was the one you turned to last night when you were hammered, and you—"

"How'd you even know where I was?" he asked, cutting me off. "Where the hell is my phone?"

"It's on the spare charger in the bedroom. I don't think you want to read your text messages though."

Ryder didn't listen to me. He stomped into the bedroom rather than coming at me to get his shirt back. I stroked the soft, worn cotton like I was petting a cat.

"Fuck!" Ah, he'd read his texts. "Pretty sure I want to die now." Most of his messages to me where random gibberish but an occasional word managed to form through his drunken tapping. I saw the words tie, baby, and get me. It was enough for me to treat it like the Bat Signal.

"No," I said, "that will come when you see your social media accounts."

"God no." I heard Ryder groaning for a few seconds as he looked through his accounts. He finally returned to stand in the doorway, looking ashen and ashamed. I couldn't help it. I rose to my feet and crossed the room to stand in front of Ryder. "That's how you found me. I'd detailed my night at Vibe with my stupid hashtags."

"Stupid is a relative term," I said gently, caressing his cheek. When Ryder didn't flinch or pull away, I got a little bolder and stroked my thumb over his full bottom lip. He sucked in a sharp breath and held it for a few seconds before taking a step backward, breaking our contact.

"Stupid is the kissing cousin to dumbass," Ryder said, trying to dig up a smile.

"You're neither stupid nor a dumbass. You've been dealt one too many blows and decided to release some steam. It makes you human, Ry."

"I told you not to call me that."

"Get over it."

Ryder opened his mouth to argue, but a knock on the door saved me.

"Ah, saved by room service," I said, crossing to the door. I opened it without looking through the peephole, which was a big mistake. "Fuck me."

"My my my," Percy said, peering over his sunglasses. "I do love the way you greet your company. Sorry, honey," he said with a flourish then shoved past me. "I'm a one-man man now. Dev and I decided it's best if we don't sh—" Percy's words suddenly died when he caught sight of Ryder leaning in the doorway to the bedroom. Ryder appraised him in return, wearing a crooked grin on his face. Who could blame him? Percy wore purple velvet jeans with a matching jacket over a frilly ivory shirt. He'd paired his ensemble with high-heeled black leather ankle boots, giving him a few extra inches of height. "Share," Percy finally said, finishing his sentence. "Who, pray tell, are you, darling? Wait!" he nearly shouted when Ryder started to answer him. "This must be thee Ryder Jameson."

"Percy, did you buy that outfit from Prince's estate?" I asked him.

"Maybe he stole it from the Rock and Roll Hall of Fame," Ryder suggested.

Percy snorted then said, "Oh no, honey. Do I look like the kind of guy who can blend in anywhere?"

"Good point," Ryder conceded.

"Speaking of points," I said, "would you like to get to the reason for your visit? It's not like you to drop by without calling first?"

"I did call," Percy told me. "Several times in fact, and I'm not the only one."

"Banks?" I'd left my phone turned off in the bedroom. There was no one I wanted to talk to other than Ryder.

"He's on a warpath, babycakes. You might want to check in with him sooner rather than later. Especially before he finds out this one," Percy said, pointing to Ryder, "is back in the picture."

"I'm not back in the picture," Ryder said firmly to Percy before turning to face me. "Who is Banks?"

"He's part of the explanation I owe you. I thought we'd do that over breakfast," I replied.

"Oh! This sounds so much better than what Deverish has planned." Percy moved toward the sofa like he planned to join us.

"Hell no," I said, halting him. "This is a conversation for two."

"Damn it. Dev is planning to watch another boring documentary, and my ass is a bit sore from trying to distract him from his newfound love of learning how things are made."

"He's never heard of the term too much information, has he?" Ryder asked me.

"Nope," I said to Ryder, "but he is lovable." I looked at Percy. "Thank you for the heads-up. I'll take it from here."

He sighed heavily. "If you insist."

"I'm afraid I must."

Percy looked at Ryder once more then said, "I can see why you can't let this one go, Lucky. I wish you all the best." Percy's exit was as flamboyant as his entrance, and I loved every second of it.

"Lucky?" Ryder asked, pulling my attention to him.

"Please don't call me that," I said. "I loathe the nickname."

"Then don't call me Ry or love."

"Fine."

"I'm really looking forward to your 'explanation' now," Ryder said.

"The next time you use those air quotes, I'm going to—" *Knock. Knock.*

This time, I checked to make sure it was breakfast and not another uninvited guest.

Chapter Fifteen

Ryder

"**W**HAT ARE YOU GOING TO DO THE NEXT TIME I USE AIR quotes?" I asked once Lucien accepted the cart from the hotel employee and we were alone once again. His gravelly tone of voice said Lucky had something sexy in mind. Lucky, huh? It suited him whether he liked it or not.

"Use them and find out," Lucien flippantly replied as he placed our breakfast on the small dining table in the suite. His devil-may-care smile dared me to find out. I wanted to really bad, but I wouldn't. Not yet.

I stopped lying to myself that I could resist him around the time I deliberately watched him jacking off in the shower. If he stayed in town long enough, I would find myself back in his bed. The only unknown factor was if I'd feel happy or remorseful afterward. The answer to my question would be found in his *explanation.*

"You just mentally did air quotes," Lucien accused. "I can see it on your face."

"It doesn't count."

"Yes, it does," Lucien countered, lifting a silver dome off one of the plates. "Here's your burnt-to-a-crisp bacon and cooked-to-death eggs, which is exactly how I ordered it. I hope they're to your liking." He recovered the plate then slid it over to me.

I was slightly concerned he was telling the truth, and the meal he described didn't sound remotely appetizing. "What did you get? So-chewy-it's-barely-warmed-through bacon with a just-give-it-to-me-raw eggs?"

"I'd love to give it to you raw, *love*, but you only want us to be professional."

"You won that point, *Lucky*, but don't think you'll win them all." I opened my dome and found my breakfast perfectly cooked. "You remembered my love for English muffins."

"I did, although I'm highly doubtful they're half as good as the ones you find in Europe." *Elitist snob.* "I remembered the orange marmalade too," Lucien said, pointing to the crystal jar on the tray. "One never forgets the fine details when it matters."

"And I matter to you?" I asked. My voice was free of anger and derision for once. I sounded...hopeful and uncertain.

"You matter more to me than any person in the world. You may never believe me, but I will not regret the time I had with you. I can only hope you'll feel the same way about me someday."

Fuck. That sounded awfully close to goodbye. I realized there was a part of me that always knew I'd cross paths with Lucien again someday because never seeing his face wasn't a viable option. I just wasn't sure how to act on those feelings without opening myself up to more heartache. I took a sip of coffee to wash down the lump of sadness lodged in my throat. "I'm ready for answers."

"I'm ready to give them to you."

"Start at the beginning," I instructed, smearing marmalade on one half of my English muffin.

"You're steering this ship. You ask the questions, and I'll answer them to the best of my ability."

"Meaning there will be some you refuse to answer?" I tried not to gag when Lucien cut into his egg and yolk oozed all over his plate.

"There will be some I *can't* answer because my life isn't the one at stake."

"Oh," I said, unsure of how to process that. "Let's start there. I assume you didn't willingly become the Robin Hood of the art world."

Lucien snorted and nearly shot his orange juice out his nose. "I'm not Robin Hood, Ryder. My actions aren't noble. And yes, I didn't willingly enter this line of work."

"You were recruited?"

"Unwillingly, yes."

"Is your tenure some type of punishment?" I asked.

Lucien pursed his lips, and I suspected he was trying to think of how he could answer the question without giving away too much. "You could say that."

"Would *you* say it?" I set the knife down and focused my attention on him. "Tell me what you can about how you were forced into this… career."

"*Career*," Lucien repeated, looking like he was deciding if he liked the way it tasted on his tongue. "I guess you could say it has been a lucrative career, even if it wasn't my choice."

"You're well-compensated then?" Damn, the bacon was cooked to perfection—crisp without being burnt.

"I am, not that I ever have time off to spend my money," Lucien said sheepishly. "I've seen some beautiful places and met some remarkable people." The intensity of his gaze made me flush. "I want out, Ryder. I'm tired of traveling. I miss my family. I don't want to spend the rest of my life alone. I feel like I'm sixty-five instead of thirty-five."

I hated that Lucien sounded so lonely, but the thought of him growing old with someone other than me ignited the slumbering green monster within. I took a bite of bacon, hoping to appease the beast so I didn't make a fool of myself like I was prone to do around this man.

"Anyway, here's what I can tell you about my background. Another lifetime ago, I was once a British SAS officer who fell in love with another SAS officer. I was out to my family, but he wasn't out to his. We got careless, and photographs were taken and used to ensure my cooperation." The green monster stirred again. How much had Lucien loved this man? It must've been a lot.

"Why you and not him?" I asked, setting my fork down. I knew I wouldn't be able to eat another bite until I learned more.

Lucien set his fork down also and wiped his mouth with the linen napkin. "Banks knew there was no way he could force this man to work for him, but he could threaten to out the man to keep me under his thumb. He knew I'd do everything I could to protect his reputation."

"The guy was at risk of losing his family?" I asked. "How selfish was this guy that he thought it was okay for you to sacrifice your life to protect his secret? I don't get it. Did you love him that much?"

"At the time, I did love him very much. Later, I realized what I had actually felt was lust and infatuation. I know the difference now between love and lust." The tender look in his eyes made me want to cry, scream, and fuck things up. "He is someone I respect, and ruining his life would never be okay with me."

"Ruining his life? That sounds so extreme."

"Ry, in some cultures, they execute gay men. You must know this."

"I do, but you said he was a British officer, and they…"

"He was born in the UK, but his family wasn't." Lucien looked out the window, looking lost in thought, but I knew his mind was working overtime wondering how much he should or could tell me.

"Lucien," I said, pulling his attention back to me. "You have no reason to believe me, but I'm going to say this anyway. What you tell me will not leave this room, and I'd never use this information to hurt you or anyone else you *care* about."

A wry smile crept across his face. "I love it when you get jealous."

"Shut up." I forked fluffy scrambled eggs into my mouth while Lucien thought things over.

"He is a blood relative of a foreign leader who would rather see him dead than lie with another man. He could be a king someday, Ry. I cannot be the person who destroys that for him." Sensing we were on surer ground, Lucien took a bite of his limp bacon.

"Do you mean in the Middle East?" It was obvious he wasn't talking about Queen Elizabeth's throne. I didn't think they were launching anyone off the tops of buildings in European nations for being gay.

"Yes, and it's all I'm able to say," Lucien said.

"I'm okay with not knowing more about the guy," I assured him then groaned at his knowing expression. "I'm *not* jealous."

"You are, and it gives me new life."

"You know what you can do with your—" My hands froze in the air when I realized what I had been about to do. "Never mind."

"It's only a matter of time," Lucien said smugly.

Ignoring him, I said, "Okay, this Banks guy used the images to blackmail you to work for him, right?" Lucien nodded. "He's clearly an unsavory type, so how can you trust he's telling the truth about these supposed stolen artifacts? How do you know he isn't the one with forged documents?"

"It's a very valid question, and I'll show you the evidence after we finish eating."

I had to admit, the part of me that cherished the *Indiana Jones* movies and played Where in the World is Carmen Sandiego games until my eye crossed was intrigued to know more. Every time I thought of a question, two more popped into my head.

"Hey," Lucien said softly. "This isn't one of those games where you have limited time to complete your tasks. If you think of a question tomorrow, then you'll ask it."

"What about next week?"

"Then you'll ask it."

"And next month?" I asked. Lucien opened his mouth to answer, but I held up my hand. There was no way in hell he could guarantee he'd answer my questions at some distant spot in the future. If he had that kind of freedom, he wouldn't have disappeared without a trace in Paris or Cairo. "Let's focus on today." I stamped down a wave of desperation to focus my energy.

I forced myself to finish my breakfast even though I'd lost my appetite after realizing nothing had really changed between Lucien and myself, except I learned he hadn't chosen this life.

"Come take a look at this," Lucien said, rising from his chair.

I followed him over to the sofa and sat beside him. A laptop and a thick file were on the coffee table, and I watched in awe as Lucien opened the laptop and placed his thumb over a glass window next to the mousepad. I could see the soft green light glowing as the scanner came to life. On the laptop screen, a rendering of Lucien's thumbprint showed up seconds before it beeped and displayed a message: Good afternoon, Lucky.

"Banks monitors our computers, so I need this to look like I'm accessing the normal case file. Banks knows I'm investigating potential leaks in the latest case. I need to be careful about accessing additional files unless I can come up with an excuse that ties them together."

"Me," I said. "I'm your common denominator."

"That's the last thing I want Banks to find out, love." Lucien was so busy typing he hadn't noticed he'd called me love. I wanted the slip to mean the endearment came from a deep place inside him incapable of lies and subterfuge, but I was still afraid to believe. Then I realized the rest of what he said.

"What do you mean?"

Lucien's face morphed into his how-much-do-I-tell-him expression again.

"If it pertains to me personally, then I need to know."

Lucien stopped typing and looked at me. "Banks found out I'd

100

fallen in love with you in Paris and sent me away before I could complete the recovery mission."

"How'd he find out?" I asked, fighting the urge to touch him. I saw the truth in Lucien's eyes. He had loved me every bit as much as I loved him. Love, not loved. The feelings were still there between us just as strong as the first day we met.

"I must've tipped him off somehow. Maybe he heard it in my voice when I reported back to him, or he noticed a pattern in delayed responses to his emails."

"You mean like when we went on our weekend getaways?"

"Precisely."

"Lucien, if he tracks your computer then he surely tracks your expenses. I assume he provided you with a means of paying for your trips."

"Every job comes complete with ID and credit cards in the name of my alias."

"Wow," I said, then bit my lip because I hadn't meant for it to slip out.

"I don't have a spending limit. I buy or do whatever it takes to convince my contact I am who I say I am," Lucien told me, and that's where my awe stopped. "What?" he asked after seeing the wonder fade from my face.

"Is sleeping with your 'contacts' something you often do?" I asked, unable to keep the bitterness from my voice.

"Damn, love, it didn't take you long," Lucien said huskily, and I realized we weren't on the same page at all. I was fuming mad while he was licking his lips.

"What the hell are you talking about?" I demanded.

"You did the air quotes. I am aware it isn't the right time to claim my prize, but I won't forget about it either."

Ignoring him, I asked again, "Is sleeping with your contacts something you often do?"

"Before I met you, I had sexual relationships with two others.

They were brief affairs initiated by them which I didn't turn down."

"When in Rome…"

"Indeed. You were different, Ryder. *I* pursued *you* because I want-ed you. Yes, at first, I wanted you to slake my lust, but then I real-ized there would be no quenching my thirst when it came to you. I only craved more and more of you," Lucien said. "I want you to know something, and I feel like this is very important."

"Okay."

"Banks never paid for any of our trips. I used *my* funds, not his. There was no way he could track my expenses to know where I was going."

"How did you pay with cards in a name other than Sebastian Deveraux?" I asked.

"Think back. Did you ever see me make purchases with a credit card or did I pay with cash? Didn't I always find something for you to look at or do while I checked us into our hotels or bed and breakfasts?"

He had always paid with cash, and I was never with him when he checked us in or out. He'd found logical things to distract me from the fact he was using a credit card with Lucien Clarke on it instead of Sebastian Deveraux.

"I've never had an intimate relationship with another contact since you. I won't pretend I've gone without sex during our entire separation, but we both know you can't say it either. I've never come close to finding anyone who's made me feel a fraction of what you do. I think it's also true for you."

It was pathetic just how badly I wanted to believe him. I wished I could say he was wrong about me and my feelings for him, but why waste the energy with a lie he could easily see through? I needed to focus on the glaringly obvious truth Lucien overlooked. "Lucien, I'm sure there are sides to you I don't know well, but I don't see a former SAS soldier acting like a lovesick sap during his phone conversations or in his emails. I bet you didn't leave a notebook sitting around that was covered in hearts with LC + RJ written in the center of them."

Lucien tipped his head slightly to acknowledge my point. "Which means one thing."

"Two, actually," I countered. "Someone on the inside fed Banks information, or he employs spies you're not aware of to track you."

"Either is a possibility," Lucien admitted. "Both of them infuriate me."

"If it's an inside guy, who could it be? Percy or that guy Dev?"

"No," Lucien said firmly.

"Do you want it to be true or do you know it's true."

"Neither Deverish nor Percy worked for Banks when I met you in Paris. Besides, I trust them, which is why they know about you."

I wanted to hit on that and find out exactly what he'd told them about me, but there would be time for me to ask later. "This Banks guy doesn't seem the type to relinquish his hold and let his men go easily, so who on the team has been around long enough to cause you trouble then and now?"

"There are several," Lucien admitted. "I need to discuss this with Dev. He will have a clearer picture than I since I'm too close to the situation."

"I'm a situation now, huh?" I asked, trying to lighten the mood.

"You're the best part about this situation, and as far as I know, Banks isn't aware you're in Cincinnati. You're not listed as a director on their website, or else he wouldn't have sent me. He'd expected me to be over my infatuation with you by the time he sent me to Cairo. It didn't take him long to realize his mistake." Lucien looked away suddenly to pull up two photos side by side on the screen. "I want to show you how we knew the provenance for the fanyi ritual wine vessel was fake." We were back to the job once more.

I watched as Lucien highlighted several sections on the two documents. There were too many glaring discrepancies for me to doubt his claim. For additional proof, he pulled up a copy of the true owner's driver's license issued by the state of California and compared his signature there to the one on the supposed selling agreement. It was a close forgery, but there was no denying someone stole the fanyi vessel from Dennis Wong and forged his name on the selling agreement.

"The new owners loan the pieces to the museums without realizing they're fake. The original owners hire your company to steal them back?"

"I assume so, but I don't ask a lot of questions. I validate the provenance was falsified, and the item was indeed stolen, then I recover the artifact, hand it over to my transportation guy, and I get out."

"Where do the insurers come in? Is it possible the insurers hire Banks to recover the property? The recovered items would become theirs once they pay the claim, right? I would think the insurer retains the item unless their client returns their money."

"That's very logical," Lucien said. "Insurers would have the kind of money to hire Banks."

"Anyone who can pay a quarter of a million dollars for a painting should be able to afford Banks too," I countered.

"True."

"Have we scratched the surface on the deception, or do we now have more questions?" I asked.

"We?"

"You're not investigating this without me. My name in on the line here too." I was going to say more, but my cell phone rang. I looked at the display and saw it was Ezra. "Oh damn. I should've called him already." I recalled a horrifying memory from the night before and groaned.

"What?"

"I screwed up and used your real name in front of Ezra, didn't I?"

"Yes," Lucien said.

"Oh no. What do we do now?"

"You answer the phone so he'll stop worrying, then I'll have to kill him and make it look like an accident." Lucien laughed when my eyes nearly bugged out of my head. "I don't kill people, love. Answer the phone."

"Hey, Ezra," I said into the phone. "I'm sorry I haven't called yet. I slept late."

Ezra laughed. "I imagine so. You sound great. How do you feel?"

"Good as new." It wasn't exactly true, but I wasn't going to whine about my headache. I'd brought it on myself. "Um, listen, about last night…"

"Hey, shouldn't you be using that speech on the guy who picked you up from the club?" Ezra asked.

"I might have posted some silly photos on my social media account that could make our mothers believe we're a couple. I deleted them as soon as I woke up, but I'm worried the damage is already done."

"Yep, it is," Ezra confirmed. "We'll weather it out together. Don't worry."

"They've sent out save-the-date announcements, haven't they? Oh man, I think it would be safer to marry you than—" A rumbling growl from my left cut me off. I turned to look at Lucien and was immediately absorbed by dark eyes gleaming with possessiveness.

"Ry, are you there?" I heard Ezra ask. "It sounds like you're about to be devoured by a wolf."

"Uh huh. Devoured." I couldn't fucking wait.

Lucien lifted my left hand and took my first two fingers into his mouth wetting them; then he shoved his sweatpants down his legs. I knew exactly what he wanted me to do with two of my air-quote fingers.

"Gotta go, Ez. Call you later."

Chapter Sixteen

Lucien

RYDER DISCONNECTED THE CALL AND TOSSED HIS PHONE TO THE side. The hunger lighting his blue eyes made me even bolder, and with his fingers still in my mouth, I quickly moved to straddle his thighs.

"Oh God," Ryder groaned, working the two digits in and out of my mouth getting them even wetter. "I've been thinking of this ever since I woke up with your dick in my hand."

I tightened my hold on his wrist. If I'd known he was awake… Our morning would've started completely differently. I pulled Ryder's fingers out of my mouth and moved his hand between my spread thighs, past my balls, and over my taint until his fingers grazed my pucker. "You can take it from here, right?" I whipped my—his—shirt over my head and tossed it to the floor next to my sweats.

Ryder responded by circling his wet fingers around the crinkled rim. "Oh, I think I can." He pressed the middle finger on his right hand harder against my pucker, teasing me. I lowered my hips, slowly impaling myself on his finger.

"Easy, Lucky." I discovered I liked the nickname when Ryder said it in his husky voice. "What plans do you have for the other half of my air-quote fingers?" Ryder lifted his hand and inserted the other two fingers in my mouth, wetting them also. "This?" he asked, circling one nipple then the other. "Or this?" Ryder traced a wet path down my chest and stomach until he reached the base of my cock.

I grunted with pleasure when he curled his wet fingers around my cock, teasing the rigid length. Ryder leaned forward and sucked a nipple into his mouth, lightly grazing it with his teeth.

"Love," I said, sliding my hands inside his hair. "I need…" I needed so much I couldn't formulate a single response.

"Lube if we're going to do this right," Ryder suggested, looking into my eyes. "I want to do this right. Do you?"

"More than anything."

Rather than jump off his lap and drag him to my room, I cupped his face in both hands and kissed him. I knew the moment was too important to fuck up. It was also too soon to hope that Ryder had forgiven me completely, but we'd taken a giant leap in the right direction. While I didn't see the same open adoration in his eyes as I did in Paris, he no longer looked at me like I was something squishy he stepped in and needed to scrape off the bottom of his shoe.

I packed as much emotion into our kiss as I could—the joy of reconnecting, relief everything was finally out in the open, and hope it was the beginning of something new and beautiful. Ryder matched my languid pace, seemingly unhurried by the passion pulsing through our bodies, and satisfied with only his finger inside me.

Ryder broke our kiss and leaned his forehead against mine. "Why don't we move this to your bed because it's where we both want to be."

"Are you sure, Ry? We can wait."

Ryder placed a soft kiss beneath my ear then licked a trail to my pulse point where he could feel how desperate I was for him. I meant what I said; I would wait for him. He chuckled against my neck then hummed happily in the back of his throat. I was putty in his hands, and he knew it. I tilted my head back, exposing my neck further to his hungry lips and tongue. Ryder rewarded my surrender by licking over to my Adam's apple then sucking it into his mouth. The gentle nip of his teeth came next before he continued licking and nibbling a path down to my collarbone. Then Ryder licked a straight path up the other side of my neck until he reached my ear and bit it sharply, making me hiss.

"We won't be able to concentrate on clearing our names unless we get *this* out of our systems," Ryder whispered.

"Is that what we're doing? Working off some sexual tension so we can get back to work?"

"What else could it be?" Ryder teased, pulling back and smiling at me.

"You started it with your groping hands," I countered.

"I was horrified at first," Ryder admitted. "But I got over it pretty quickly, especially since I could tell by your breathing you were awake."

"Who the hell could sleep through that?" Then more seriously, I said, "There will never be a day where I don't want you, but I need to be sure this is what you want. I can't have you get angry at me in a day or two and throw this in my face. I'm trying to do the right thing here."

"I'm a man who knows what he wants, Lucien. Right now, I want to touch, kiss, lick, and fuck you like I should've been doing all these years. If it's not what you want—"

I slammed my lips against his, cutting off what was surely going to be the silliest thing he'd ever said. My kiss was hungry, possessive, and left no doubt about who or what I wanted. I didn't let up until I heard the familiar little whimpers in Ryder's throat. I slid off his lap and extended my hand to him.

We kissed between removing Ryder's clothes until we were both fully naked. Perhaps I should've been worried about making out and touching each other in front of the window, but by that point, I was daring the world to take its best shot.

Ryder walked me backward to the bedroom, our mouths still fused and our tongues still teasing. Once we reached the bed, we resumed a similar position to the one on the sofa, except Ryder sat on his knees in the center of the bed amidst the tangled sheets. It was so much hotter when we were both naked. I cupped Ryder's head with both hands while he gripped my ass cheeks and held me tightly against him.

"I've missed you so much," I whispered against his lips. "I'm." *Kiss.* "Never." *Kiss.* "Letting." *Kiss.* "You." *Kiss.* "Go." *Kiss.* "Again."

"You didn't let me go, Lucien," Ryder said softly. "You left me."

"It won't happen again," I promised.

"See that it doesn't."

"I missed your smell," I whispered against his throat. *Kiss.*

"I missed your dragon," Ryder said, his mouth hovering over the head of my tattoo. *Kiss.*

"I missed the way you whimper in the back of your throat when you need me." I chuckled when Ryder answered with the sound I cherished. "Just." *Kiss.* "Like." *Kiss.* "That." *Kiss.*

"I missed the feel of you stretching me open and making me yours," Ryder said, using his powerful thighs to rise and push me to my back before kneeling between my spread thighs. "You were the first and the only man I've given my ass to, and I need you, Lucky."

"Whatever you need, love."

"I want to kiss all the other places I missed first."

We took our time touching, kissing, and exploring until every nerve ending felt frayed, and holding out became impossible. I retrieved the condoms and lube, expecting Ryder to tease me about my preparedness, but he only wore a sexy smirk when he took the condom from my hand. He wasted no time rolling it on my cock then lay back down on his back and spread his legs.

My hands shook when I tried to flip the lid open on the bottle of lube. Ryder ran his hands up and down my thighs to soothe me. I was known for my calm demeanor under intense pressure, but I was on the verge of unraveling during a crucial moment.

"Want some help?" Ryder asked, smiling smugly and taking great pleasure from my fumbling.

I flipped the lid open and held the bottle proudly in the air. "I've got it."

"Good. Stretch me open, slick your cock, and fuck me, Lucky."

I took my time massaging Ryder's pucker with a slick finger before I added more lube and slid it inside him. God, his ass was so fucking tight. "Mine." It drove me insane to know this was a part of him he'd only given to me. If I had my way, it would stay that way forever.

"Y-y-yes," Ryder moaned, arching his neck.

My cock said I needed to hurry, but my heart demanded I slow down and savor every fucking second. Ryder had always loved ass play, and I would happily finger his ass until he was pliant in my arms. He kissed me hungrily, clinging to my body while I continued to work him open by adding a second finger. Ryder gasped from the added pressure, so I slowed down to allow him time to adjust. His left thigh rubbed restlessly against mine; the friction ignited a firestorm of memories of the times I'd made love to Ryder. There was always a part of him that had to move like he either was running from the pleasure or chasing it. Was it too much or was it just beyond his grasp?

"More," Ryder demanded, his voice crackling with frantic need. He thrust his hips upward, impaling himself faster and deeper on my two fingers. I captured his mouth, parting his lips to capture the gasp bursting from him when I rotated my wrist and crooked my fingers to peg his prostate. "Mmmmm."

I lifted my head, hovering my mouth above his and staring into his pleading blue eyes. *In. Out. Twist. Peg.* "Do you want my cock?" *In. Out. Twist. Peg.*

"Yes, Lucien."

I briefly closed my eyes because my name rolled off his tongue like a silky caress I felt straight to my balls. "Say it again."

"*Lucien.*" He'd known what I meant.

I removed my fingers from Ryder's ass and pressed the head of my dick to his entrance. "Again."

"*Lucien.*"

I wanted to taste his gasp when I entered him, so I reclaimed his mouth once more then pushed past the first ring of muscles. Ryder cried out and dug his fingers in my ass cheeks. I couldn't tell if he wanted more or needed me to wait before pushing forward until he ripped his mouth from mine.

"Deeper," Ryder said, shifting his legs again.

"Say it again."

"*Lucien.*"

I pushed forward another inch deeper inside Ryder, fighting the urge to bury my dick to the hilt inside him.

"More."

"Say it."

"*Lucien.*"

Ryder sounded as desperate as I felt. Need clawed at my guts, threatening to tear me apart. I pushed deeper inside and was rewarded when Ryder arched his back beneath me. One of his hands tangled in my hair while the other slid down my back to tease the crack of my ass with his wicked fingers.

"*Lucien,*" he whispered against my ear before he bit it.

My control snapped, and I slammed forward, burying my dick as deep as it would go. Ryder laughed victoriously until I repositioned our bodies so his knees pressed against his chest.

"So deep," Ryder said. "So full."

"Again."

"*Lucien.*" This time, my name was a desperate plea I couldn't ignore.

Drops of sweat dripped from my hair and rolled down my back as I powered in and out of Ryder's tight, greedy ass. The way I claimed him was animalistic and primal, but it wasn't fucking. I made love to him; I laid claim to him.

Ryder started stroking his cock in short jerking motion as I continued pegging his prostate. *"Lucien!"* he cried as he came all over his chest, abdomen, chin, and even his lips.

I lowered his legs then leaned over him, licking the cum off his face and thrusting harder and faster. With a grunt, I flooded the condom and continued rutting against him while Ryder's spasming clench milked every last drop out of me. Ryder gripped the back of my neck and pulled my head down for a kiss, tasting himself on my mouth. Outside the bedroom, Ryder was a reserved man, but he had zero inhibitions once we were alone.

I carefully pulled out of Ryder but stayed in his arms, kissing and caressing him. Neither of us seemed eager to leave the bed and return to an uncertain reality.

"It felt different this time," Ryder whispered. He could've meant the physical act of sex, but I knew better. Different could be good, or it could be really bad; I was afraid to find out which way he leaned. Ryder chuckled because he could read my thoughts. "Paris was the excitement of new love, but it wasn't real. Cairo felt like a second chance, but it wasn't real either." I started to argue because everything we felt for each other was genuine, but Ryder stopped me with a brief kiss. "The emotions we felt for each other were authentic, but they weren't true. How could they be with so much secrecy between us, Lucien? The truth is out in the open now, even the ugly parts, and I want you more than ever. I can tell you feel the same way."

"What does it mean for us though?" I was afraid to hope.

"It means, I'm not giving you up again without a fight. I'm not saying one afternoon of confessions followed by amazing sex has solved anything, but it's a start. If we're going to fail again, it won't be because a manipulative asshole decided we didn't belong together. We're going to figure this out together, and we're going to get you out of this Banks's evil clutches."

"Evil clutches?" I asked, fighting off a laugh. "Are you picturing some faceless, cartoon villain?"

"Maybe," Ryder said with a shrug.

"I assure you he's far more dangerous," I said, rubbing my nose alongside his. "You make me believe taking him down is possible."

"Good," Ryder said. "It's time we form a game plan with this Deverish guy and Percy." He wiggled out from under me and stood up next to the bed. "We need to get cleaned up and dressed."

"Are you sure this is what you want to do on your day off?"

"Day off?" Ryder asked, slapping my ass. "I'm out of a job, remember?"

"Suspended with pay," I countered.

"That won't last long if I can't clear my name."

I rolled to my side and took his hand in mine. "Ry, this isn't a spy game or an action-adventure movie. People could get hurt, and lives get ruined. Are you sure it's something you want to get tangled in?"

Ryder scrunched up his face and took a step back, pulling free of my grip. "Don't you want me by your side? I thought—"

"Yes, I want you by my side. I also want you going into this with your eyes wide open. I have no idea what kind of dirt Banks has on Deverish and Percy, but I'm willing to bet it's every bit as salacious as mine."

"Consenting adults falling in love isn't salacious," Ryder said.

"It's salacious in the right hands," I countered. "My point is, people will go to great lengths to protect themselves or people they care about. Getting the truth won't be easy or without risk. I will not allow any more harm to come to you because of me, so if I ask you to step away from our crusade, then I want you to promise me you'll listen."

"I will listen," Ryder vowed. "I'm aware I'm out of my league here."

"I'm going to work every day to earn your trust so you'll believe I will always find a way back to you no matter what happens."

"I want to believe," Ryder said, brushing the back of his hand against my cheek.

"One day at a time."

"The first step is a strategy meeting with your partners in crime." Ryder began walking toward the bathroom. "Spit spot, Lucky," he said in a butchered British accent.

I groaned. "Love, we've talked about this. No one other than Mary Poppins says that."

Ryder's laughter echoed in the bathroom, putting the sappiest smile on my face. God, how I missed him.

Chapter Seventeen

Ryder

IT WAS A SILLY THING: SMILING LIKE A LUNATIC BECAUSE WE ARGUED OVER something as mundane as who owned the Versailles T-shirt. Lucien reminded me that possession was nine tenths of the law. At first, I was pissed when I saw him flaunting his stolen treasure, but then I realized *why* he took it. Lucien had wanted to keep a piece of me with him always. It was hard to stay pissed about it, and then I was bummed I hadn't thought of it too.

"Do you know I mourned the loss of that shirt more than I have the passing of acquaintances?" I asked him during the elevator ride up to Deverish and Percy's room.

"Blood relatives even," I added. They were blood relatives I hardly knew, but I wasn't ready to concede just yet.

Lucien grinned evilly and stroked the front of the well-worn fabric beneath his open jacket.

"First my T-shirt, then my tie. What's next? My underwear?"

"You're wearing mine now," Lucien reminded me. "Those happen to be my lucky briefs too."

I looked at him skeptically, but I was keeping them just in case it was true.

Percy was waiting for us by the door. He'd changed out of his purple suit and high-heeled boots in favor of silk pajamas. I had a feeling Percy didn't do anything in small measures, including his choice for lounging clothes.

"You're just in time, mates. We're about to order in Chinese food and find out how they make wood slat baskets," Percy said with mock-cheerfulness. He stepped aside and gestured with a flourish for us to enter.

"I love *How It's Made*," I told him. "Have you seen the one about glass faucets?"

I jerked to a stop when I reached the sitting room. I was excited to meet this Deverish guy, and I had pictured a younger version of Elton John to match Percy's colorful personality. Birds of a feather and all that. Imagine my surprise when I saw a younger version of Colin Firth instead. It was like I was looking at Mr. Darcy. Oh, how I loved watching the *Pride and Prejudice* series on DVD with my mother. We both crushed on Colin so hard. My infatuation remained a secret for several years, but Colin Firth and Jane Austen novels were things Mother and I could always agree on.

Colin—er—Deverish sat elegantly on the sofa wearing silk pajamas too, but they were a sophisticated dark teal compared to Percy's bold cheetah print.

"Oh, that sounds interesting," Deverish said, rising to his feet. The bulky cast on his leg made his movements awkward, but instead of ruining his elegant appearance, it made him appear even more charming and real. "You must be Ryder," he said extending his hand as I approached. His grip was firm but friendly.

"I am, and you must be Deverish."

"Please call me Dev," he said, gesturing for me to take a seat on the adjacent sofa while he inelegantly dropped down on the sofa cushion he'd vacated to greet me. "I feel like I know you so well already."

My face heated. Was I blushing? He wasn't really Colin Firth, even if the resemblance was uncanny. "You have a distinct advantage over me then, sir. I'm afraid Lucien has been a bit greedy with information." I leaned closer and lowered my voice, feeling Lucien's intense regard from across the room. Why hadn't he joined me on the sofa? "You'll have to tell me what he's said about me."

Dev laughed then blessed me with a charming smile. "All lovely things, I assure you."

I looked up and saw Lucien leaning against the wall with Percy by his side. Neither man looked jealous; they looked amused. Percy was probably used to people fawning all over his man, and Lucien knew damn well who I wanted. I patted the sofa for Lucien to join me. The look in his eyes shifted from humor to heat in the blink of an eye. Lucien slowly straightened then walked across the room to sit beside me. I expected him to be reserved with me in front of his friends, so I was a little surprised when he placed his hand on the back of my neck. The warmth and gravity of his touch grounded me, and I naturally leaned into it.

"What do you guys want to eat?" Percy asked while he tapped away on his phone without looking up.

"I want moo shu pork and crab rangoon," Deverish told him. "Sweet tea if they have it, or water if not."

"I know what you like, baby," Percy said then made a purring sound. "Lucky?"

"I'll take General Tso's chicken, but I prefer fried rice instead of white. Can I get two eggrolls and a Coke, also?"

"Certainly," Percy replied primly. "How about you, Ryder?"

"Beef and broccoli, white rice, two egg rolls, and I'll settle for a Coke."

"Settle?" Lucien said. "Coke is the supreme soda in the universe."

"I'm a Pepsi guy," I reminded him.

Lucien snorted. "I remember." Of course he did.

Percy entered my order then joined us in the sitting room. Dev lifted his arm and Percy tucked himself beneath it, pulling up his legs and tucking them against his chest.

Dev looked at Lucien with desperate eyes. "I need to get this cast removed and get moving again before I gain fifty pounds. Sweet tea, Lucien. Who drinks that amount of sugar in a beverage? I do now. I'll pack on the pounds from eating takeout food continuously, and I'll have no teeth from sugar rot."

"According to Percy, your cardio game is on point," Lucien responded. I lightly jabbed him in the ribs for saying such a tacky thing.

"Yes, well, I do the best I can with what I have to work with," Dev said, winking at Lucien.

"You have *plenty* to work with, dear," Percy added, smiling at his lover.

"Behave, pet," Dev said, dropping a kiss on top of Percy's head.

Percy and Deverish were a study in contrasts. Looking at them individually, you couldn't fathom these two men fitting together. Dev was tall, dark, and handsome with nearly black hair and dark eyes. Percy was much shorter, lean, and shamelessly beautiful with his blond hair styled in a modern pompadour and twinkling, mischievous blue eyes. Where one was elegant and suave, the other was bold and brash. Seeing them together, leaning into one another, they formed a beautiful work of art. Deverish was the neutral canvas allowing Percy's bold splashes of color to shine. In return, Percy could flourish without fear because he had the assurance of Dev's sturdy support. Separately, they were attractive, but together, they were stunning.

"So, Lucky," Percy said, breaking into my thoughts, "you've been in America for what? A month?"

"Give or take a few days," Lucien replied. "Why do you ask?"

"You're just looking more casual than usual," Percy said, eyes appraising Lucien's choice of clothes.

"I don't want to hear it from you," Lucien said. "The two of you are living in pajamas and bathrobes."

"We've been infected also."

"Infected?" I asked, feeling a bit insulted.

"Oh, I didn't mean to offend you," Percy rushed to say. "Casual clothes are fine, but I'm not used to seeing Lucky dressed *that* casual."

"What does his casual wear usually look like?" I asked, intrigued to know how Lucien had changed over the years.

"He dresses like he just stepped off a Ralph Lauren runway," Dev added.

"And you don't?" Percy countered. "While I admire both of your taste in quality clothing, I would prefer you wear something a little bolder. Our pal Lucky has gone too far in the opposite direction."

"Really?" I asked, turning to look at Lucien. "Polo shirts and khaki pants? What happened to T-shirts and jeans?"

"He does wear jeans, but only dark denim," Percy said.

"I don't wear fussy stuff all the time," Lucien told them. "Normally when I run into you guys, I'm playing a part. This," he said, gesturing to his—my—shirt and sweatpants, "is what I wear when I'm not on a mission."

"So, you've given up the hunt then?" Deverish asked.

"No," Lucien replied quickly. "I just don't see the need for business casual wear when I'm working from my hotel. I don my Inspector Somersby suits when I need to."

"I can't believe people fell for the phony title and fake mustache."

"Not all of us fell for it," I told Dev. "I did admire the size of his balls for walking into my parents' home wearing the pitiful disguise."

"You like my balls." Lucien stated.

"This conversation is going sideways," Dev said while Percy rubbed his hands together in glee.

"Right," Lucien said, pulling his mind off his balls and back to the conversation. "About the case, Ryder pointed out something I'd overlooked."

"Do tell," Percy said, sitting up straighter and lowering his feet to the ground.

"I think there's more going on behind the scenes than we know about," Lucien said, then recalled that portion of our conversation for them. "How in the hell did Banks even know about Ryder and me? I used my money to pay for our trips, dinners, and gifts. I never missed a check-in or failed to provide him with updates."

"Something he heard in your voice, maybe?" Percy asked.

"No," Dev said with a faraway look in his eyes. "Lucky's too well-trained to make a rookie mistake like that."

"I'd like to think so," Lucien said. "I never spoke to Banks when Ryder was near, so he couldn't have overheard anything in the background either."

"He probably hacked the camera in your laptop so he could keep tabs on you every time you had it open."

"That's fucking creepy," Dev said, with an exaggerated shiver. "It sounds like something the bastard would do though."

"Yes, but I never had my laptop out either when Ryder visited my hotel, and I kept it locked in the safe in my hotel room when we took trips."

"You had it open today," I whispered, feeling sick to my stomach. If Percy were right, Banks, or whomever was spying on Lucien, would know we had reconnected.

Lucien lowered his hand from my neck to my thigh, squeezing it to reassure me. "Percy was just teasing or throwing ideas out there."

"I wasn't joking," Percy said softly. "Sure, you mostly see those forms of stalking in television shows or movies, but the technology is real. Any decent hacker could do it."

"Fuck," Lucien said, rising to his feet. So much for allaying my fears. "Why would he do it?"

Percy and Deverish looked at each other for a few seconds before facing us once more.

"We've been talking about your situation too," Percy said, looking at Deverish for encouragement. Dev nodded for him to continue. "I may not possess the stealthy skills that you two do, but what I have is my own superpower." Deverish chuckled beside him. "Not that,"

Percy admonished and rolled his eyes. "I see people."

"Are they alive or dead?" Lucien wanted to know.

"Ha ha ha," Percy said dryly. "I mean, I can read people, a crowd, or a situation. I'm better at it when I'm face-to-face, but I can get a feel for someone over the phone once I'm familiar with their tells."

"Tells?" I asked.

"Peculiarities or quirks," he clarified. "We *all* have them. In a crowded room, I can look at someone's body language and tell it doesn't jive with what they're saying or how they're saying it. For example, someone may speak loudly and seem gregarious until you notice their stiff posture or a tick of some kind like fidgety hands or licking their lips repeatedly. People don't take me seriously because I'm fabulous and flamboyant. People erroneously believe with me, what they see is what they get."

I realized just how wrong they were. Percy had layers and depth. His brash clothing choices could be part of his personality, part of his cover, or both. "I can see how people might make false assumptions about you based on outward appearances alone. Since they don't see you as a threat of any kind; they let their guard down around you."

"Indeed," Percy said. "Total strangers say the most personal things both directly to me and around me."

"It's true," Dev said, wearing a smirk. "You appear harmless and friendly."

"I am those things, Dev," Percy corrected, "but I also have a keen grasp on what's going on around me." When Dev snorted, Percy elbowed him. "Okay, so I misread you on occasion, and it caused us a lot of grief. I was afraid to believe in us, and I messed up." Percy looked at Lucien. "I didn't have sex with him."

"Huh?" I asked then looked at Lucien. Him who? Dev thought Percy and Lucien had sex?

"Him who?" Lucien asked, echoing my thoughts.

"Don't try to protect him, Lucky. I know Dev told you about the supposed cheating incident."

121

"I found you sleeping in bed with another man." Oddly, Dev didn't sound accusatory; he sounded amused. "It was a natural assumption, pet."

"Sleeping is the keyword, Dev."

I looked at Lucien for answers, but he was too busy watching the show Dev and Percy were putting on to notice.

"I traveled for twenty-four hours straight so I could get home in time for your birthday. I had these big plans to take off my clothes and slip in the bed beside you and wake you up with soft kisses I would trail—"

"We get the point," Lucien said. "I want to hear the rest of the story. I admit I didn't expect the two of you to make up. I told Banks your freak accident was probably caused by Percy pushing you down a flight of stairs."

"Stairs?" Dev asked him, sounding insulted. "You thought I clumsily fell down a flight of stairs? Is that what Banks told you?"

"Banks referred to it as a freak accident," Lucien said. "When I pressed him further, he wouldn't provide additional information. He turned the conversation to the job. After the failed recovery, I learned Percy was here also and made the comment about him pushing you down the stairs. I was only joking," Lucien said to Percy, who winked at him.

"I have thought about it a time or two," Percy said.

"Wait a minute," I said loudly. "One damn story at a time. We started with Percy telling us about his superpowers, but before he could finish, Dev went off on a tangent about a supposed affair, and now we're changing directions again to talk about Dev's accident."

"Fine," Percy said. "From the top, but don't be mad at me if I drop some bombs then make you wait to learn more because it would be 'changing directions.' As I was saying, I'm really good at—" He didn't get to finish his sentence because Lucien and I leaned into each other, laughing over his usage of air quotes. "What's so funny?" Percy demanded to know.

"It's the air quotes," I said, wiping moisture from my eyes. "It's just a thing between us."

"Kids, can we focus?" Percy asked, clapping his hands. "Our dinner should be here any minute, and I don't want to ruin it with a discussion about unsavory characters. Ryder wants the details given in order, so let's give them to him."

"Okay," Lucien and I said.

"I've talked to Banks enough times to know something is different in the way he speaks about Lucky and how he micromanages him. Dev and I were talking about it after you left the other day, Lucky. I—"

Dev cleared his throat.

"*We* think Banks is obsessed with you," Percy said. "It's no accident you work for him, and it's no accident he's tried to keep you away from Ryder. He knows Dev and I are a couple and doesn't care."

"Really?" Lucien asked. "You didn't get the spiel about relationships destroying your focus?"

"He only said he didn't care as long as I kept my head in the game," Dev said.

Percy grinned slyly and said, "Your head is *always* in the game, darling."

"Maybe I misunderstood what Banks was surprised about when we talked about the two of you working together. I had no business mentioning it anyway."

"It's okay, Lucky," Dev assured him. "I trust you."

"*We* trust you," Percy corrected. "While we let the new information settle, let's clear the air about my supposed 'affair.'"

"Do you want to jump him too?" I whispered when Percy used air quotes again.

"No, love."

Percy waved us off and continued. "Dev, I can't believe you didn't set Lucky straight once you learned the whole story."

Dev brushed away a nonexistent piece of something on his pajama bottoms before looking up and smiling wickedly. "Lucky already had a low opinion of you, dear. I thought it would be worse if he learned I'd found you in bed with your cousin."

"Kinky," Lucien said.

"Quite," Dev agreed.

"Shut up, the both of you," Percy said, turning pleading eyes on me. "We weren't naked. We were simply sharing a bed like we've done since we were babies. Our mothers delivered us three days apart. I've bathed and slept with Quinton more times than I can count." Beside me, Lucien started to laugh. "I haven't seen him naked since we were small children. Anyway, I was pouting because Dev was out of town and going to miss my birthday. Quinton took me out to celebrate, we both got drunk, and tumbled into bed with our clothes on. Dev came home early to surprise me and jumps to all kinds of conclusions."

"So, what happened?" I asked.

"I snuck out without waking them and took another assignment right away so I could lick my wounds in private."

"I just happened to be his partner for the next recovery mission," Lucien added. "We had to pose as a married couple, which we managed to pull off."

Deverish threw his head back and laughed. "We were supposed to be a suave, sophisticated couple, but I was still so mad at Percy and kept picking fights with Lucky."

"One lady said it was nice to see same-sex couples had the same troubles as straight couples did," Lucky added. "We used it to our advantage and staged bickering to distract those around us. I didn't know they had patched things up until I stopped by to see Dev after the botched recovery and Percy answered the door."

"I was furious with Dev for thinking so little of me and doubting my feelings for him. He tried to speak to me about what happened once he'd had time to calm down and think about what he really saw, but I was too busy being petty to listen. Let's just say Dev's hit and run accident opened our eyes," Percy said, caressing Dev's cheek. "I could've lost you."

"You didn't," Dev said, capturing Percy's hand and kissing his palm.

"Hit and run?" Lucien asked in a grave tone.

"My freak accident was no accident, Lucky."

"Fuck," Lucien said. "Someone tried to take you out, but we're not sure if it was to kill you or take you out of the game. I happen to be the only recovery specialist available to fill in on short notice. Carmen Sandiego appears without warning and steals the fanyi vessel but without her usual tactics."

"Don't forget Ryder is here," Percy said. "Why would Banks send you here if he wanted to keep the two of you apart? It goes against my theory, and I know I'm not wrong about his infatuation."

"A test?" I asked.

"I don't think Banks knows Ryder is here," Lucien said, then stated why he'd formed the opinion. Yeah, it hurt like hell when my name was deliberately left off the website, and when the museum didn't welcome me to the team with an article in the arts and leisure section like they usually did. Had it not been for the silly article about my mother in the society section, Lucien might not have discovered I worked for the museum either.

"Well, one thing is clear," Dev said. "As smart as the four of us are, we won't find these answers sitting around this hotel room."

"We need someone with tech skills," Percy said. "I know a guy we can trust."

"Whom?" Deverish asked, sounding suspicious.

"Quinton."

"Your kissing cousin," Lucien teased.

"Do you remember the incident where an anonymous hacking group created all kinds of chaos by releasing proof of parliament members' fraudulent activities?" Percy asked.

"That was Quinton?" Lucien asked.

"And his friends. There's nothing more he'd like to do than take down Banks."

"I know this isn't really any of my business, but why are you still allowing a sadistic asshole like Banks to control you when you have a resource like Quinton to help get you free of him?" I asked Percy. It made no sense until I saw the way Percy looked at Deverish.

"I wanted Dev more than I wanted my freedom. Now I want both."

"We'll have it, pet," Dev whispered huskily to his lover.

I shifted my attention to Lucky. "What about you? Have you tried to free yourself?"

"Of course," Lucien scoffed. "Do you think someone as powerful as Banks makes it easy?"

"He's trying to tell you he has limited computer skills," Dev mock-whispered.

"It's not a secret," Lucien admitted with a wry grin. "I don't have a simple yes or no answer for you, Ry. I was resentful when I first started working for Banks, but then I became addicted to the adrenaline. I got all the excitement of secret missions without the death and destruction I saw as an officer." Lucien reached over and gently touched my face. "After hurting you in Paris, I went to a really dark place. I wouldn't allow myself to believe I deserved a better life. Then we reconnected in Cairo, and it fueled my desire to be free. I didn't believe I'd ever have a chance to make things right with you, but it made me fighting mad. I tried digging up dirt and following the money trail to find a smoking gun, but all I ever found were roadblocks. This line of work doesn't exactly breed trust," Lucien said, looking at Dev and Percy. They nodded in agreement. "There was no way to know how high his connections went in the government or who was on his payroll. I recently threw caution to the wind and reached out to an old family connection who I thought might be able to help me. He said he has a contact who might be able to get the information I need. I'm hoping to hear something soon."

"Fair enough," I said. A brief knock on the door startled me.

"It's just dinner," Lucien said, rising to his feet. "I'll get it."

"Do you mind calling Quinton after we eat?" Dev asked Percy.

"Sure, but Q doesn't always answer his calls, and he's shitty at returning messages promptly if he's tied up on a job."

"It's worth a shot, pet."

Lucien returned with heavy sacks of food. We all eyed one another's choices and joked about ordering the wrong thing until Percy retrieved paper plates from the cabinet and set up the takeout buffet style on the coffee table. We gorged ourselves until we were nearly sick, but I didn't regret it. I hadn't felt this alive since the last time Lucien appeared in my life.

As Percy predicted, Quinton didn't answer his phone, and he hadn't returned Percy's message by the time we were ready to leave.

"Don't worry," Percy said when he walked us to the door. "I'll allow him some leeway since there's a five-hour time difference. I'll call Q's mum if he hasn't returned my call by tomorrow afternoon. He might ignore the rest of the world, but he never ignores his mother. Have a good night," Percy said, air-kissing us both before closing the door.

When we got back to our hotel, there was a large bouquet of red roses on the table next to a bottle of Laphroaig, Lucien's favorite whisky.

"What the fuck?" Lucien asked.

"Banks?"

"Not in a million years," Lucien said confidently, striding to the table. He picked up the card nestled in the bed of roses. "This has Carmen written all over it."

"The art thief sends you flowers and expensive whisky?"

"Only when she wants my attention."

"Well, she has mine," I told him.

Lucien opened the card and read: "Uncle Vernon sends his regards. You and I might play for different sides, but that doesn't mean I want to see you hurt. There's a place called Sal's in Little Havana on Calle Ocho. They make the best ropa vieja and Cuban sandwiches outside of Cuba. If you see Renaldo, tell him I sent you."

"Who is Uncle Vernon?" I asked.

"He's the family friend who's trying to help me dig up dirt on Banks. I've called him my uncle as long as I can remember even if we're not related by blood."

"What are we going to do?" I asked.

"We're going to pack our bags and fly to Miami."

Chapter Eighteen

Lucien

I WAS USED TO PACKING MY STUFF AND LEAVING IN A HURRY, SO IT TOOK me less than ten minutes to pack a carry-on bag before we drove to Ryder's apartment. He, on the other hand, wasn't used to speedy exits and paced between his closet, bathroom, and dresser, looking indecisive.

I lay in the center of his bed watching the show, too amused to be annoyed with the delay.

"What's the temperature in Miami right now? Should I pack T-shirts and shorts? Do I need a hat and sunglasses for a disguise?"

"Love, we're not going on a safari nor are we robbing a bank. We need to blend in by looking like the other tourists. You can pack them, and we'll see what we end up needing. I have no idea how long we'll be gone. Pack for a few days, and we can buy more clothes if we need them. Same goes for any toiletries you forget," I said, eyeing his leather shaving bag stuffed to the brim with stuff. "Just so you know, I'll be perfectly happy if you don't shave. I love it when your scruffy beard rasps against my inner thighs."

That got his attention, and Ryder stopped what he was doing to rub his chin and jaw. His blue eyes looked smoky as he gauged how many days it would take to reach optimal scruffiness. "It's not as if my employer can bitch about me growing a beard."

"No, they can't."

"I'm going to grow a beard," Ryder said, taking his shaving bag back into the bedroom. "Have you booked our plane tickets yet?" It was the fifth time he asked in the past thirty minutes.

"Not yet," I said patiently.

Ryder came to the bathroom door and stared at me with a confused expression on his face. "What are you waiting for?"

"For you to at least pack one outfit in your carry-on bag. Items are lying around it, but not in it. I can't tell if you're having a hard time making a decision on what to pack or you're panicking about going?"

Ryder relaxed and leaned in the doorway. "Let me tell you a secret about me."

I tucked my hands beneath my head to get comfortable. "Go on."

"I'm used to structure and methodical planning." He released a long sigh of relief. "There, I said it."

"You don't say," I replied wryly. "I never would have guessed it about you."

"It requires great patience and a knack for tedious details to restore paintings and artifacts. I can't just go into my lab with a power washer to blast off decades of dirt, debris, and grime."

"How does that relate to packing on the fly?"

"It doesn't explicitly apply to the situation we find ourselves in right now; I'm just explaining how rushing through things, even packing, goes against my nature. I take great care in all things."

"I've known you to take excellent care of things in a hurry when the situation required it," I said, stroking my hand over my groin. "I seem to recall us sneaking away from our guided tour of Versailles." I placed my two fingers against my temple and scrunched up my face

130

like I struggled to remember the specific details. "It's coming to me in spurts." Ryder snorted. "I'm seeing velvet curtains and two men. One is on his knees with the other man's dick in his mouth."

"I don't think I've ever come so hard in my life," Ryder said huskily. "You should feel terrible about 'coming in spurts' all over the polished floor."

"I don't feel an ounce of guilt about it, but you're going to regret whipping out those air quotes again."

"I am?"

"You might if it causes us further delay. I saw the excitement in your eyes when I announced we're going on an adventure."

Ryder grinned. "I love Miami, and some might consider it an adventure, but it's not quite the same as repelling down into an unexplored cave to search for a pirate's hidden treasure."

"Maybe Miami is only the first stop on our journey. Carmen does nothing in small measures."

"You mean we could go to this Sal's place on Calle Oche and ask for Renaldo, and he'll give us our next clue after we tell him Carmen sent us?" He looked so excited by the prospect; I almost hoped it happened like that.

"Bring your passport along just in case."

It turned out the lure of adventure was the key to getting Ryder to focus on packing for our trip. He stopped wondering what he should pack and stuffed reasonable and comfortable clothing in his carry-on bag. When he retrieved his shaving kit from the bathroom, I could tell the bag was much lighter.

"You did pack deodorant, right?"

Ryder nodded as he dropped the kit in his bag. "Toothbrush, toothpaste, deodorant, lube, and condoms."

"We're all set then."

The first available flight to Miami wasn't until noon the following day, which allowed us to get a good night of sleep. I insisted Ryder inform his parents and sister of his plans so they wouldn't report him missing. He texted Iris then called his mother as soon as we cleared security and made it sound like a spur-of-the-moment trip with friends. He skirted her attempts to get more information out of him, by announcing they were calling our flight. We still had an hour to go before we boarded the plane, but it was as good of an evasive tactic as any other.

"How'd your mother take it?" I asked when he hung up.

"She sounded excited and happy for me. She probably thinks Ezra and I are flying to Miami to elope. I bet she called Simone as soon as we hung up."

"Are you deliberately trying to rile me up before our flight?" I asked.

"Not this time," Ryder replied flippantly, reading an incoming text message. "Airport bathrooms aren't sanitary enough for the type of problem-solving we prefer."

"True."

"Iris is wishing me a safe trip and reminded me to pack protection."

"Did you remember sunblock?" I asked, quirking a brow when Ryder gave me an incredulous look.

"Of course, but it isn't the kind of protection she meant. You already know I have us covered there." His phone chimed again, and a huge grin spread across his face. "I was right. Ezra said his mother was heartbroken to learn he wasn't making the trip too."

"The sooner you tell your mother that you and Ezra will never be a thing, the better it will be for everyone."

Ryder quirked a brow. "Better for everyone or your green monster?"

"Ry, do you think it's fair for your mum to get her hopes up about your relationship with Ezra? Is it fair to Ezra when he gets a phone call or text from his mum after every conversation you have with yours? Let's not forget about Simone; she thinks she's going to land you for a son-in-law."

"You're right. I've behaved selfishly and without regard for any-one else's feelings, but I don't believe for a second that you're concerned about my mother, Simone, or Ezra."

"I *am* worried about what your mother thinks. I hope someday you will reintroduce me to Celeste as someone important to you."

Ryder's eyes widened. "You do?"

"I do. I hope its sooner rather than later, but I'm willing to wait until I've earned the privilege."

"Are you also hoping to introduce me to your family in the same way?" Ryder asked softly, hopefully.

"I am."

"Oh."

"Doesn't this please you, love?"

Ryder slid his fingers between mine and squeezed. "It makes me very happy, Lucien. I guess it's still hard for me to visualize the kind of future with you that allows us to live freely and openly. There are so many things we have to figure out. I don't even know the first thing about your family."

"I'll tell you whatever you want to know about my family." My phone rang, and I groaned when I saw Banks was calling me. I held it up for Ryder to see and he acknowledged it with a nod. He tried to ease his hand from mine, but I held it tighter. I needed the connection. I accepted the call and said, "Banks."

"Is there something you'd like to tell me, Lucky?" Banks asked.

"I don't have anything concrete to tell you," I said. I purchased the plane tickets with a personal credit card. If Banks was monitoring my personal bank accounts and credit cards, he'd know it. I needed to bait Banks into revealing something I could use—either proof there's a mole in the group or I have someone trailing my every move. "I'm tracking down a lead right now." I refused to consider the bomb Percy dropped the previous day.

"Where?"

"Does it matter?" I asked.

"It does if I'm paying for it."

"Have you seen any travel expenses coming through on my Somersby accounts that indicate I'm traveling?"

"No."

"There's your answer then."

"You're telling me you're still in Cincinnati?" Banks asked. I could hear the hardness in his voice. He knew damn well I was on the move but couldn't admit it without showing me his hand.

"Technically, I'm in Covington, Kentucky, but I won't be here much longer." As if an answer from above, our boarding call came over the speakers. "Got to go, Banks. I'll be in touch soon."

"Luc—"

I hung up before he could finish and pocketed my phone. "He must be monitoring my credit cards."

"We'll use mine from here on out," Ryder said. "If he doesn't suspect we're together then he won't bother trying to hack into my records." He held up my hand when I scowled at the idea of him funding our trip. "I have plenty of money to fall back on. I've been saving it for an adventure of a lifetime, and here we go."

"To Miami," I reminded him.

"A wise man once said it might only be the first stop on our journey."

"True," I conceded. "They're boarding the premium seats now. That's us."

We stood up and walked to the gate to board the plane. Once we stowed our bags and sat in our seats, the flight attendant took our drink orders.

"At least the Jack Daniel's will make the Coke less painful to drink," Ryder told me.

"You could've chosen water or something else," I said.

"Nope. I'm going to need alcohol to get through this flight," he said, closing his eyes and breathing deeply.

"You don't like to fly?" I never knew that about him.

"I like to fly okay, but I prefer to sit in the back of the plane."

"Why? Your legs are much too long for you to sit comfortably back there." I noticed the death grip he had on his armrest and knew he wasn't yanking my leg.

"Have you ever heard of planes backing into things?" Ryder whispered.

"No."

"See," he said, "it's safer to sit back there."

"Here's your drink, sir," the flight attendant said.

"Oh good," Ryder said, sounding relieved. "Thank you." He accepted the cup and took a long drink. "Let's find an in-flight movie to watch. Something with an adventure to distract me." I just sipped my screwdriver and smiled as Ryder looked through the options. I adored learning these new facets about his personality. "Here we go. Action, adventure, *and* romance."

I looked over and saw he'd chosen *Romancing the Stone* with Kathleen Turner and Michael Douglas. "I haven't seen this movie in years. It's one of my mum's favorites."

"Mine too," Ryder said excitedly. "She used to practically swoon over Jack T. Colton. We both wanted to be Joan Wilder." He took another drink and laughed. "This movie made me want to write romance novels."

"Really?" I asked. "What did Celeste say about it?"

"She thought I should find something with a more reliable income. She told me very few authors reached the level of success that afforded them the opportunity to write books full time."

"Love, please tell me you have a closet full of steamy novels you've written but never published."

"I'll never tell."

"Yes, you will," I countered. "You can read the stories to me naked in bed."

Our conversation was tabled so we could watch the flight

attendants instruct us on what to do in case of an emergency. Well, I watched Ryder studying her intently while chewing on his bottom lip until I couldn't stand the abuse any longer. I gripped his chin between my thumb and forefinger, turning his face toward me. Ryder released his bottom lip, and I kissed him briefly.

"I'm quite fond of your lips, so stop abusing them."

"Okay," he said softly.

Takeoff went smoothly, and Ryder started playing our movie as soon as we leveled off. I expected *Romancing the Stone* to seem cheesy through the eyes of an adult like it did with most movies I had liked when I was younger, but I still found it as witty and charming as ever.

"That Jack sure is something," Ryder said appreciatively.

"He's okay."

"Are you jealous of a fictional character?"

"Don't be silly," I said unconvincingly.

"I wouldn't choose him over you." Ryder slid his fingers through mine. "You're all the adventure I need."

I kissed him again. How could I not?

The weather was sunny and seventy-five degrees when we landed in Miami, which was a far cry different from the rainy, cold weather we left behind in Cincinnati. The benefit of packing light meant getting out of the airport faster instead of waiting for checked baggage.

"Is it wrong if I hope our clue-finding mission takes a few days?" Ryder asked. "This weather is incredible. The water temperature stays in the seventies during winter months. I'd love to spend a day on the beach with you."

"We can make this trip whatever we want it to be. Carmen didn't say I had to be at Sal's on a certain day or a certain time. Let's check into our hotel and decide what we want to do."

"Lucien, her note implied you're in danger. Dev told you his freak accident wasn't an accident, although he didn't state how he knew it. Your safety is more important to me than anything. Let's find Sal's so we know exactly what we're facing. We'll come back to Miami someday when we don't have Banks's threats looming over us."

As if he heard his name mentioned from half a world away, Banks sent me a text. *Don't forget your place, Lucky.*

I tilted my phone so Ryder could read the message. "You're exactly where you belong," he told me.

I stopped in the middle of the airport, cupped his neck, and pulled him toward me for a kiss. "With you," I said.

"With me," Ryder agreed.

We picked up a sleek, silver Jaguar F-Type convertible before heading to the Four Seasons Hotel. I'd made both the reservation for the car and the hotel under my real name, which unfortunately meant Banks would know where we were staying. I would deal with the fall-out later.

Our suite was toward the top of the high-rise hotel and offered the most stunning views of the Atlantic Ocean. "It's hard to think about work and missions when faced with something so beautiful, isn't it?" I asked.

"I was just thinking the same thing," Ryder said huskily. I turned and saw he was looking at me, not the stunning ocean on display. "Do you think our adventure can wait just a little longer?"

"Adventure is a relative word, love. I'm more than happy to get into mischief with you right here and now."

Ryder pulled his shirt over his head and tossed it to the floor. "Let the exploration begin."

Chapter Nineteen

Ryder

AFTER WASHING OFF THE TRAVEL GRIME, WE TOOK OUR TIME EX-ploring each other. I'd worshiped Lucien's body many times, but I was still learning new things about him. The latest lesson was discovering how sensitive he was behind his knees when I began my journey of kisses at his ankle and worked my way up toward his delectable ass. Lucien twitched slightly when my lips skimmed over the crease behind his knee.

"Hmm," I hummed against his flesh, making him squirm. "Here?" I licked across the crease and enjoyed the clench of Lucien's ass cheeks as he tried and failed not to react. I discovered a light touch tickled and a firmer one made him moan in pleasure. I filed the knowledge away for future use and continued my journey to the promise land.

Lucien learned my armpits were a previously unchartered erogenous zone when he ran his tongue across them. Unlike him, I didn't try to hide my reaction; I gripped his hair and kept him there. Lucien growled and mastered me as no one else could.

The biggest turn-on for me was the way we spoke to each other and continued to kiss while making love. It was about so much more than fitting my body inside his or vice versa.

"It's like coming home," Lucien said when he entered me. "Warm, welcoming, and fits me perfectly."

I was on the verge of telling him I loved him, that I had never stopped loving him, but the words froze in my throat. My mouth hung open and I gasped. Lucien could've mistaken it as a sigh of pleasure, but he must've seen the truth in my eyes.

"I know, love."

We left the Four Seasons ninety minutes later, both of us sporting new love bites beneath our clothing and wearing sated smiles.

"I could get used to this," Lucien said, shifting gears on the powerful sports car.

"The city, the sun, or the snazzy car?"

"I like all those things, but I was referring to traveling and experiencing things with you."

"Charmer," I teased.

Lucien glanced over at me, and I allowed him to see the sappy smile he put on my face. No more games. "It's the truth."

"I've been to Miami many times, but I feel like I'm seeing it for the first time. How did I overlook the beautiful contrast of pastel art deco buildings mixed in with sleek, high-rise hotels and businesses? It reminds me of Deverish and Percy. Shouldn't work but somehow does."

Lucien threw his head back and laughed. "Your analogy is pure perfection, love. I've never met two men with less in common than Dev and Percy. I've known Dev for several years now and didn't realize something was missing until Percy arrived and clicked into place like a wayward puzzle piece. It was like Dev looked at Percy and said, 'Ah, there you are. I've been looking everywhere for you.' Then he panicked."

"He wouldn't be the first, and he definitely won't be the last."

"I envied them," Lucien said after a few seconds passed. "They didn't have to make up excuses of where they were going or why they couldn't turn up on time for an event. They understood the job. No secrets. No subterfuge. I thought it made things easier for them, but Banks breeds a culture of mistrust, and if something seems too good to be true, then it most likely is. It's no surprise Dev jumped to the wrong conclusions about Percy, but at least they worked things out."

"Do you ever wonder what Banks has on them?"

"All the fucking time," Lucien said as he made a right turn.

"What do you think they did before coming to work for Banks? I bet Percy was a card shark, and he got busted for counting cards."

Lucien nodded. "I like it. I bet he has one hell of a rainy-day fund."

"And Dev? He's as urbane and polished as you. I already know you were an SAS officer, but what about him?"

Lucien smiled then began humming the theme song to James Bond.

"No way," I said. "Really?"

"I wouldn't be surprised," Lucien said. "Close your mouth, love, or you'll be eating bugs for a pre-dinner snack."

I laughed instead of reminding him the windshield protected me from bugs. "You sound jealous again."

"You should've seen the look on your face when you met him. Are you a Colin Firth fan?"

"I am," I admitted. "You're still my favorite 'recovery specialist,' Lucky."

"Do I spy air quotes from the corner of my eyes?"

"Maybe."

"This time, I'm going to wet two of your fingers and slip them in your ass while I blow you. You can use the other two fingers to tease your nipples."

"God."

"No, love, this is all my idea." Lucien parked the car and killed the engine. "Sal's is down the road on the left."

"Is it wrong for me to hope Renaldo isn't available?"

"Even if he is, I have a special night planned for the two of us."

"You do?" I asked. "When did you have time to make plans?"

"I reserved a table at Edge Steak & Bar at the Four Seasons when I booked our room. The rest I thought of during our flight."

"I have some surprises of my own," I said.

"I can't wait. Let's check in at Sal's first."

The very air around us pulsed with life and activity. Street musicians entertained the tourists and couples who danced to the lively rhythm. Beneath the shade of palm trees, older gentlemen played dominoes while appearing to hold deep conversations. From the open doorway of restaurants, mouth-watering aromas and more music spilled out onto the sidewalks.

"This is going to be an eating holiday," I told Lucien. "I want one of everything."

"Sounds good to me."

Sal's was a café located in a row of stucco buildings; each one painted a different pastel color. Sal's was pale yellow with robin's-egg blue trim. Judging by the long line, it was a popular place to eat.

"Shall we," Lucien asked, gesturing to the back of the line. "Our dinner reservation isn't until seven thirty so we might as well get a bite to eat. It feels like a million years ago since we ate the chicken pecan salad sandwiches on the plane."

"I'm famished," I agreed.

"It's the sunshine and lively atmosphere," said a short woman at the back of the line. She was barely over five feet tall and wore a large straw hat and oversized sunglasses to protect her eyes and face from the vibrant sun. "A combination that puts me in the mood to eat every time."

"I'm always in the mood to eat," said the man holding her hand. He was only a few inches taller than the woman. He wore a snazzy white Panama hat with a black band above the brim.

"It's true," the woman said then giggled.

"We were just saying that we're making this an eating vacation," Lucien told them.

There wasn't a trace of the accent I loved in his voice. It was all I could do not to stare at him in shock. I realized I needed to let him lead so I didn't make any wrong moves.

"We're the Watsons," she said. "I'm Desiree, and this is my husband, Dennis. We're celebrating our wedding anniversary. Are y'all in town for business or pleasure?"

"A bit of both," Lucien said. "My name is Lucien, and this is my boyfriend, Ryder." He'd decided to stick with real names, but I guess it made sense. We weren't there to steal—er—recover anything. Why did he hide his accent then?

Boyfriend, huh? I liked it. If the Watsons were shocked by Lucien's openness, they didn't show it.

"Where are you boys from?" Dennis asked.

Lucien placed his hand at the small of my back, which I took as a cue to field the question. It would look odd to them if Lucien did all the answering. "We're from Cincinnati," I said, deciding to stick to the truth as best I could.

"We're from Atlanta, but we've been to Cincinnati several times to watch the Braves play. Great America Ballpark is cute." Cute? Kittens are cute.

"I'm a huge Reds fan," I told them. "I do admire the Braves organization. They've mastered the art of staying competitive for decades."

"Yes, but we just can't seem to go the distance," Dennis said.

"Oh, Cincinnati fans know the frustration well."

"Is this your first trip to Miami?" Desiree asked.

"It's not, but this is our first trip to Miami together," Lucien said. "So, it feels like the first time in many ways."

"We come a lot," Dennis told us. "Would you like some recommendations for great places to eat? The best restaurants don't show up in those online articles."

"Sounds great," I told them, pulling out my phone to make notes. I heard Lucien chuckling beside me, but he'd appreciate my thoroughness later.

"We're in line to eat at our favorite place, but Versailles is a close runner up," Dennis said.

"Versailles, huh?" Lucien asked, winking at me.

"Oh, yes," Desiree said. "I know most of the world associates Versailles with France, but in this part of the world, we think of an amazing restaurant in Miami that offers Cuban cuisine."

"Sounds amazing," I said. "I think we should try it."

"They only serve lunch and dinner," Dennis told us. "For breakfast, you need to eat at Little Heaven Café. Oh my goodness. Thick ham, fried eggs, and a plate of delicious fruits."

"Papaya," Desiree added.

They spoke so fast I had a hard time keeping up with them, but they kept us entertained while we waited to get inside Sal's to ask for Renaldo. I was so hungry after talking to them, I practically drooled on my phone while taking notes. Noting Dennis's nice hat and traditional guayabera shirt, I pulled him off to the side to get some other recommendations for the plans I'd made for Lucien and myself.

"It was lovely meeting you," Desiree said when we reached the counter.

"Likewise," I said. "Happy anniversary."

"Thank you, honey."

When it was our turn to order, Lucien wasted no time asking if Renaldo was in. The young lady working behind the counter looked like she'd worked five hours over her scheduled break time. Her crooked name tag read Dulcie, and her expression told us she thought we were idiot tourists. "Renaldo won't be in until five o'clock tomorrow night. And no, I don't know where you can find him." It sounded like Renaldo was quite a popular guy. Who the fuck was Carmen hooking us up with?

"Okay, thank you for your help," Lucien said calmly.

"We'll take two orders of the ropa vieja and two Cuban sandwiches to go," I told the lady. To Lucien, I said, "There is no way I'm leaving here without food after standing in line for forty-five minutes." I handed my credit card to Dulcie. "The smells are incredible, and I've heard that no one beats your food."

"Damn straight," she said. "Do you want drinks too?"

I smiled evilly when I saw the beverages available. "We'll take large Pepsis."

"You got it." Dulcie added the drinks, swiped my card, then returned it to me with a slip for me to sign. "You pick up your food at the other end of the counter. Have a great day."

"You too," I said. "Finally, an opportunity to drink quality soda."

Lucien frowned but followed me to the end of the counter to wait for our food. "Where do you want to eat?" he asked once our order was ready. I picked up the drink carrier so he wouldn't be tempted to *accidentally* spill my precious elixir. Lucien picked up the paper bag and smirked at me. He either knew what I was thinking or knew I was using mental air quotes again.

"There's a great spot nearby called Maximo Gomez Park, but we locals call it Domino Park," a young man wearing a Leo name tag told us. "It's a great place to chill and eat your meal."

"Where is it?" Lucien asked.

We headed in the direction Leo sent us, holding hands and soaking up the sunshine. I could immediately see how the park had earned its nickname. Teams of two men dotted the park, studying the tables between them. We found an empty table in the shade and divided the food and drinks. The meal was out of this world, but we could've gotten by with a single order of both and split it. I loved the tender beef and peppers in the ropa vieja, and even though I wasn't a fan of mustard, it was the perfect complement to the pork, ham, and swiss cheese in the Cuban sandwich.

"I might order this again tomorrow when we go back to speak to

Renaldo," Lucien said, looking around the park.

"I want this to be me when I'm sixty-five," I said to Lucien, gesturing to the men playing dominoes like they didn't have a care in the world.

"I don't even know how to play dominoes. I may not offer up much of a challenge," Lucien told me.

"I don't either," I confessed. I sure liked the idea of Lucien sitting across from me thirty years in the future. "I bet we could get some of these nice gentlemen to teach us."

For the next hour, José and Roberto gave us our first lesson on how to play dominoes. Unsurprisingly, Lucien caught on faster than I did because he could accept that a rule was a rule, where I wanted to know why it was a rule. Roberto got a kick out of my attention to detail, and José patiently explained things to me.

After we thanked José and Roberto for their graciousness, I googled the store Dennis told me about to check if it was in walking distance. I'd hoped so because I could use the exercise to burn off the calories from the rich food. Luckily, Diego's Fine Couture was two blocks away. Without telling Lucien what I had in mind, I told him I wanted to give him his surprise then instead of waiting.

We strolled hand in hand, noting many of the places the Watsons mentioned to us and making plans for the following day. "Here we are," I said when we reached Diego's. "There is no way in hell we're going out on the town without dressing properly."

Lucien looked at the display of fedoras and Panama hats, guayabera shirts, and linen pants in the window and grinned. "This is going to be so much fun," he said.

"Hola," a friendly man said when we entered the boutique. "I'm Diego, and this is my shop."

"Perfect," I said. "You're just the man we need to see. We want some special clothes for a night out."

"I'm the man for the job."

"I don't want him to see my outfit until tonight though," Lucien told Diego.

"Fine, but this is my treat," I insisted then looked at Diego. "We need to be outfitted from top to bottom."

Diego clapped his hands. "Rafael," he yelled loudly.

A tall, elegantly dressed man stepped through the red velvet curtains in the rear of the store. "Yes, dear?" he asked.

Diego told Rafael the situation in rapid Spanish then both men assessed us. "One of you will go with Rafe, and the other with me." I sent Lucien with Rafe because I knew he wouldn't play it safe with colors and patterns.

An hour later, I met Lucien on the sidewalk in front of the store after paying for our date clothes. He smiled happily and looked more relaxed than I'd ever seen him.

"I have an idea what we can do for the few hours we have left before our dinner reservation," Lucien said, wrapping his arm around my shoulders and steering me toward the direction where we left the Jag.

"Surprise me," I said, leaning into him.

Chapter Twenty

Lucien

WHEN WE GOT BACK TO OUR SUITE, I INSTRUCTED RYDER TO change into his swimwear. "We are going to try their swinging hammocks."

"Whoa," Ryder said when I pulled on my swimsuit. "Is that what you're wearing to the pool?"

I looked down at my navy blue swim boxers then back at him. "Is that what you're wearing?" I asked, gesturing to his nude body. "Believe me; no one will notice me standing next to you."

"They're so little and leave nothing to the imagination."

I walked over to the mirror and checked out my reflection, feeling Ryder's eyes on me the entire time. They were short and tight but modest compared to a lot of swimwear I'd seen. "What's wrong with these? Everything is covered."

"It's your entire package," Ryder said, groaning.

"My junk is tucked away safely in a mesh lining. Neither of my balls will fall out the leg holes."

Ryder was still naked as the day he was born when he joined me at the mirror. "I wasn't talking about just this," he said, cupping my cock and balls. "The entirety of *you* is a delicious package. There's something about your poise that challenges people to unravel you. Your sexy tattoos and devil-may-care grin make people think about doing very naughty things to you."

"We can't help the things people think about us though, can we?"

"No, but we don't have to put so much on display."

"Are you calling me a slut?" I asked.

"No."

"Attention whore?"

"Come on, Lucien."

"A narcissist then?"

"No, damn it. I don't like the idea of people seeing Dudley and wanting to lick him as I do."

"You named my dick Dudley? Why am I just now finding out about this?"

"I thought you said your dick was going to be covered?" Ryder asked in frustration. "I was talking about your tattoo." He traced a finger over my chest, making my nipples harden.

I looked at the dragon inked on my chest and thought he was fierce and ferocious. Ryder looked at it and thought he should be named Dudley. No self-respecting, fire-breathing dragon would choose that for a name. "Dudley?" I asked in disbelief.

"I don't know why I chose that name. It just came to me," Ryder said, sounding embarrassed. "You were supposed to be thinking about me licking the dragon and not get hung up on the name I assigned him."

Ryder's words evoked memories of him lazily licking and kissing the dragon to arouse me before sex, and afterward, he cleaned the cum he made me shoot all over my chest with his tongue.

"Now, you're remembering," Ryder said huskily. "Remember the one time you came so hard you nearly put Dudley's eye out?"

"We're not calling him that," I said firmly. Then I noticed the tiny amount of material he held in his hand. "What's in your hand? One of those little cock pocket sling thingies?"

Ryder loosened his hand and held up a turquoise blue triangle for swim trunks. "It's a Speedo."

"And how are you going to get all of that," I said, gesturing to his well-endowed genitals, "inside the tiny triangle."

"Not very easily now since you've made me recall my fondest memories with Dudley."

"Should I go down and grab us a hammock so you have time to get your dick under control and stuff it in your trunks?"

"I'll be just fine. Put on a T-shirt or something," Ryder said, sitting on the bed to slide his Speedo up his long, toned legs.

"Yes. I know just the thing." I retrieved my favorite shirt and said, "There. All ready."

Ryder looked up and noticed my Versailles shirt. His blue eyes went soft, and a sweet smile stretched across his face.

"I'm going to get a toothache just from looking at your smile," I told him. "It's not quite as fun wearing this shirt when you don't want to rip it off me."

"Lucky, I want to rip it off you but for totally different reasons."

"I don't think the reasons were that different the other day. Sure, you were pissed I took your shirt, but you were pretty damn eager to take it off to get to…."

"Dudley," Ryder said. "Among other things." He stood and tugged his Speedo up until it was in place. He reached inside his swim briefs to situate everything, and a soft whimper escaped my throat. "Later, Lucky. Let's go down to the pool."

"At least my swim trunks cover the love bite you left on my inner thigh," I told him, tracing the curve of the bruise I'd left on his hip bone. "Yours is on full display."

"It's barely showing."

"It will draw every eye right to it," I said, sounding like a pouty brat.

"Only you get to touch and taste," he said, appeasing me.

Ryder pulled on his own T-shirt, and we both put on shorts to cover our trunks for the walk through the hotel lobby. The Four Seasons' large swimming pool was separate from the shallow section of water weaving around palm trees. Tied to the trees were swinging hammocks big enough for two, but you had to wade through the water to reach them. We stripped down to our swimwear and left our discarded clothes on a lounge chair then hopped into the water and waded over to a hammock.

"This seems sexy, but I wonder if getting in it will be harder than it looks?" Ryder asked, studying it.

"Only one way to find out," I said, deciding I'd go first. I sat carefully on the edge and waited for it to stop rocking then turned my body while swinging my legs up and over. The hammock swung hard the other way and dumped me into the water with a splash. I stood up, sputtering because water had gone up my nose. "You think you can do it better?" I asked Ryder, who was doubled over laughing at me.

"After watching you? Yeah." Ryder started like me, but he swung one leg over at a time, keeping his plant foot on the bottom of the pool until he was balanced. Then he tucked his arms under his head and aimed a cocky smile at me. "Piece of cake."

I wanted to wipe the smugness from Ryder's face, so I gripped the edge of the hammock, pulled it up fast, and dumped him out on the other side.

Ryder stood up, shaking the water from his hair and glaring at me. "I'm going to get you back for that."

My eyes landed on the way Ryder's Speedo clung to his package, and I figured seeing him and not being able to touch him was punishment enough. "Do your worst, love."

The third attempt was successful. Ryder and I lay at opposite ends of the hammock so we could eye-fuck each other. I mapped out everything I was going to do to him as soon as we were alone again.

I reached for the foot closest to me and began massaging it. Ryder's eyes grew heavy-lidded, but he still reached for my foot to return the favor. I shook my head, and a knowing smile crossed his face. I expected Ryder to reach for my foot and test his theory, but he stroked my calf instead until he fell asleep. I was nearly there too but fought to stay awake so we wouldn't miss our dinner reservation.

I didn't have my watch on, but I could tell from the sun's position we only had about an hour to get up to our room, shower, change, and be at the restaurant. I wanted to crawl across the hammock and kiss him awake, but we'd both end up in the water and potentially drown Ryder in the process. I pinched his big toe then scraped my thumb along the arch of his foot until his eyelashes fluttered open and his gorgeous baby blues looked at me.

"Time to go up and get ready for dinner, love."

Ryder smiled and stretched which caused the hammock to swing. It wasn't enough to tip us over, so I leaned my body to help it along. *Splash.* Our laughter echoed off the concrete and carried on the wind by the swaying palms. *Lord, how much I missed this man.*

I pulled Ryder into my arms and kissed him soft and slow like we didn't have a care in the world. We deserved to have one night where we didn't think about Banks and the threats he held over me. We could dress up, eat, and have fun out on the town without thinking about why we were there in the first place. I kissed Ryder until he hummed happily.

"We better get going," Ryder said. "You made plans for me, and I don't want to miss them."

We showered together but mostly kept our hands to ourselves because neither of us wanted to rush the plans we'd silently made in the hammock. Ryder stayed in the bathroom to get dressed while I stayed in the bedroom. I had to admit, Rafael picked bolder colors for me than I would've chosen, but I loved the way I looked.

"Is it safe to come out?" Ryder asked from the other side of the bathroom door.

"Yep. I'm decent."

Ryder pushed open the door fast to get my attention then sauntered into the bedroom, turned like a runway model, then raked his eyes over me from head to toe. "Oh, you went with a fedora," he said, adjusting his straw Panama hat with a white band.

I ran my hand over the camel-colored brim of my hat then performed a circle for him to check me out too. "You like what you see?"

"I love it," Ryder said. "You look like you were born to wear those clothes."

Rafael had suggested a peachy-coral color, four-pocket shirt with white pineapples embroidered in the pleating down the front of the shirt. I had to admit; it looked good with my dark coloring. Ryder's shirt was made of pale blue linen and had classic, unadorned pleats. We both chose white linen pants and brown leather oxfords.

"Damn, love," I said huskily, "everyone is going to want to steal you away from me."

"I was just thinking the same about you." Ryder closed the distance and placed his hand on my pecs then slid them higher to wrap around my neck. "They can look all they want, but that's as far as it goes."

"Ready for dinner?"

"Yes. I can't believe I'm going to say this after our huge meal a few hours ago, but I'm starved."

The Edge Steak & Bar was elegant and quiet, allowing us to talk over drinks before our food arrived.

"This is going to sound odd, but I didn't think of you as having parents," Ryder said after sipping his martini.

I nearly swallowed my Scotch down the wrong pipe. "Did you think I came here from an alien planet like Superman?"

"I assumed you had parents at one time," Ryder said, then discreetly looked around to see if anyone was within hearing range. "I just figured Banks would prefer agents without familial ties. Until you mentioned your family today, I assumed your parents were no longer living or you were estranged from them. What kind of questions do your parents ask when you leave suddenly or miss holidays?"

"I've told them I work for a secret agency and leave when I'm required."

"They think you're James Bond," Ryder said, grinning slyly.

"They've never said as much, but I guess it's possible. Many SAS officers go on to work clandestine jobs. We do have unique skillsets that come in handy and make us overqualified for many careers."

"Do you ever carry a gun?" Ryder asked, sounding uncertain.

"Not in this line of work. Banks is about us recovering stolen artifacts, not eliminating targets. I did enough of that as an SAS officer, and I never want to hold a gun in my hand again if possible. The thing is, Ryder, Banks is a legitimate businessman and uses his company as a cover. To anyone looking, I'm acquiring antiquities on his behalf. My parents would have a very hard time believing I would choose that job over serving my country. So, it's not a cover I employ."

"Do you have any brothers or sisters?" Ryder asked.

"No. I'm an only child. My father is an investment banker like yours. His name is Jenson. My mother, Katherine, is a very distant cousin to the queen. Something like a twelfth cousin twice removed or some silliness. She's very active in causes and committees. She always has someone to meet and someplace to be. Celeste reminds me a lot of my mother, except she's warmer than mine."

Ryder snorted. "I bet my mother could freeze water just by looking at it. She's warmed up a lot since the gala, and she's trying hard to repair our strained relationship. I realize she needs to be needed. Mother was very involved in our lives when we were little, but once we went to college, she filled her days and nights with activities and committees to make up for our absence. My parents have never had a loving marriage, but they were at least friends once. Our absence made the strain more apparent and they turned away from one another instead of toward each other. My mother was extremely lonely, but I was too selfish to see it. She's trying to get back to the mother I worshiped. As I told her, it's not too late for us."

"I have to admit; I'm dying to meet Iris. I saw her at the gala. She looks like a magnificent force to be reckoned with."

"She is that, and speaking of Iris, I need to pick her up some good cigars while I'm down here. I'll ship them home if we don't head back right away."

"Iris smokes cigars?"

"And she drinks expensive bourbon and cusses like a sailor."

"I'm going to adore her."

"She'll feel the same about you."

"Ryder, what have you told your family about me?"

"They know nothing about you, Lucien."

"Sebastian Deveraux? Have they heard about him?"

"They don't like him much, so it's a good thing he doesn't exist. I don't know what the feds have said to Mother about Lucien Clarke, but I haven't told her Lucien and Sebastian are the same person. We can keep it that way."

"I don't want to build our lives on a lie."

"You want to build a life with me?" Ryder asked, smiling shyly.

"More than anything. That wasn't my dick doing all the talking for me the other day. I won't let you go again."

Ryder traced the rim of his cocktail glass, and I could tell he was thinking hard about something, like he wanted to ask me a question but was afraid to hear the answer. I thought I knew, so I took a stab in the dark. "After I left you in Paris, I was in terrible shape. My mother knew something was horribly wrong and wouldn't stop badgering me until I talked. I told her I'd fallen in love with someone in Paris, but it could never work out because of the line of work I was in. She looked at me and said 'Lucien Clarke, it's not like you to give up without a fight. If you really love this man, you'll find a way to make it work.' At the time, I didn't believe it was possible."

"And now?" Ryder asked softly.

"You make me believe anything is possible."

Ryder was on the verge of telling me he loved me just like he'd been earlier in the day. I didn't need the words then, and I didn't need them sitting across from him in a fancy restaurant. I saw how he felt about me.

"I know, love," I said softly.

Our waiter showed up with our dinners before either of us could say something else. "Does everything look okay? Is there anything else I can get you? Sour cream for your baked potatoes?"

"No, but thank you," Ryder and I told him.

"Okay. Enjoy your meals. I'll check back in a bit."

I ordered the ribeye and lobster tail, and Ryder ordered the filet and crab legs. We didn't do a lot of talking once we tucked into our food. I liked my steaks on the rare side while Ryder liked his cooked to death, so neither of us was keen on trying each other's steaks, but we did share our seafood.

"Glad to see you still like your steak moving," Ryder said.

"I'm not surprised you still like yours as tough as shoe leather," I countered.

After dinner, I took Ryder to Fuego. It was a multilevel, gay club offering a little bit of everything to suit everyone's needs. When we arrived, they had one hell of a drag show going on with laser lights, fog machines, queens on rope swings sailing over the crowd while dropping glitter, and barely clad go-go dancers in gilded cages.

"I want to dance with you," Ryder yelled when the show ended and the DJ cranked up the club music. "It's something we've never done together."

"How do you know I can dance?"

"You move so gracefully. There's no way in hell you can't dance."

"I have no rhythm," I told him.

"Lies!" Ryder grabbed my hand and led me onto the dance floor. He turned my body, aligning my back to his chest, then lifted my arms and looped them behind his neck. Ryder gripped my hips and started to move, guiding me to sway with him. "See, you have beautiful rhythm."

"You're doing the real work. I'm just letting you lead me."

Ryder kept one hand on my hip while slipping the other beneath my shirt to caress my stomach. My dick hardened beneath my thin linen pants, matching the hard-on pressing against my ass. Ryder trailed kisses up my neck, and I tilted my head back, granting him more access. Our hats made it harder to make out, but I wasn't going to risk losing his gift.

When the next song started, I turned in his arms and pressed my chest to his so we could dance facing one another. Ryder grinned and sang along with the music as we danced, burrowing himself deeper in my heart. *God, how I love him.*

"I know, Lucky," Ryder said, reading my emotions.

We leaned in to kiss and bumped hats, nearly knocking them off. We removed them so we could kiss and sway to the music unencumbered.

"I'm going to make things right, Ryder. I promise you."

"I know you will."

A flash of scarlet caught my attention, and I turned. "So much for tracking down Renaldo tomorrow," I told Ryder.

He turned to see who'd grabbed my attention, and his eyes widened when a tall, sexy brunette wearing a scarlet halter dress, stilettos, and a red fedora hat approached us.

"Holy fuck. Carmen Sandiego is in Miami," Ryder said, staring at her in awe.

"Close," Carmen said with a smirk. "Carmen Santiago at your service. Welcome to my town, fellas."

"Hello again, Carmen," I said, leaning forward to kiss her offered cheek.

"It's always nice to see you, Lucien. Shall we go someplace quieter to talk?" Carmen turned and walked away without a backward glance because she knew we were going to follow.

Chapter Twenty-One

Ryder

WE FOLLOWED CARMEN TO A NEARBY MERCEDES SEDAN IDLING in front of the club. Next to the passenger door stood a bald, muscular man who looked like he was carved out of a mountain. I was no expert, but I suspected he was more than her driver because he had a gun strapped to his massive body beneath the black Tom Ford suit jacket he wore.

As we approached, Mr. Mountain opened the passenger door and pointed to Lucky. "You're up front with me. Miss Santiago always sits in the back."

I tightened my grip on Lucien's hand, not wanting to be separated from him.

"I'll be fine, love. They had plenty of opportunities to make trouble for us today if that was their objective. He's just protecting Carmen. I respect that."

"Draco has no intention of hurting either of you," Carmen said then looked at me over her shoulder. "Neither do I."

Draco opened the back door for Carmen, and she gracefully slid inside the car. "Around the other side," he snarled at me.

"You're not going to open the door for me too?" I asked, earning a glare. "I get no respect." I could hear Carmen's rich laughter spilling out of the car before Draco shut her door. He stood watching me with narrow eyes as I rounded the back of the car and got in beside her. "I can't believe he didn't pat me down first," I told her.

"I like you, Ryder Jameson," she said. "I think we could be great friends."

"No," Lucien said from the front of the car. I looked away from my stunning, new bestie and met Lucien's gaze. He grinned at me. "I want to be the one to give you all the adventures you crave."

"Aww," Carmen said, covering her heart. "I'm so grateful to be part of such a touching moment."

"You *interrupted* our touching moment, and we'd like to get back to it," Lucien told her.

"I bet the two of you are stunning together," Carmen said.

"We are," I agreed. "But we don't put on shows for anyone."

"I'd never ask for something so tacky," she said, sounding affronted. "I wanted you here in Miami so I could help you."

"Which one of us?" Lucien asked.

"Both, of course," she replied.

"Why?" I asked her.

"Why not," she answered flippantly.

"Carmen, you do nothing if it doesn't benefit you," Lucien told her. "How do you know Uncle Vernon?"

"A lady never tells, Lucien" She threw her head back and laughed warmly at the scowl he aimed at her. "You are my favorite nemesis," Carmen told him. "You Brits are blunt and to the point. I like it."

"Then return the favor and get to the point," Lucien said. "Where are we going, anyway?"

"The only place in the world I trust."

Draco drove us away from the hustle and bustle until the real estate spread out a bit more and the property values escalated. He pulled into a driveway and stopped at a gate. Instead of reaching toward the box to punch in a code, I saw a blue light pop on above the camera angled toward the driveway. I looked for a barcode sticker on the windshield for it to scan but didn't see one. Within seconds, the gates opened, and Draco drove forward.

"It's a sophisticated biometric scanner," Carmen said from beside me. "It recognized Draco's face, retinas, and even his body temperature. The last one is a bit tricky for most because it changes based on outside stimuli, but Draco's changes so little that I'm starting to doubt he's human."

The big man behind the steering wheel snorted, indicating he had a sense of humor. I forgot all about him when I caught sight of the huge white mansion overlooking the sea. Exterior lights strategically placed on the grounds bathed the home in a soft blue glow.

"Not red?" I asked Carmen.

"I prefer the serenity of blue lights."

"Your home is stunning," I told her. "The ocean breeze must be amazing."

"Thank you, sweetie," Carmen said, reaching over and patting the hand I rested on the seat between us. "You'll get to see for yourself. I think our conversation calls for fresh air and a fine bottle of wine."

"I prefer Scotch," Lucien said, sounding surly.

"You can pick your poison, Lucky."

Lucien groaned. "Not you too."

"Why? The nickname suits you," Carmen told him.

"Until recently, I haven't felt very fucking lucky."

"Well, I promise tonight will change your opinion of the word forever. It's your *lucky* night, I suppose," she teased as Draco stopped in front of the house. Up close, it was taller and more imposing than I first imagined.

"Who cleans all those windows?" I asked randomly.

"Not me," Carmen said. "That will be all for the night, Draco."

"You don't want me to drive the gentlemen back to their hotel later?"

"Yes," Lucien said at the same time Carmen said, "No."

Carmen opened her door and said, "Come on, boys. We have work to do."

I got out and walked around the car to join Lucien and Carmen on the sidewalk. Lucien pulled me close for a quick kiss as if he needed to assure himself I was okay.

"The only lucky time in my life was when I met you, then I proceeded to fuck up for the next six years."

"Maybe *our* luck has started to change."

Linking our fingers together, we followed the lady in scarlet up the walkway and into the foyer of her home.

Carmen was immediately greeted by two gorgeous German shepherds who flattened their ears and growled low in their throats when they spied us. The enormous dogs bared their teeth and crept toward us.

"Halt, Günter and Hans," Carmen said, and the dogs stopped. "Sitz." Both dogs sat but didn't look happy about it. "Freunde," she said next, identifying us as friends. They stopped growling, and their ears returned to an erect position.

"You speak German?" I asked.

"I only know bits and pieces of German—mostly to command the dogs—but I am fluent in many languages."

The stunning animals whined low in their throats until Carmen nodded, then they rose and walked over to us.

"Can I pet them?" I asked her.

"You can now," she teased.

I knelt and extended my hand. One of the dogs held back while the other ventured forward. "What a magnificent beast you are," I said, scratching behind his ears.

"Hey," Lucien said. "I thought you only used that line on me."

"Sorry," I said, smiling up at him. The other dog decided he wanted his ears scratched too and closed the distance. I gave him a good rubbing too then rose to my feet. "They're gorgeous animals."

"Loyal, loving, and fierce," Carmen said. "Too bad I can't find those attributes in a man." She turned around and headed deeper into the home. "Follow me."

Lucien reached for my hand, and we quickly followed behind Carmen. I glanced around the rooms we passed through and noted the elegant white furnishings and cobalt blue accents. A huge watercolor painting of the ocean caught my eye, but it wasn't the right time to ask for a better look at it.

Carmen stepped through an open French door onto a patio. It was smaller than I expected but packed a punch. She had a rectangular infinity pool front and center and an inground hot tub off to the right. The water in both features was a dark greenish-blue color, which made me think they'd used teal-colored tiles to accomplish the effect since the underwater lighting was subdued and romantic. The view to the ocean was unrestricted because the perimeter fencing consisted of glass panels supported by metal rails on the top and bottom. How amazing would it be to float in the pool or relax in the hot tub while staring out into the ocean?

Lucien squeezed my hand to get my attention. I wasn't even aware I'd stopped and gawked at the sight before me.

"Wait until you see the sunrise," Carmen said. "Talk about heaven on earth."

"We won't be here to see the sunrise," Lucien said firmly. "If Draco won't drive us back to our hotel, then we'll walk to the gate and hire a Lyft."

"You think?" Carmen asked. She walked to the table where a cobalt blue ceramic bowl overloaded with fruit sat in the center. Carmen picked up a grape and lobbed it at the glass fence around the perimeter. The grape hit the top rail and exploded. "Think bug zapper for humans," she said. "Until I'm ready to turn off the perimeter fences, you won't make it out of here alive."

Lucien stiffened, and his hand tightened around mine. "What do you want from me, Carmen?"

"I don't want anything from you, Lucky. You're here because I like you, and I want to save your life." She pulled out a chair and gestured for us to join her. "I mean no harm to either of you. I have the solutions to both your problems, and I'm extending a guest room to you as a courtesy and sign of respect. Do you think I invite just anybody to my home?"

"I suppose not," Lucien said, softening. "I already have someone making demands and telling me what I will and will not do. I don't need another one, Carmen."

"Don't look at me," I said when she turned a raised brow to me. "You know the source of his problems."

"I do, just as I know yours."

"Up until recently, I thought Lucien was the source of my problems," I told Carmen.

She blessed us with another throaty laugh. "Keep him this time, Lucien. We're not given many chances at happiness."

"No, we're not," he agreed.

"Drinks before we begin, or do you want me to give it to you straight?"

"Straight," we both answered at the same time. Then we looked at each other and laughed.

"It's not often I request a straight version of anything," I teased.

"I like my drinks straight up sometimes," Lucien countered.

"My parents spent a lot of money on braces so I could acquire straight teeth. I'm quite partial to them," I admitted.

"I like your teeth a lot too." Lucien's gravelly voice let me know he was thinking about the marks I left on his body.

Carmen cleared her throat to gain our attention.

"Oops," Lucien said. "I forgot where I was."

"Sorry," I added.

Carmen placed her elbows on the glass tabletop and steepled her fingers. "Tomorrow morning, FBI agents Kiphart and Marshall will receive an anonymous package containing the evidence they need to arrest the person responsible for stealing the fanyi ritual wine vessel from the Cincinnati Art Museum."

"Okay, maybe I do need a drink," I told her, earning another laugh.

"Lucky wants a Scotch on the rocks, but what's your poison?"

"Vodka martini, please. Extra dirty."

Carmen purred as she rose to her feet. "I adore you."

I waited until I was alone with Lucien then asked, "What the hell is going on?"

"I don't know, but we're going to find out."

"I bet this place is wired for sound," I said, looking around like I might be able to spot a bug. I'd obviously read too many spy thrillers and watched too many movies.

"You're so fucking adorable," Lucien said, pulling me to him for a kiss. "Of course this place is wired for sound and video. You better keep your hands to yourself in our guest room unless you want us to show up as a viral video on PornHub."

"Don't insult me," Carmen said, returning to the patio without our drinks. She did have a laptop and two manila envelopes though. "Oh, you thought I was making the drinks myself? How cute. Stephan will bring them out shortly along with a cheese tray."

"We're not hungry," Lucien said, scowling at her.

"I could eat," I told Carmen, wondering where exactly I was putting all the food I'd consumed the past ten hours.

Carmen slid the envelope across the table to me. "Here you go, sweetheart. This is a copy of everything I sent to your FBI friends."

I accepted the envelope and opened it without hesitation. If she'd wanted to hurt me, she would've done so already. I pulled out a stack of documents including glossy photos of Daniel Perez having lunch with an attractive woman wearing a scarlet business suit. The woman's face wasn't showing in the photo, but I recognized her proud posture and the curly dark hair cascading down her back.

"I knew he was involved," I growled. "He was too eager to throw me under the bus. I bet he hired me solely because of my history in Paris and Cairo."

"Yes," she said softly. "I believe Perez called you his patsy."

"Son of a bitch," Lucien said angrily. He'd leaned over so he could see what I held in my hands. Anger rolled off him in waves. "What else is in the envelope?"

"A flash drive with copies of email correspondence between Perez and my alias, along with financial records showing the money leaving his account and landing in mine. The feds can trace the transaction numbers to the accounts. You're welcome to use my laptop to validate what I'm telling you, but I enclosed printouts so this conversation would go quicker."

"This is all the proof I need," I said, holding up the documents in my hand. "Perez paid you out of his personal account?" I asked incredulously. "Surely he wasn't that stupid?"

"No," Carmen said, "but I included the documentation they needed to attach Perez to the shell company who paid Lolita Dominguez to steal the vessel. Before you ask, the vessel is safe and sound in a safe-deposit box in Fifth Third Bank on Fountain Square. I've enclosed the key for them to retrieve it."

"Why are you helping me?" I asked Carmen.

"I'm not helping you so much as I'm doing my job."

"You were hired to catch Perez in the act," Lucien stated. "By whom?"

"That part isn't important. Unlike you, I'm an independent contractor. I take jobs from governments who want back what was stolen from them. I'm hired by insurance companies to recover items stolen from their clients, and therefore them, and sometimes I even consult with law enforcement agencies around the world to bust people like Daniel Perez."

"Forget telling us who hired you," I said, waving my hand in the air. Judging by the wealth surrounding us, Carmen's services were in high demand, and her jobs paid well. None of it mattered to me. "The important thing to me is how he ended up on their radar."

"Let's say I've been watching him for a long time. He didn't willingly leave the Smithsonian, Ryder. A few of their acquisitions turned out to be fakes or stolen, and although they couldn't prove he was involved, it was apparent he hadn't done his due diligence by checking provenance."

"Wow," I said, sitting back in my chair.

"Perez was a wily one, but he couldn't resist Lolita's charms." She smiled wickedly at me. "That solves your problem, sweetheart; now we need to save Lucky from Banks."

"And how do you propose we do this?" Lucky asked.

"I have an envelope for you too."

Chapter Twenty-Two

Lucien

I WASN'T AS EAGER TO OPEN MY ENVELOPE AS RYDER HAD BEEN. IT TRIG-gered a flashback to a time when Banks had dropped one just like it on the table where I'd waited to meet Hiram for lunch. We'd both been on leave at the time, so why not meet in Italy for a brief lovers' getaway?

Banks had handed me a business card when I glanced up from the envelope to meet his cold gaze. "Call me within twenty-four hours, or I release those photographs to the press." I'd risen to my feet, ready to challenge him right then and there, but his cold smile had stopped me in my place. "While those images may not cause harm to you, they'll destroy your lover and may result in his death. Call me."

Banks had walked away with his head held high because he knew he'd had me by the balls. A part of me had already known I could nev-er have a life with Hiram, but I never thought our relationship would end that way. I snatched up the envelope and immediately left the restaurant before Hiram arrived. I checked out of the hotel I'd booked and got as far away from him as I could within the time frame Banks had allowed. Hiram had called my phone dozens of times and left messages ranging from concerned to frantic to angry. I didn't know what to say to him, so I didn't say anything. I waited until the twenty-third hour before I opened the envelope. I cried when I saw the color photos of us engaging in passionate sex on a balcony or kissing in the rain on a faraway street where we didn't think anyone watching would care.

We'd been so wrong; and it changed the course of both of our lives. I never spoke with Hiram—not to say goodbye and certainly not to tell him about the photos. I allowed him to believe he'd meant nothing to me. I didn't think I could hate Banks any more than I already did until I met Ryder.

"Lucien," Ryder said softly, pulling me back to the present. "Are you okay?"

"Yeah, I just…" My words trailed off.

"Lucky," Carmen said just as softly as Ryder. "I'm not out to hurt you. The things inside the envelope can't hurt you, but they could hurt someone very special to me. I'm trusting the two of you with information that very few people know."

"Why?" I asked, coming out of the daze.

"Because you and I both want the same thing: to take down Charles Banks. My reasons are personal and extremely painful, but I can't bring him down without your help. I must warn you the information inside the envelope is devastating and disturbing. I've had to wait more than a decade to obtain the hard evidence needed to exact my revenge." A decade? I placed Carmen in her late twenties if that, meaning she'd had a vendetta against Banks since she was a teenage girl. *Oh fuck.* I felt like I was going to be sick. "I need your help, Lucky. Please."

"Okay," I said, opening the envelope. The first paper on top was DNA results, and it took me a minute to realize I was looking at a paternity test. I saw the results at the bottom of the page and jerked my head up to meet Carmen's direct gaze. "He's your…" I couldn't even form the words.

"Father," Carmen said for me.

"Whoa," Ryder whispered breathlessly. "I'm so sorry to hear that."

Carmen grinned adoringly at him. "Can I keep you?"

"No," I said firmly, "but you can have visitation rights."

"Fair enough," she said, tipping her head in acknowledgment. "There's a lot of information in the envelope, which you're welcome to look at later if you choose, but I'll give you an overview." Carmen started to say more but stopped when a guy I presumed to be Stephan stepped onto the patio with our drinks and a plate of cheese. "Ah, thank you, Stephan. Perfect timing as always."

"Anything else, miss?" Stephan asked, looking from Carmen to us. One side of his face was disfigured and scarred from burns. Half of his mouth was locked in a permanent sneer and one of his eyes had a milky white iris completely devoid of color.

"That will be all. You can turn in if you like. I can take care of anything my guests might need."

The man studied Ryder and me, and I could tell he was curious about our relationship to Carmen. Then again, maybe he just wasn't used to her having company. Stephan nodded politely to us then looked at Carmen. "Goodnight then, miss."

"Grab your drinks, fellas; you're going to need them."

"I'll drink to that," I said, holding up my Scotch in a mock toast. I took a healthy drink and welcomed the burn that followed. "Good stuff."

"Only the best," Carmen said then took a drink of wine.

Ryder just looked between us like he couldn't believe we could converse so calmly after Carmen dropped the large bomb on my lap. Me? I knew bigger hits were about to come, and I needed the alcohol to brace myself.

"Drink up, love," I said, pushing Ryder's martini toward him.

Ryder blinked a few times before he did as I suggested. Then he released a hum of pleasure and said, "Pure perfection."

Carmen smiled her approval then shifted her eyes to the stack of documents sitting on top of the envelope. "My mother was a victim of human trafficking. She was taken from her home in Cuba when she was only fourteen years old and sent to live at a special school in England."

"Carmen, I can read the documents. You don't need to put yourself through telling me."

"I want you to understand how deeply my hatred for this man runs. I need someone who understands his treachery to listen to me."

"I'm listening, Carmen," I said gently. "I'll hear whatever you want to say." Beneath the table, Ryder reached for my free hand and linked our fingers.

"My mother didn't speak or understand a word of English. Can you imagine how frightened she was?" Carmen asked.

"I bet she was terrified," Ryder said gently.

"She learned to read and speak English and took comportment classes so she could be a proper lady. While some men would like a wild and untamed beauty, they didn't bring as much money. My mother was sold to the highest bidder at an auction for the United Kingdom's wealthiest and most perverted men. Do you know who purchased my mother's services? Who raped her without regard for her virginity? Who cast her aside like garbage when her pregnant condition became known?"

"Banks?" I said in a voice so low and mean it was barely audible. With every word she spoke, I got angrier and angrier.

"Lucky and smart," Carmen quipped. "I learned the truth about him when I was an angry teenager. I'd demanded to know who my father was and acted out when my mother refused to tell me. After she'd had enough of my wild behavior, Mama told me the truth."

"And you've bided your time since then," Ryder said.

"Yes, I have. Infiltrating the human trafficking ring was the hardest thing I've ever done, but I did it. The bastards who were caught will hopefully never take another easy breath. Many of the perverts covered their trails well, but you can never fully erase your digital footprint. It's taken me another two years to find proof Banks is a child-raping, sick son of a bitch and get his DNA to prove he is my father."

"How'd you get his DNA?" I asked. "The man never eats or drinks in my presence, and he's always wearing those thin leather gloves."

"I paid his favorite whore to hand over his used condom after one of his weekly visits."

"Why aren't you taking Banks down? Why do you want me to do it?"

"It will be me who takes him down, but I thought you might like to get in on the action too. I'd include Deverish also, but he's laid up with his adorable lover for now."

"I'd love to help you," I told her. "What's your plan?"

"The two of us will travel to London and set a trap for Banks— one he won't be able to resist," Carmen said.

"Two?" Ryder asked. "What about me?"

"Love, I need you to be someplace safe so I can do whatever it takes to bring this fucker to justice. I can't do it if I'm worried about you."

"Why can't you just release the information to the authorities like you did with the fanyi and Perez?" Ryder asked, sounding panicked. "Why is there need for anyone to get hurt?"

Carmen leaned forward and covered Ryder's hand. "If you want to take on the lion, you must be willing to enter his den. I have the weapon to destroy him; I just need the bait to do it."

"Me?" I asked. "Dev and Percy are convinced Banks is obsessed with me. Are you saying you agree with them?"

"Without a shadow of a doubt. I've also included evidence to back up the theory. It's in the envelope if you wish to see for yourself."

"Just tell me," I snarled.

"Lucien," Ryder admonished softly. "I'm not happy about this either, but Carmen's giving us the opportunity to eliminate the one person preventing you from having a happy life."

"Tell me, Carmen," I said in a softer tone.

"He keeps a file for every one of his *employees*. I'm not talking about your tax withholding information or bank account details for direct deposit; I specifically mean the information he uses to wield power over you."

"You've seen the photos then?" I asked.

"I've seen the photos of your affair from a decade ago, but more importantly, I've seen the five dozen or more images he's kept of you since you started working for him. Eating, fucking, meeting with contacts, sleeping, and—"

"Fucking?" Ryder asked.

"Sleeping?" I questioned.

"Who shall I answer first?" she asked herself.

Carmen pointed to me. "You were sleeping in a lounge chair by a pool. Your eyes were closed, and your face looked relaxed in a way that indicated your brain was at rest."

"Fucking?" Ryder asked again.

"Oddly, he didn't save any photos of the two of you, sweetheart. I think he knew there was something special between you, and he couldn't handle seeing it." Carmen looked at me then and said, "I would've expected someone with your experience to know when he was being tailed."

"Fuck!" I spat out, running both hands through my hair. "These types of photos weren't in the other employees' files?"

"Not a single one. I don't know if Banks wants you for himself, has penis envy, or both, but his obsession is singular, and you are the object."

"Don't go to London," Ryder said urgently. "There has to be another way."

"There isn't, sweetheart," Carmen told him. "You can't always dial things in from far away. I promise we'll be careful."

"This isn't adding up," I said, grasping for straws.

"Because he raped my mother, he can't also be interested in men? You're assuming when I said whore, I meant a woman. It's incredibly sexist of you, Lucky. He's an equal opportunity sadist and employs both male and female prostitutes." Carmen leaned forward. "In case I haven't been clear, every single one of his male prostitutes look eerily similar to you." The urge to vomit returned.

"Why do you think Lucky's in danger?" Ryder asked her. Thank God one of us was still thinking.

"Dev's *accident* was no accident," Carmen said. "I don't have proof yet, but I can feel it in my bones. I was already in the city when it happened. I overheard police officers discussing the hit and run while I was in line to get coffee the day after. They mentioned the traffic cameras had malfunctioned on that side of the city which they found odd. They also never found the SUV that hit Dev, and it had to be one hell of a crash. Unless they were driving an armored truck, the SUV would've sustained significant damage."

"Which meant the driver had help stashing it," I said, rolling it over in my head.

"It probably left the city in the back of a semi-truck trailer," Carmen said.

"Jesus," Ryder said, sounding like he was finally at the end of his rope. "Why would Banks want to kill Dev?"

"Because he's Lucky's only friend."

I tried to deny it but couldn't. My line of work didn't allow many friendships, and it fostered paranoia instead of trust. It took everything I had to suppress the urge to doubt Carmen even with the evidence in my hand.

"Lucky, what I'm going to say next is going to be painful, but you need to know how serious this is."

"What?" I asked shakily.

"News broke right before I came to get you at the club. There was a boating accident off the coast of Maldives, and—"

"No," I said, shaking my head vigorously.

"There were no survivors, including Hiram Chandio."

"No, Carmen." I stood up from the table so fast my chair tipped over. "No." I saw the truth in her eyes, and I lost the battle to calm my riotous stomach. I walked a few feet away and vomited in the perfectly maintained flowerbed.

Ryder followed me and placed his hand between my shoulder blades. "I'm sorry, baby," he whispered, rubbing my back. I rose to my feet once I had nothing left to purge, and Ryder took me in his arms. Even his body heat couldn't thaw the chill caused by Carmen's shocking news.

"It can't be real," I told her, approaching the table. I downed the rest of my Scotch to kill the nasty taste in my mouth. The burn was ten times worse on my raw throat. "Why would Banks kill the only leverage he had over me. Why try to kill Dev and send me to Cincinnati?"

"Because of me," Ryder said, stiffening against me. "He knew I was there all along, and he wanted to hurt me. He probably meant for you to get arrested while stealing the vessel."

"Recovering it," I corrected.

"'Recovering it.' Sorry." Ryder's eyes widened when he realized he'd used air quotes, but did he remember what I said would happen next time? Even with all the shocking discoveries, I hadn't forgotten. "Later, Lucky," Ryder said, waving me off. He remembered.

My heart sped up, reminding me I was alive, and more importantly, so was Ryder. I needed to keep it that way. I had to focus on what needed to be done instead of the things I couldn't change.

"I knew from the start something was off about the Cincinnati job. Banks's demeanor made me suspicious, and I started looking for the reason why. When I saw Ryder had been hired to work at the museum, I assumed Banks didn't want me to know, or didn't know himself. He wanted me to get in and get out."

"Banks knows everything you do. If I didn't know better, I'd say he planted a tracking device in your ass."

"He never got close enough to plant one," I countered dryly.

"Yes, or there'd be plenty of photographic evidence in his Lucien Clarke spank bank."

"Come on, Carmen," I said, feeling extremely uncomfortable. "I feel like my head is about to explode."

"I'm sorry. Let's wrap this up, and we can turn in for the night and regroup in the morning." Ryder and I both nodded. "I do not have any proof Banks tried to kill Dev, set up Lucky for the fall in Cincinnati, or sunk the boat carrying Hiram and his friends, but I've studied everything I could about the man, and my gut tells me he's behind it all. He wanted to eliminate everyone you care about so you can spend the rest of your days wallowing in prison." I wanted to deny everything she said, but I couldn't when she laid the truth in front of me. "We also need to assume Banks knows you're in Miami with Ryder. Assume the worst."

"And hope for the best?" Ryder asked.

"Hoping only gets you so far, sweetheart. By assuming the worst, we plan for all contingencies, and it makes us better warriors."

"Warriors?" he asked Carmen weakly.

"We are going to war; make no mistake about it."

"I'll go with you to London on one condition," I said suddenly.

"Name it," Carmen replied.

"You keep Ryder safe while we're gone."

"Lucien, no," Ryder said.

"If everything you say is true, there's not a single person on this planet who means more to me than him, Carmen. I want your guarantee Ryder will be safe."

"You have my word, Lucky," Carmen said, reaching across the table to shake my hand. "He'll stay here, and my people will keep him safe. I already have a team in place who are keeping an eye on your parents."

"You've left no stone unturned. I'm impressed."

"I have worldwide reach just like Banks does, but my people enrich lives, not destroy them."

"You have yourself a deal, Carmen."

"Lucien," Ryder whispered.

I rose to my feet and pulled him up with me. "Where is our room?"

"Take the hallway off the right of the great room. Your bedroom is the second on the left. I'll see you both in the morning."

"Goodnight." I gripped Ryder's hand firmly in mine when he started to resist me. I turned to face him so he could see the resolution in my eyes. "You'll come with me now so we can discuss this in private. You can walk, or I can carry you. What will it be?"

Ryder swallowed hard and gestured with his free hand for me to head inside the house.

Chapter Twenty-Three

Ryder

I WASN'T OKAY WITH CARMEN AND LUCIEN'S PLANS, BUT I WAS POWERLESS to persuade them. Even thinking of robbing them of the chance to make Banks pay for his crimes felt selfish and wrong. Too many horrific things were revealed to justify delaying the inevitable longer than necessary for Carmen and Lucien to get into position and spring their trap.

Trap. Bait. Fuck! I just wanted to howl at the unfairness of it. I just got my Lucky back, and he was being ripped away from me again.

"Hey," Lucien softly said once we were alone in our guest room. "Your brain must be working overtime right now because you squeezed my fingers hard enough to dislocate a few of them."

"Damn, Lucky. I'm so sorry."

Lucien spun around and cupped my face with both hands. "Say it again."

"I'm sorry."

"Not that; use the nickname. I only like it when you say it."

"I am sorry for so many things, Lucky," I said, stepping closer so

Lucien could wrap his arms around me. I traced my fingers over his lips. "I'm sorry I punched you in the mouth and hate-fucked you. I'm sorry I didn't give you the chance to explain right away because we lost valuable time we can't ever get back. I'm so fucking sorry for the loss of your friend."

"Love, you don't have to apologize for any of those things. I deserved getting punched in the mouth, and I enjoyed the angry fuck more than words can describe. You didn't assault me." Lucien lifted his hand and stroked the back of his fingers over my cheek. "You also deserved time to consider if you were willing to trust me again after everything I put you through." He leaned forward and brushed his lips against my jaw. "You aren't responsible for what happened to Hiram. I'm not responsible for what happened to him either. In a few days, the person who is responsible for all the things you're trying to apologize for will reap what he sowed. I will be free to build a life with the man I love more than anyone in the world."

I jerked back and looked into his dark eyes. They shone with love and determination, but there was also sadness lingering in their depths.

"Too soon?" Lucien asked softly.

I shook my head. "I love you too, Lucky. I always have, and I always will. I fucking hate that we're going to be separated, but I'm going to prove how much I trust and respect you by doing what you ask. I'm going to stay safe and wait for you to return to me so we can have our fresh start."

I could see how much my words meant to him, but they weren't enough to chase away the shock and sadness. Lucien's body remained as stiff and unyielding as it was when he heard about Hiram's boating accident. I wasn't jealous; I ached for him. I wanted to ease him any way I could.

"Shower with me before we go to bed?" I asked.

"I'm not passing up a chance to get wet and naked with you," Lucien replied, but his usual lusty gaze lacked its typical vibrancy.

I didn't need sex to be intimate with Lucien, and I'd prove it to him. I took his hand and led him to the bathroom. Releasing his hand, I opened the glass shower door to turn on the faucet. The rainfall showerhead had an LED light which turned the cascading water a lovely shade of blue.

"I'm so glad there are spare toothbrushes and mouthwash in here," Lucien said from behind me. "I'm not surprised though; Carmen seems to think of everything." He unwrapped a toothbrush, squirted toothpaste on it, and began vigorously brushing his teeth.

"Maybe tomorrow she'll tell us how she knew where we were."

Lucien pulled the toothbrush from his mouth and spat. "She had people tailing us once we left Sal's."

"What? You didn't tell me?"

Lucien opened the mouthwash, tipped the bottle to pour the liquid into his mouth, and swished it around. When he bent over to spit the mouthwash in the sink, I saw the stunned expression on my face in the mirror. "I didn't want to upset you," Lucien said. "Carmen's people are good, but I spotted a few of them. I could tell they were non-hostiles and figured they belonged to her. I just didn't know what her game was."

"When?" I asked, turning to look at him. Then wished I hadn't, because Lucien had already unbuttoned his shirt. I was immediately distracted by his hot body and sexy ink.

"I suspected Desiree and Dennis at first, but figured I was paranoid." *Desiree and Dennis?* "I picked up a tail in the park when we were hanging out with José and Roberto, another one outside the clothing store, and I was pretty sure someone followed our Lyft driver when we went to Fuego."

"I never noticed and didn't realize you had."

"Years of training." Lucien got quiet. "Which is why I don't understand how I missed Banks's goons trailing me."

"Maybe Percy was right, and most of the photos came from hacking the camera in your laptop or cell phone? He could've also rigged the peephole in your hotel room door with a camera. It happened to a sports reporter. A sicko was able to predict which events she would cover, stalked her, and rigged the peephole in her door to spy on her."

"I think I remember reading about that," Lucien said, sounding like he was a million miles away. I took over undressing him the rest of the way so we could get in the shower. "The setup man working for Banks probably planted all types of devices in my room for each of my jobs." Lucien gasped when I dropped to my knees to unlace his oxfords before pulling them off.

"How would he know which room the hotel assigned you?" I asked, rising to my feet and reaching for the top button on my shirt. "You check in with the desk, right?" Lucien knocked my hands away and took over the task.

"Yeah. Even if we were stupid enough to check in using an app, we'd still have to stop by the front desk to pick up our key. Never once have I been told someone already picked it up." Lucien kissed along my collarbone as he slid the open shirt down my arms then reached for my pants next. Lucien knelt to remove my shoes as I'd done for him, then he tugged my underwear down so I was as naked as he was.

"Which means Banks's goons stick around long enough to see which room you're in, then they plant the cameras and leave."

Lucien leaned forward, pressed his nose to the trimmed curls at the base of my cock, and inhaled deeply. "Mmmmmm."

I fought the urge to grip his hair and hold him against me. Instead, I whispered, "Lucky."

Lucien rose to his feet, smiling wickedly. "The setup crew had to stick around on occasion though. How else would they catch me lounging by a pool?"

"Hack the exterior hotel security cameras?" I asked.

"It's a real possibility, and as creepy as it sounds, I prefer it over not realizing someone was tailing my every move." Lucien's expression said the option couldn't possibly apply to all the images Carmen described. "I need to know how I ever wound up on his radar in the first place."

"You'll get your chance to ask him," I pointed out, shivering hard with the realization.

"Hey," Lucien said softly. "I'm going to be okay, love."

We stepped beneath the cascade of water, and the tension faded from my body when Lucien pulled me into his arms. My brain and body were exhausted from the tsunami of information we'd received. I needed time to process and come up with the remaining answers, but it didn't have to be right then. My dick hardened and length-ened against Lucien's, proving at least part of me wasn't exhausted. Remembering my vow to choose intimacy over sex, I ignored its demand.

"Are we just going to act like we don't have hard-ons?" Lucien asked, cupping my face.

"I thought sex might not be appropriate in light of everything we learned tonight," I said. "There are many ways we can be intimate without having sex." I traced the spine of Dudley. "Draco would've been a great name for your dragon."

"Let me be clear here," Lucien said, sliding his hands down and firmly gripping my ass cheeks. "The only name you will call out during any sexual act involving our hands, mouths, and cocks will be mine. No Dudley, and definitely no Draco."

"Got it," I said, sliding my hands up into his wet hair. "Lucky."

"As for your other thought, can you tell me a better way to live in the moment than mutually gratifying orgasms?"

"No," I whispered, tilting my head back and baring my neck for his kisses.

"Can you think of a different way you want to celebrate the fact we're still alive and together?" Lucien murmured against my wet skin.

"Lucky," I pleaded. Lucien answered by sliding a wicked finger in the crease of my ass.

"Do you think I'm leaving here without you marking my flesh again?"

It was my turn to answer with actions instead of words. I sank my teeth in Lucien's pectoral muscle above Dudley's curled tongue. He grunted in pleasure, and I began to suck hard, pulling the blood to the surface of his skin. I licked to soothe him then struck again until an angry mark bloomed dark against his tan flesh.

"I want to mark you too," Lucien said, fisting his hand in my hair.

"In the bedroom," I told him. "You need room to work."

I shut off the water and Lucien grabbed two fluffy towels from the rack. We hurriedly dried ourselves off then went into the bedroom to strip the duvet and the top sheet to the end of the bed. Neither of us knew how long it would be before we were in each other's arms again, so rushing through sex was the last thing on our minds.

Lucien rolled me to my back and left a love bite on my other hip before he slowly worked my cock with his talented mouth. He worked me to the edge then pulled back, evading my grasp when I reached for him.

"You don't think I'll take what I want?" I asked, hoping he would say no.

"I'd like to see you give it your best shot."

Lucien was more muscular, stronger, and more skilled than I was, but I had a point to prove. I would not go down without a fight, I wouldn't give up just because something was a challenge, and I had no problem fighting dirty. When Lucien had me pinned to the center of the bed, I reached down and tickled the back of his knee, surprising him enough to loosen his grip on me. I rolled out from under him, twisted my body, and wrapped an arm around his lower legs, pinning his calves against my chest.

"You wouldn't," Lucien panted from the opposite end of the bed.

"I would." I began tickling his feet, tightening my hold around his legs when he bucked and tried to get away. "Say uncle."

"I don't have an uncle," Lucien said between gasps.

"What about Uncle Vernon?"

"Honorary uncles don't count," Lucien quipped. I rewarded his obstinance by digging my fingers deeper into the arch of his foot. "Uncle! Uncle! Uncle!"

I released his legs and crawled up his body until I straddled his face, my cock dripping precum on his lips. Lucien licked my salty essence while daring me with his dark eyes. I gripped the head of my dick and smeared more precum on his lips then pushed against them until he opened for me. Gripping the headboard, I slowly rocked forward until I felt the tip of my cock nudge the back of his throat. I pulled back out then rubbed the sensitive spot beneath the crown against his tongue.

Lucien dug his fingers into my ass cheeks, urging me to bury my dick in his mouth. I fought the desire to give in because I wanted to make this last. *Slow push in; slow drag back.* Lucien slapped my ass hard enough to startle me, but I didn't speed up. *Slow push in; slow drag back.* Lucien released my ass cheeks; one of his hands fondled my balls, and the other disappeared farther down his body. I glanced over my shoulder and watched him lazily stroking his dick up and down, using his precum to ease the way. I rocked my hips faster, increasing the tempo, and the hand wrapped around his cock sped up too. The wet suction around my dick and the masterful way Lucien massaged my balls made me forget about tormenting him and drawing out our pleasure. I needed to come; I wanted him to come with me.

Lucien hummed approvingly when I snapped my hips forward and began fucking his face. I could hear his hand shuffling up and down his dick as he kept pace. The vibration against my cock had me roaring and coming down his throat seconds before I felt the splash of Lucien's release on my ass and lower back.

I scooted down his body, smearing his spunk all over his lower abdomen, not giving a damn we'd most likely end up glued together. Kissing Lucien would always be my favorite way to begin and end any lovemaking session or a conversation. Once our hearts returned to their normal paces, I rose from the bed to turn off the lights then covered our bodies with the sheet and duvet when I returned.

Lucien tucked me against him, and we lay there quietly listening to the ocean waves crashing against the shore. Neither of us spoke for several minutes until I broke the silence.

"Lucien, promise you won't leave on your mission without saying a proper goodbye."

His body stiffened against mine for a second, and I wondered what horrible memory I triggered in his mind. I started to apologize, but he relaxed and placed a lingering kiss on my forehead. "I won't do that to you again." Lucien's voice was thick with emotion.

"Lucky, I wasn't talking about Paris and Cairo. I understand now. Your abrupt departure probably saved my life." If what Carmen said was true, and I had no reason to doubt her, it was a miracle I was still alive. My guess was Banks was saving killing me for a rainy day.

"It wasn't just you I pulled the disappearing act with," Lucien said. His grip on me tightened, and my heart broke when I realized who he meant. *Hiram.* "I never told Hiram goodbye; I got as far away from him as I could so Banks wouldn't hurt him. I ended up being the one who hurt Hiram. I knew our relationship wouldn't last. I thought it would run its course, and we'd go our separate ways; both of us feeling like better men for having known each other. I regret hurting Hiram, and I'll never have a chance to apologize and explain."

Lucien had succinctly stated Banks was the one who hurt Hiram earlier, but he didn't need me to remind him what he'd said. He needed his lover and friend to hold him while he worked through his pain. I let him talk, kissing and touching him until we fell asleep in one another's arms.

He woke me up just as the sun started to rise above the ocean. "Carmen thinks of everything," he said, brandishing a bottle of lube and a condom packet. "When I get back from London, what do you think about getting tested so we can lose the condoms?"

"I think it's the best idea you've had since you introduced yourself to me in Paris," I replied.

"Me?" Lucien asked innocently. "You were the one who offered to help the lost tourist find the restaurant he was looking for by walking him there and invited yourself to join him for a drink."

"Your eyes dared me to do it."

"What do my eyes dare you to do now?" Lucien asked.

I took the foil packet from him, ripped it open, and slid the latex down his erection. "Fuck me, Lucky."

He made slow love to me instead, and I knew it could be the goodbye I both cherished and dreaded.

I was starved by the time we showered and dressed in the clothes we found in the closet and drawers. My nose detected the delicious aroma of breakfast the minute we stepped out of the bedroom. I followed the scent to the patio where we last saw Carmen the previous evening.

We found her sitting in the same seat, and if not for the wardrobe change, I would've thought she never left. Carmen smiled when she saw us. "Sleep well?"

"Surprisingly, yes," Lucien said. "I could've used a few more hours though."

"I'm afraid it's a luxury we can't afford today," she said softly.

"Why aren't you wearing red?" I asked, gesturing to the white and blue maxi dress she wore.

"I hate red," she said with a wry smile. "My name and looks so closely resemble the fictional character that I dressed as her for Halloween one year and it stuck."

"She only wears red when she wants to appear powerful and mysterious," said a familiar voice from behind us.

I whipped my head around. "Desiree?" I asked.

Beside me, Lucien snorted and said, "I knew it."

"I call her Mama," Carmen said, rising to hold out her arms for the older woman. "Gentlemen, this is my mother, Manuela Santiago. The gentleman you met with Mama yesterday really is Dennis, and he's my soon-to-be stepfather." I was dying to know how Manuela escaped to safety, but it wasn't my place to ask.

"You didn't just happen to be in the neighborhood when we showed up at Sal's, I bet," Lucien said.

"Nope," Manuela said. "Dennis and I staked the place out and got in line when we saw you approach."

Lucien looked at Carmen, and she shrugged. "I knew there was no way you wouldn't get on the first plane to Miami after receiving my note, Lucky. It was easy enough for me to figure out which flight you'd choose too. I decided not to bother tailing you from the airport, because curiosity would send you to Sal's soon after landing and checking in at your hotel. From there it was easy, but I'm certain you knew you had a tail."

"I did," he admitted. "I knew they weren't hostile, so I allowed it to play out."

"When do you leave?" I asked Carmen.

"Our flight leaves at seven forty tonight. It takes approximately eight and a half hours to get to Heathrow, and with the change in time zone, that puts us landing in London tomorrow morning at nine fifteen," she said. "If it helps, you won't be alone here, and your every need will be looked after."

"Not *every* need," Lucien countered.

"Of course not, Lucky," Carmen said, rolling her eyes.

I noticed Manuela didn't leave us to talk; she scooted back the chair next to her daughter and lowered herself into it, smiling to reassure me. As much as I appreciated her effort, nothing would comfort me until Lucien returned safely to my side.

"The rest of our team should be arriving with Draco any minute now."

"Rest of our team?" Lucien asked.

No sooner had he asked, I heard familiar voices inside the house. "Oh, this should be interesting."

"Indeed," Carmen said with a wink.

Chapter Twenty-Four

Lucien

"**H**OW DARE YOU JET OFF TO PARADISE WITHOUT US," PERCY said, stepping onto the patio and pinning me with an irritated glare. "I thought we were a team."

"We are," I said. "Our team has grown unexpectedly."

Carmen rose from her chair and walked to Percy then exchanged air kisses. "Welcome to Miami, Felix and Oscar."

"Felix and Oscar?" Ryder and I both asked.

"Can you believe the aliases on our new IDs she sent along with our tickets?" Percy asked in disbelief. "She made us leave our cell phones and electronics behind. Is this an intervention? If so, I don't want to be unplugged."

"If by intervention you mean saving your life, then yes," Carmen said.

Beside me, Ryder laughed heartily. I couldn't imagine what he found so funny. Carmen's laughter join Ryder's, and I realized the aliases she'd chosen were significant somehow.

"Felix and Oscar," Ryder repeated, wiping the tears from his eyes

"Oh, that's a good one. You have a delightful sense of humor." Ryder looked at me and said, "Felix and Oscar are the names of the lead characters in *The Odd Couple*. I think the original movie came out in the sixties, and they released a sequel in the nineties."

"Oh, how perfect," I said. A person didn't need to see the movie to understand the reference.

Percy gave me the middle finger then looked around the property in awe. "Your home is stunning. I could get used to this."

"Consider this your home during your stay," Carmen told him.

"You're going to regret saying that, my dear," Dev said, hobbling through the door on his crutches. "You'll never get him out of here." Carmen gave Dev the same air kisses as Percy then introduced both men to her mother.

"You didn't write; you didn't call," Percy proclaimed dramatically. "Lucky for you, *Lucky*, I already had this magnificent outfit in my suitcase. I was saving it for the perfect occasion." Percy put his hand on his hip and turned around for us to see him in all his glory.

"I don't think I've ever seen a flamingo-pink suit," Carmen said.

"Linen for warm climates," Percy replied then gestured to the white T-shirt he wore beneath the open jacket. "When in Miami…"

"You dress like Sonny Crocket and Elton John's love child?" Ryder asked.

"Oh, that's a good one," Dev said to Ryder. He wore a polo shirt, jean shorts, and one boat shoe since he still wore a cast on his other foot. "It's good to see you, mate," Dev told me, dropping onto the vacant chair on the other side of me.

"I should've let you know we were leaving," I told him. "My lack of communication had nothing to do with not trusting you."

"I'm sure you've been busy," Dev replied, winking at Ryder. "A lot has happened since we last talked."

"How much does Dev know?" I asked Carmen.

"She promised me a free vacation and a sexy cabana boy, so I hobbled onto the first plane to Miami," Dev teased.

"Lucky for you, *Lucky*, I just happen to have the perfect cabana boy ensemble."

"Damn, I'll have to hide in my room the entire time," Ryder groused.

"I packed an outfit for you too when I learned you were going to be here," Percy teased.

"I don't fucking think so," I said, reaching beneath the table to place a possessive hand on Ryder's knee. I recalled the cartoon-heart-eyes Ryder made at Dev when he first met him.

"I guess you better hurry back then," Dev challenged playfully.

"What's the plan?" I asked Carmen.

"We are—"

Manuela tsked and held up her hand. "Breakfast first."

"Listen to your mama," Percy said to Carmen.

After we ate, Manuela excused herself from the table so we could talk privately, and Carmen brought Dev and Percy up to speed. Hearing Carmen share her mother's story and mention the attempt on Dev's life and Hiram's murder was just as painful the second time around.

"Why obsess over him?" Deverish asked, hooking his thumb in my direction. "I'm much better looking."

It was exactly what I needed to dispel the rising tension. "I'm just as perplexed, Dev. I have no idea how the hell I even landed on the man's radar, but you can bet your sweet ass I'll find out."

"I do have a very sweet ass," Dev admitted.

"We need to assume all your electronics were bugged and tracked prior to stepping inside my home. I had you guys leave your devices in Cincinnati so Banks doesn't know you left," Carmen said to Dev and Percy. "Inside these walls, Banks's childish attempts at espionage won't stand a chance against my state-of-the-art technology. I'm providing us with new phones, laptops, and tablets so we can communicate without worry of discovery until we want to be found. Lucky, be sure to pack the phone Banks provided you. We'll use it to our advantage."

"Um, Carmen," Ryder said hesitantly. "I know it's safer to stay here, and I have no problem being a prisoner in paradise, but I'm concerned about getting zapped if I accidentally touch something I'm not supposed to."

"Zapped?" Percy asked, sounding alarmed. Carmen bounced another grape against the upper railing, and it exploded. "Fuck me!" Percy shouted. "I want to avoid that at all costs."

"That's the first stop on our tour this morning," Carmen said, rising to her feet.

We followed her to a large office deep in the house where Draco sat behind a computer. Three walls consisted of computers, monitors, and various other pieces of equipment I'd never seen before. The fourth wall was glass and overlooked a high-tech conference room featuring a navy blue and white marble table with a teleconference station in the center. Around the table were eight white leather chairs with a laptop and tablet placed in front of each one. A large flat-screen television took up nearly half of one wall. It was one hell of a command center. Carmen Santiago wasn't playing around.

"Draco will run scans and updated our system to identify you as friendlies, and you won't get 'zapped' as Ryder puts it."

"I nominate Percy to test out the fences first," Ryder said.

"Damn, this is starting to sound like a *Jurassic Park* movie," Dev said dryly.

"No fucking way," Percy said to Ryder. "You go first. You're much bigger and can sustain more voltage before your heart explodes. I'm dainty and precious."

"Just use some of the gunk you put in your hair as a barrier," Ryder said. "That way your fingers slide right off."

"Yeah, right. With my luck, it would act as a conduit."

Draco stared expressionlessly at the two men like they were part of a circus act for a few seconds before an odd rumbling noise came from his chest. I started to think Carmen was right when she said he might not be human. The noise got louder, pulling everyone's attention to him. Draco's head fell back, and the noise burst from him, and I realized it was laughter.

Dev leaned into me and said, "How long do you suppose it's been since the last time the man has laughed? My grandfather had a very old car he liked to tinker with, and it made that same rusty sound when he fired it up."

"We don't get much entertainment around here," Carmen said. "All work and no play has made Draco a very dull boy."

"After this, I think you need to take your people on a long holiday," Dev suggested, nodding at Draco. He'd knocked the rust out of his pipes and sounded almost human while continuing to laugh over Percy and Ryder bickering back and forth.

"I'll test the fence," I said, breaking up the argument. "Time is wasting, and I have better things to do than listen to you guys argue."

"Okay," Percy said, shrugging.

"Works for me," Ryder agreed.

It took another hour for us all to get scanned into Carmen's fancy system then we all went back out to the pool area. Ryder walked with me to the far side of the pool but stood a few feet away.

"Good luck, baby," he said.

I looked over my shoulder at Carmen, who gave me two thumbs up and said, "No worries, Lucky. I have bigger fish to fry."

"Ha ha ha," I said drolly. I took a calming breath, said a prayer, and slowly reached toward the fence.

"Wait! I love you, Lucky."

"Aww," I heard Dev, Percy, and Carmen say.

"I love you too," I replied.

"This is better than a movie," Percy said. "Let's hope it's not a tragedy."

"Use the back of your hand so your fingers don't accidentally grip the fence if it doesn't recognize you. I'm prepared to knock you off the fence in case of an emergency," Ryder told me.

I had a choice to make: quickly touch the fence to demonstrate it's okay or put on a show. There really was no decision. I grabbed the fence, started making a loud buzzing noise, and convulsed like a powerful current was going through me.

"Not funny," Ryder said tersely.

Percy and Dev laughed their asses off while Carmen just shook her head.

"Why are you mad?" I asked him once I released the fence. "I'm the one who should be upset."

"How do you figure?" Ryder countered, crossing his arms over his chest.

"You didn't knock me off the fence."

"I'm thinking about knocking you out."

I walked toward him with purposeful strides. Just as I reached him, he gripped my biceps and pulled me into the swimming pool with him. Ryder wrapped his arms around me and dragged me to the bottom of the pool, where we playfully grappled until the need for oxygen urged us toward the surface.

"You shit," Ryder said, pulling me toward him.

"Drown him," Percy said, urging Ryder on.

"You had it coming," Dev told me.

"Come on," Carmen said, "let's give these guys some time alone. Dinner is at five, then we'll head to the airport."

Her sobering words reminded us we had limited time together. For once, sex took a back seat, and we spent the afternoon wrapped in each other's arms talking about everything that came to mind—both of us trying to make up for the wasted years. We made lists of movies we wanted to see, the places we wanted to travel to, and concerts we wanted to attend. We planned for our future while staying connected in the moment with touches and kisses.

"This won't be goodbye," I said, brushing a lock of hair off Ryder's forehead. "I'll be back as soon as I can."

"It won't be soon enough," Ryder teased, rolling me to my back and making love to me.

Chapter Twenty-Five

Ryder

SAYING GOODBYE TO LUCIEN WAS ONE OF THE HARDEST AND SWEETEST things I'd ever done. I was worried, and I would miss him like crazy, but I saw the determination in his eyes that said, "I will finish this, and I will come back to you." Lucien's resolve fueled mine to show him I believed in us.

Our goodbye at the front door wasn't dramatic; we'd said everything we needed to say privately. A hug, a lingering kiss, and a softly exchanged "I love you." That was it; then he was gone.

"Come on, mate," Percy said, hooking his arm through mine and leading me away from the front door. It was probably a good thing too, or else I'd end up looking like the German shepherds, who still sat staring after their mistress. "Let's go see what kind of mischief we can get into to take your mind off missing your guy."

"How do you do it?" I asked Percy.

"We Brits are made of stern stuff," Dev said, falling into step behind us on crutches.

"Don't listen to him," Percy said. "The difference between you and me is I'm used to it. Dev and I met under these circumstances and both of us went into our relationship with our eyes wide open. It's been terribly difficult at times, and I miss him like crazy sometimes, but I've never been blindsided like you have. Hopefully, you won't have to worry about getting used to this life once Carmen and Lucky complete their mission."

"I don't exactly see Lucky taking up permanent residence in a rocking chair anytime soon," Dev teased. His words were like an arrow straight to the heart.

"Dev," Percy admonished, tipping his head in my direction. Had I gasped out loud, or did he feel me tense because our arms were linked? "It's not like those are Lucky's only two options."

"Of course not," Dev agreed. "I didn't mean to imply Lucky wasn't willing to settle down and find a tamer job. There are many careers he could choose that would permit him to be home more often."

I wanted to be petulant and demand he name one. I recalled the conversation I had with Lucien about men like him. They tended to take on clandestine jobs because their skillset made them overqualified for many careers. Was that code for too mundane to sustain him? Hell, he wasn't even gone fifteen minutes, and I was already worried about not being enough to make him happy for the long haul. He had to survive before we could have a future.

"Great job," Percy whispered angrily. "See what you did? Dial down the good ole British bluntness a notch or two."

"What did I say?" Dev asked, sounding perturbed. "I didn't tell him Lucky would be bored with him after five minutes or anything. I just implied he wasn't ready for the rocking chair."

I couldn't imagine finding humor in anything while Lucien's life was in danger, but Dev and Percy proved me wrong. My body shook with silent laughter, pulling Percy's attention to me.

"Oh, God. I think he's having a fit or something. Withdrawal from the cock has already set in."

My laughter erupted from me then. "Fuck," I said when I could finally breathe. "The two of you are bickering back and forth like two old women. I'm not sure if I'm entertained or annoyed."

"Both," Percy and Dev said at the same time.

"Ryder, the only thing I can say for sure is I don't see a future for Lucky that doesn't include you."

"Thank you, Dev."

"Baby, that's so sweet," Percy said. "I knew you had it in you."

My cell phone rang, which meant someone outside this circle was calling me. Carmen had assured me it was okay to use my phone if my family, friends, or colleagues called me. We'd been waiting for breaking news about Daniel Perez's arrest all day, but nothing had come across the wire. Carmen figured the FBI would take steps to validate the data and recover the vessel before they arrested the scumbag and held a news conference.

"It's my mother," I told the guys. "I'll just take this in my room. Want to meet by the pool for a relaxing swim after I'm finished?" Dev pointed to his cast. "Um, Percy, would you like to go for a nice swim while Dev watches?"

Percy purred. "Kinky, I like it."

I heard them bickering when I answered the phone and hastened to get away so my mother didn't overhear them. I wasn't sure how to explain Dev and Percy to her. "Hello, Mom," I said.

"You haven't called me mom in a long time," she said softly. "I should encourage you to visit Miami more often. Are you having a great time with your *friends*?" She knew all the usual suspects I'd vacation with and probably deduced none of them went with me. I admired the restraint she showed by not asking.

"It's been eye-opening," I replied noncommittally. "Most of the trip has been amazing."

"That's wonderful to hear, darling. Listen, I have some big news I want to share with you, but I need you to promise me you won't say anything to anyone until after the news conference tomorrow."

"Of course. What's this about a news conference?"

"Daniel Perez was arrested by the FBI today, and they recovered the fanyi ritual wine vessel. He's been on someone's radar for several years now, and they set up a sting operation to catch him."

"Who'd you get the information from? The Inspector Somersby guy?"

"Agent Kiphart called me. Do you know what else he told me?" I had a good feeling I did. "He said Interpol has agents not inspectors, and they don't send them out to solve crimes around the world. Can you believe it?"

"Then who does Agent Kiphart say this man is?" I asked.

"He thinks he's involved in the sting operation. Maybe he was looking for additional dirt to nail Daniel's coffin shut. The nice agents said they weren't at liberty to discuss it with me, but they just wanted to give me a heads-up they'd made an arrest and would be holding a conference tomorrow morning. Isn't it great news?" Mom asked.

"It's wonderful news." I'd tried to sound ecstatic but failed miserably.

"I expected you to be thrilled," Mom said, sounding confused. "It means you're cleared and can go back to work."

"I am ecstatic the FBI recovered the vessel and my name will be cleared of any wrongdoing."

"But?"

"I'm not sure I'm a good fit at the museum," I admitted. "I loved the idea of working there because of our family's longstanding connection to the museum, and I wanted to be close to you, Dad, and Iris, but I never felt comfortable there." On the other hand, if I hadn't taken the job, would Lucien and I have reconnected? Carmen and Lucien's role would be unchanged. She was on a mission, and Lucky was her best weapon to achieve it. If not Cincinnati, their paths would've crossed someplace else. The question was: would Lucien have sought me out once he was free of Banks?

"I know they didn't welcome you with open arms, but that was

Daniel's fault for creating an environment of mistrust and paranoia. Please give them a chance to get to know you."

"I promise to think about it," I assured her.

"It's all I can ask."

"Mom, do you remember how much we loved watching *Romancing the Stone*?" I asked, changing the subject. "I watched the movie on the flight yesterday and thought of you."

"Oh my goodness, yes. Jack T. Colton was *the* man."

"Remember how I wanted to be a romance novelist like Joan Wilder?"

"Then you wanted to be an archeologist like Indiana Jones." She released a long sigh. "Did I squash the adventurer in you with my speeches about practicality?"

"What? I didn't bring this up to critique your parenting skills, Mom. I just wanted to talk about a fond memory. Yes, you preached about choosing practical jobs and seeing the big picture, but you never called me or my ideas stupid."

"Good to know I wasn't too terrible," she said. "I'm dying to know who you went to Miami with, but I refuse to press. I only want you to have good things in life. I want you to find your Jack T. Colton or Indiana Jones."

"I have found him, Mom."

"I knew it! This is the happiest I've heard you sound since Paris when that Sebastian jerk broke your heart." I chuckled, which must've tripped her mother's intuition. "You're on a lovers' getaway."

"Yeah, you could call it that." As much as I trusted Carmen and her technology, I wasn't going to risk telling my mom any details over the phone, especially with so much hanging in the balance. I also wouldn't tell my mother anything about Lucien without his prior approval.

"When can we meet him?" she asked.

"It's complicated right now."

"Ugh. I hate that Facebook status," she teased. "You're a grown man, and I won't pry, even though it's killing me. It's enough for me to know you're happy."

"Thanks, Mom. I do hope to introduce him to you and Dad very soon." I didn't say reintroduce because she'd never met the man I love. She'd heard of Sebastian, met Christian, but she'd never had the pleasure of knowing my Lucien.

"You're not just happy; you're in love."

"I am."

"Whoa. I wasn't aware you were even seeing someone."

"Well, this is…"

"Say no more," she said suddenly. "You told me you're not able to discuss it right now, and I'm going to honor that. Besides, I want to talk about this in person."

I groaned. "Please don't plan a dinner party or anything. I just want my guy to meet my parents and sister in a relaxed environment without feeling like he's on display."

"Fair enough. I love you, Ryder. I don't say it enough."

"I love you too, Mom."

We chatted a while longer about other things going on in our lives, and I assured her I'd give my job at the museum a lot of consideration. After we hung up, I went in search of Percy and Dev. They were easy to spot relaxing by the pool, although relaxing was a relative term. Percy was straddling Dev's lap, and they were locked at the lips. Either Percy was completely naked, or his swimming trunks were so tiny they were hiding beneath the large hands gripping his ass. I could see the fellas had found a way to entertain themselves while waiting for me. I was glad to have their company but seeing them cuddling reminded me of who I was missing.

I followed the sound of happy humming to the kitchen where Manuela stood at the sink washing dishes. "Can I give you a hand?"

"Oh!" she exclaimed then pivoted around, clutching a hand over her chest. I felt like the worst kind of human being for startling her. "Don't feel bad," she said, reading my expression. "I'm the world's jumpiest person. I should probably have the distinct honor put on a shirt or coffee cup."

"I'm still sorry. Why don't you let me make it up to you by allowing me to help?"

"You're a guest here, Ryder. I could never ask you to do dishes."

"You didn't ask; I offered."

Manuela nodded her head to acknowledge my point. "You can dry." She removed the towel slung over her shoulder and handed it to me. I began drying the dishes and putting them up where she directed me. "Carmen has provided me with the best of everything, but sometimes I still like to wash the dishes by hand. Sometimes the hot water helps me think, and sometimes it helps me relax."

"I bet Carmen would prefer you used the hot tub to relax instead of scrubbing dishes."

"You're coming to understand my daughter well," she said, smiling serenely.

"She's an incredible woman, Manuela. You've done a remarkable job raising her."

"Not always," she said. "We had some major battles during her teen years, but it was the foundation of who she is today: fierce, loyal, and a justice fighter. I couldn't be prouder of her. I ask myself where she gets her determination."

"Really?" I asked. "You don't just look in the mirror and recognize the same drive inside you?" I again wondered about her journey and hoped someday she might trust me enough to tell me.

Manuela's cheeks turned pink, and I felt horrible for bringing up her tragic past even in a roundabout way. She was a fucking survivor, and she raised one hell of a warrior. She needed to take credit where it was due. "Yes, I can see the similarities in our personalities. You know, I regretted telling her the truth about her conception for so long, but it made us both stronger. I hope she doesn't end up paying the price. I cannot lose my girl."

I wrapped my arm around Manuela and pulled her into a hug.

"She and Lucky are going to kick that bastard's ass for all the malevolent acts he's committed. Then we're all going to live happy lives free of his shadow. I'm not a betting man, but if I was, there's no way in hell I'd bet against Carmen and Lucky."

"Thank you, cariño. I know you're right, but I still worry about her. I'm glad she has Lucky."

"They'll make a dynamic duo for sure."

Once we finished tidying the kitchen, I kissed her cheek and decided to head to my room. The sheets would still smell like Lucky, and I could find something to entertain myself on the laptop Carmen provided to me. I spotted Günter and Hans lying in their beds in the great room, looking sad.

"Günter, Hans," I said firmly. They lifted their heads, looking suddenly alert. "Hier," I said then headed to my bedroom. I wasn't sure they would obey me, but I heard the clicking of their toenails on the tile as they rose from their beds and followed me. I sat on the bed and patted the space beside me. "Hier." They tilted their heads to the side. "Hier," I repeated, patting the bed again. The shepherds jumped on the bed and immediately made themselves comfortable up on my pillow. It was fine with me because I preferred to use Lucky's so I could breathe in his scent.

I rested my head on the pillow beside the gorgeous dogs then decided it was the perfect situation for a selfie. I grabbed the phone Carmen gave me and snapped a picture. I sent it to Lucien's secure phone with a message that read: *No one can replace you, but these guys are giving it their best shot. Be safe. Hurry back. Love you.*

Chapter Twenty-Six

Lucien

I DIDN'T SLEEP WELL ON THE FLIGHT TO HEATHROW, AND I WASN'T THE greatest company when I followed Carmen to a Land Rover where Draco's identical twin waited for us.

"There's two of them?" I asked once we stopped at Costa Coffee to caffeinate. Draco 2.0 stayed in the car and kept the car warm while we dashed in. One of the things I admired most about Carmen was the way she treated her employees. She didn't just assume Draco 2.0 had his fix already; she asked if he wanted anything. I expected the stoic man to pass on the offer, but he asked for a chai latte instead. His voice sounded as gravelly and unused as his brother's.

"Yes, and you'll never guess his first name?" Carmen asked, humor lacing her words.

I knew how much she loved irony, so I took a good stab at it. "Harry."

"Yes, Draco and Harry."

"Can they perform magic too?" I teased.

"Yes," Carmen replied then lowered her voice, "but not the kind you're thinking of. One is a retired SEAL, and the other is a retired Green Beret. Trust me when I tell you they have plenty of tricks up their sleeves."

I lowered my voice too and asked, "Where the hell do you find your employees? Is there some job service that locates positions for former special forces officers and mercenaries?"

"Why? Thinking of a career change when this is over?"

"The thought has crossed my mind," I admitted.

"It's because you're not working for the right person," Carmen said, lifting a perfectly arched brow.

"Why? Do you know someone who might be interested in hiring me?"

"I am," she said, nodding. "If you're open to the idea, I'd like to pitch a proposal to you once we deal with Banks."

"I'm open to hearing what you have to say, but keep in mind I'm not making a decision based on what works only for me."

"I know you and Ryder are a packaged deal, Lucky. I don't want to break that up. Hell, I need some pointers," Carmen said, smiling wryly.

"Don't look at me. I have a horrible track record, especially with Ryder."

"It's all going to work out in the end though. I feel it," Carmen said confidently.

"Speaking of Ryder," I said, reaching in my pocket and pulling out my phone. "I forgot to turn my new fancy phone on. I promised I'd text him when we arrived safely." I hoped he was still sleeping, but I wanted a message from me to be the first thing he saw. I was happy to find a message from Ryder waiting for me then laughed when I saw the pictures and words accompanying it. "You're in jeopardy of losing your dogs." I tilted the phone so she could see.

"No chance in hell," she said. "Those are my boys, but I'm grateful they've taken to Ryder. They tend to pout and mope for the first few days when I'm gone."

"Don't you ever get tired of it?" I asked, stepping to the side to wait for the barista to make our drinks.

"The travel wears me down after a while, but I can't stop. I don't want to stop, I should say. This is who I am; this is my life."

"It's a piece of who you are, not the sum," I countered, tapping out a message to Ryder.

Tell those boys not to get too comfortable. I'm going to want my spot back. I'll call as soon as I can. Caffeinating then strategy meeting with another team member. At this rate, it's probably my mum. A new surprise is around every corner. Then I need to crash for a bit, or I won't be good to anyone. I love you, Ry.

After we left, Harry drove in the direction of a warehouse district that had been renovated to living spaces. I had a feeling Carmen didn't rent a converted flat but owned an entire warehouse to get up to her mischief. I wasn't wrong.

"The elevator uses the same biometric scan system you saw at my front gate in Miami. Here, it's disguised to look like a typical call button," she stated, gesturing to the button. "Push the button and see what happens."

"Haha. I stopped falling for that a long time ago," I quipped. "Is this also like the perimeter fence in Miami?"

"No," Carmen said, rolling her eyes. "Unapproved visitors push the button, and it initiates the same type of intercom system you find in secure buildings where someone has to buzz visitors in. Now, put your finger on the call button and hold it down to initiate the scan."

I did as she asked, and a blue light in the glass panel came on and scanned my face while the call button beneath my thumb scanned my print. The doors opened, and we stepped inside. Instead of numbers, a button was assigned to each floor, and beside them were a digital display identifying its purpose: Gym/Pool, Training Facility, Command Center, Guest Suite, and Penthouse Suite.

"Guests granted permission to come up don't get to see the same digital displays as you and I. They see the typical floor numbers you expect to find in an elevator. For added security, the elevator will only take them to floors approved by security."

It was an impressive setup. "Training facility," I said, perking up. "Can we go there? Can we? Huh?"

"Sure. We'll take a quick tour."

The gym and pool were the typical setup and included a steam room and shower. The training facility was enough to make me weep from excitement though. Carmen covered every aspect of our job from rappelling, scaling, avoiding laser and other motion-triggered detection, cracking safes, hacking, checking for bugs, and she even had a car simulator where you could learn to lose a tail. The facility must've taken up at least three of the previous floors to permit scaling and rappelling training.

"The computer lab is over there," she said, pointing to a door on the far side of the room. "Gun range is through that door."

"Gun range?" I asked with a raised brow.

"I've made many enemies, so my bodyguards are licensed to carry."

"Makes sense," I agreed. "This is an amazing facility. I admit it seems a little over-the-top with as few employees as you have now."

"Think big picture, Lucky. I don't want to be in the field forever. That's what I want to talk to you about when our mission is over." I admit she grabbed my attention. "Ready to see the rest?"

"Lead the way."

"I'll save the command center for last since we'll be meeting Quinton there when he arrives."

"Quinton? Percy's cousin?"

"Yes," Carmen said. "While you were spending private time with Ryder, Percy tried to contact his cousin again and was able to get through. I decided to bring him in for the job."

"You've done great so far without him though," I pointed out.

"What took me two years to find probably would've taken him two months. He's probably the best hacker in the world, and I want to employ the best."

"You've met him before then?" I asked.

"No, I only know of his reputation through mutual friends."

"It sounds like he will be a great asset to our mission."

"I liked our odds before, but I fucking love them now, Lucky."

The tour continued through the guest and penthouse suites. Everything was as state-of-the-art as her home in Miami, but the décor was entirely different. Her London residence was urbane and sophisticated where her Miami mansion was peaceful and serene. Equally beautifully places; totally different vibes.

"Ryder would love this suite," I said, looking around the sitting room in the guest suite that would be my private retreat for the next few days. Black and gold marble floors, butterscotch leather sofas and club chairs, and the most incredible view of London.

"You must bring him for a visit after this is all over. You're welcome to stay whether I'm in residence or not. It would be one of your corporate perks."

Carmen's phone chimed, and she looked at the screen. She tapped a button and said, "Hello."

"I have an appointment at eleven."

Carmen tipped the phone so I could see the data on the screen identifying him as Quinton Harrison. She brought up another menu and pressed the command to open the elevator. "Come on up."

"Okie dokie," he said before Carmen disconnected.

"He doesn't sound like the world's best hacker," I said. "How'd Quinton's info come up? Surely a hacker knows how to protect his data from becoming available for anyone to access."

"He had an appointment with Harry yesterday evening so we could get the ball rolling. He checked out."

"I'm trusting your judgment. I know how to retrieve artifacts, but the technical stuff is over my head."

Quinton Harrison was the exact opposite of his cousin in nearly every possible way. He was tall to Percy's short, dark to his fair, and wore sedated clothes to Percy's flamboyant outfits. I bet his black-rimmed glasses were from necessity and not for looks like the ones Percy wore on occasion.

"Yeah, I get that surprised look a lot from people who've met Percy," Quinton said, smiling crookedly. "It's good to meet you, Lucky." He shook my hand warmly and turned to Carmen. "It's lovely to meet you too."

I glanced over at Carmen and did a double take. Carmen Santiago was blushing and smiling shyly at Quinton. She looked as equally enthralled with him as he did with her. His gaze swept over her long legs, svelte curves, and riot of dark curls cascading over her scarlet leather jacket. What an interesting turn of events.

"Shall we get started?" I asked. "I could really use a nap."

"Hmmm?" Carmen asked then seemed to jerk herself out of her trance. "Yes, let's get started.

I couldn't wait to tell Ryder about this development when I called him.

Chapter Twenty-Seven

Ryder

TWO DAYS AFTER LUCIEN LEFT, DRACO SUMMONED US TO THE CONference room. "We're going to have a conference call with Carmen, Lucky, and Q in just a bit. Things will be happening soon, and they want to bring the rest of us up to speed."

I was sure Carmen would've preferred just to set up the mission, execute it, and get back home without having to hold my hand every time she turned around. I'd said as much to Lucien the previous night on the phone, but he said she understood each of us had a lot invested in the operation. It was true. Every person sitting around the table waiting for the conference to start had been at Banks's mercy in one way or another.

I glanced to my right and saw Manuela shaking. I scooted my chair closer and wrapped my arm around her.

"I haven't been this scared since I escaped from that horrible place," she whispered so only I heard. We'd grown close since my arrival. She'd taught me to cook traditional Cuban dishes, and I helped her clean the kitchen after each meal. The more I grew to know

Manuela, the more I respected her. "My heart said he was going to kill me, and I ran while I could. They expected me to use the road since I was on foot, so I escaped through the woods in the middle of the night. I'd packed food and wore extra layers, but it still wasn't enough. I walked until I ached then I stopped to rest. All around me, I could hear things moving around in the dark and wolves howling in the distance. I thought I was walking away from the wolves, but their howls grew closer. I felt like they were stalking me and were waiting for the right moment to attack. I had no idea where I was going and was terrified I would circle right back to the grounds of the madman's house. But by some miracle, I exited the woods eight miles away from the evil place. It had taken me three days, and I'd only packed enough food and water for a day and a half. I was exhausted and dehydrated when I knocked on the door of the first house I came to. I had no reason to believe they'd help me, but I had to try for my baby."

"It almost sounds like the wolves were guiding you out of the woods," I said in awe of her courage.

"I think so too," Manuela said. "I don't even remember the door opening. I'd knocked and collapsed before the owners could answer. I woke up in the hospital a few days later. My body had gone into shock, and the doctors said it was a miracle I hadn't lost my baby."

"Carmen was a fighter from the very beginning," I said, squeezing her hand.

"She sure was," Manuela said, a faraway look washing over her features. "The police came by, but I refused to answer who I was or where I came from. I couldn't risk Banks knowing I was alive. Of course, I wouldn't know his real name for a few years when I happened to see his photo in a newspaper above an article about his antiquities business. Anyway, I wasn't much of a threat to him when I escaped, but it was doubtful he would've agreed.

"The hospital assigned a social worker to me since it was pretty obvious I was a victim of abuse. I went to live with Carmen Caraway, who ran a home for battered women and children. There were a few pregnant ladies who lived there, and it was the first time I hadn't felt scared since I was abducted on my way home from school.

"I told Miss Carmen about my family in Cuba, and she permitted me to call them. My mama and I cried when we heard each other's voice for the first time. She thought I was dead, and trust me, cariño, there were many days I wish I had died. My family was poor, and they had no money to send for me. After my Carmen was born, I found work as a maid for a wonderful family. They treated me well, doted on my daughter, and allowed me to call home to Cuba once a week. I had hoped someday my mama and papa would know Carmen from more than the pictures I mailed to them, but they were killed when Hurricane Georges hit land in 1998."

"Manuela, I don't know what to say. You've experienced so much grief in your life, yet you still smile. It isn't just for show either; I see real joy in your eyes. How do you do it?"

"How could I not? I have my Carmen, and she's the most wonderful gift I've ever received. I know people don't understand how I can say such a thing because of how she came to be, but it wasn't her fault. Carmen feared she would end up like her father after she found out about him, but I knew better. There isn't a trace of the bastard in her."

"She's all you," I told Manuela.

"Look around you, cariño. I have so much to be grateful for, so I want more than anything for our loves to finish this mission and return to us so we can move forward and leave the past where it belongs—behind us."

I looked around the room as Manuela instructed and my eyes landed on Dev and Percy. Dev had his casted leg propped on the table, and Percy had produced a crochet hook from someplace and was sticking it inside the cast to scratch Dev's leg.

"Yessss," Dev said, eyes rolling back in pleasure. "Baby, that feels so damn good. Yes, right there. A little harder. A little deeper. To the left. Yes. Oh yes! A little to the right now. Sweet Jesus!"

Beside me, Manuela giggled with delight. I was so glad Percy and Dev's shenanigans had once more saved the day.

"Faster, baby. Faster. Dig deeper. So good. You know how to work that thing," Dev said, head thrown back in abandon as Percy began scratching his leg in earnest. Then Dev began banging the table. "Yes! Yes! Yes!"

"Um, guys, do you need us to call back?" Carmen's voice asked through the speakers in the teleconference station.

"Sounds to me like he's almost finished," Lucien said. My heart melted to a puddle of goo just from hearing his voice. "Carmen, do you know Dev's nickname?"

"Nope," Carmen said.

"We call him the two-minute man."

"Shut up, you wanker," Dev said. "That's how long it takes me to crack a safe not how long I can maintain an erection. Carmen, your mother was kind enough to let me borrow a crochet hook to—"

"Whoa," said another voice I hadn't heard before. I assumed it belonged to Quinton. "I don't think any of us want to know where Percy is sticking the crochet hook."

"Hey, Q," Percy said. "How's it going?"

"Great, but it sounds like things are much more exciting on your end."

"Get your mind out of the gutter, arsehole. I'm just using it to scratch Deverish's leg beneath his cast. Then I'll give it back to Manuela."

"Keep it, cariño. It's clear the two of you are getting great joy from it."

"Hello, Mama," Carmen said softly.

"Te echo de menos," Manuela said.

"I miss you too, Mama." Carmen took a deep breath and said, "Banks has taken the bait."

"And by bait you mean he's been in contact with Lucky?" I asked.

"Yes," Carmen confirmed. "Lucky called Banks using his bugged phone and requested a meeting."

"I told him I have the evidence to prove who the mole is in his company. The bastard acted intrigued and set the time and place."

"You're just going to sit down across from Banks and show him the evidence?" I asked.

"No, love, I'm going to keep my phone on so he'll know where I am and wait for one of Banks's men to grab me."

I gasped sharply. They talked about using Lucky as bait, but I didn't think they meant for him to get abducted. "There has to be a better way."

"There isn't," Lucky said. "Banks needs to feel like he's in control until we have everything we need. If we're going to put the twisted bastard away for life, we need to get him to admit to his crimes on tape."

"How will that be permissible in a court of law? His attorneys would advise him not to lose sleep over illegally obtained confessions."

"The court of public opinion matters a great deal to someone like Banks, love," Lucien said softly.

"Ryder, there will be three of us watching Lucky. When he gets nabbed, we'll know it, and we will ride to the rescue," Carmen said confidently. "Even if they manage to slip by us, Lucky is wearing a tiny little tracking device. We'll know where he is."

"Three?" Deverish asked.

"My bodyguard Harry and I will be in the field while Quinton tracks Lucky's transmissions from our command center."

"I still don't like it," I said, "but I have faith in all of you."

"I'll keep you posted as best I can, but we'll go radio silent once we execute the recovery mission for obvious reasons," Carmen said.

"Yeah, I want your focus to be on getting my man back."

"Q, are you playing nice with others?" Percy asked. "You're so used to being the lone wolf."

"He's um...fine," Carmen said, sounding a little breathless. "A bit sure of himself, but I guess we wouldn't want anything less from someone in this situation."

"It's not arrogance if it's true," Quinton said. "I'm the best you'll ever know." *Was that a bold double entendre?*

"Is that so?" Carmen asked Q, sounding annoyed.

"Yep." *Hell yes, it was a double entendre.*

"Quinton is the perfect man for the job," Lucien said, steering the conversation back to the purpose of our meeting. "I'm happy knowing he'll have our backs while we're in the field."

I couldn't keep the smile off my face. Lucien had told me about Carmen and Quinton's reactions to one another. The attraction was obviously mutual, but neither of them was the trusting type, so they circled each other. Sometimes the unresolved sexual tension spilled over into arguments about the silliest things. Lucien laughed so hard when he recounted their spats and hearing their exchange during the conference made me doubly sad I wasn't there to witness their interactions in person.

"I don't have anything else to share," Carmen said, reclaiming control. "Send up prayers and good vibes for us tomorrow. We expect everything to go extremely well, but we'll take all the help we can get."

"May God be with you," Manuela said.

"I'm saying prayers, sending out good vibes, and I'm crossing everything I can," I said.

"I'll light a candle and call upon my goddesses," Percy said.

"Who? Prada, Lady Gaga, Chanel, and Cher?" Lucien asked.

Percy tried to look angry but couldn't pull it off. "Lucky, I would miss your insults. I hope you come back with only minimal bruising."

"Aw, thanks, kitten," Lucky replied.

"I'll be thinking of you guys and wishing like hell I could be there to help," Deverish said. "Quinton, don't edit the recordings until after I've had a chance to hear Banks beg for mercy."

"Deal," Quinton said.

We said our goodbyes, and I headed to my bedroom. I needed

some alone time to process everything or find a way to shut down my overactive brain that wanted to show me a montage of images of Lucien getting abducted, beaten, and possibly… No. I wouldn't allow my mind to go there. My two shadows came with me and made themselves at home on my bed while I picked up my laptop and opened my Word document. What started as something cute to keep my brain busy had turned out to be something I truly enjoyed. I'd just started typing when his Skype call came through.

"Hello, handsome," I said when Lucien's face filled my screen.

"I needed to see that you're okay," he said. "It's a lot to process."

"I won't pretend I'm not scared, but I was telling the truth when I said I have faith in you."

"I love you so much," Lucien said, lifting his hand and caressing my face on the screen. I could feel his phantom touch and couldn't wait for the real thing. "This will all be over soon."

"I can't wait." I didn't want to spend our time talking about Banks. I wanted to discuss normal things like other couples did, so I changed the subject. "HR called about my position at the museum earlier today. They informed me I could return anytime I was ready, and my suspension was removed from my employment record."

"Did you tell them to go fuck themselves?" Lucien asked.

"No, I politely told them I needed time to decide if working there was something I wanted."

"Good for you; although, I like my idea better."

"As do I," I admitted. "I loved seeing the video of Daniel Perez getting arrested. I might've watched it a dozen times."

"We enjoyed watching it here too."

I couldn't wait until Lucky's "we" comments referred to him and me. I knew how selfish it sounded, which was why I hadn't said it out loud. If not for Carmen, Daniel's arrest wouldn't have happened in the first place, and Lucky wouldn't be twenty-four hours away from freedom. My pity party wouldn't help anyone, including myself, so I shoved my sour thoughts aside.

"I have some fun news to share," I said.

"Yeah, what is it?"

"I started writing my first adult romance story," I said. "It's a far cry better than the drivel I wrote as a teen."

"Are there sexy parts in it?"

"There will be. The guys don't like each other much right now."

"Might I suggest an angry fuck?" Lucien asked.

"I can run it by Reed and Leo to see if they're interested," I said noncommittally, but my brain had already started creating a scenario for them.

"*Reed and Leo?*" Lucien asked. "Let me guess: Reed is the sweet guy and Leo is the dickhead."

"Wow. It's like you're peering into my head."

"Has this Leo guy stolen something from Reed?" Lucien asked.

"In a way," I said. "It's more like they're seeking the same thing and keep ruining opportunities for each other."

"Reed should bend Leo over the sofa in his hotel and fuck him until he falls in line. It's a proven method."

"Noted." Damn, I wanted to relive the moment with him again, minus the hitting part.

"Love, I can tell exactly what you're thinking."

"You can?" I asked.

"Send the dogs away, lock your bedroom door, and I'll tell you. Better yet; I'll show you."

"Be right back."

I wanted to relax and stop thinking about the mission, and he had found the perfect solution. Lucien speaking filthy things to me while we simultaneously jerked off brought tears of pleasure to my eyes. We talked for a few more hours about the most random stuff, and even buddy-watched an Indiana Jones movie until Lucien yawned loudly and said he needed to get some sleep.

"Kick that fucker's ass and come home to me," I said, hiding my sorrow and fear beneath the bravado.

"Does Carmen know you've taken over her dogs *and* her home?" he teased.

"Your heart is my home, Lucky." Man, I was starting to think and talk like a romance book character.

"You've got that right, love."

The silence that followed after we disconnected terrified me, so I located the dogs and returned to Leo and Reed's world. My fingers flew over the keyboard as their scene unfolded in vivid color in my mind. Angry fuck, indeed.

"He's going to demand royalties," I told Hans, who tilted his head like he was giving it serious consideration. Who was I kidding? I might not even finish my Lucien-inspired erotica.

Chapter Twenty-Eight

Lucien

I KEPT REMINDING MYSELF THAT GETTING CAPTURED WAS PART OF OUR master plan. It sounded all well and good until you were the one rendered unconscious from a pistol whip, shoved in the back of a van, and drove out to the middle of nowhere. We'd made a list of properties Banks owned personally or under one of his shell companies and surveilled them all to see which one worked best for torturing and killing one's obsession. It stood to reason Banks would choose one of his country properties located close enough to the city for him to easily access but far enough away his neighbors wouldn't hear me scream and beg for mercy.

Of course, I wouldn't scream and beg for mercy no matter what he or his goons did to me. Had he forgotten the rigorous training I'd endured to become an SAS officer? Or was this all a game to see how far he could push me? The blow to my head rattled my brain pretty good, but I didn't feel nauseous. I could clearly remember the events before I was struck and the times I came to in the back of the van and when they dragged me blindfolded and gagged inside one of Banks's properties. While I couldn't fully rule out a concussion without some tests, I was ninety percent sure I hadn't sustained serious injury. Banks didn't need to know it though.

I relaxed in the wooden chair I was tied to and used the senses available to me to get a picture of my surroundings. My nose detected leather, lemon polish, a faint whiff of pipe tobacco, and books. I wiggled my bare toes against the rug beneath my feet and could tell it was woven with high-quality wool. Of course, taking me to a warehouse or putting me in the basement beneath one of his manor houses was too gauche for someone of Banks's ilk. He'd want to be comfortable during my interrogation.

Because I was in and out of consciousness, I couldn't be sure how long we'd traveled in the van, but my money was on Banks's estate in Kent. I not only heard the crackling of a warm fire, I felt its heat chasing away the chill from riding in the van without a coat or shoes. Banks's goon had naturally assumed those two items would be a great place for me to stash a tracking device. They weren't wrong, but we were several steps ahead of them. I just hoped they hadn't scanned my body while I was out cold and located the tiny tracking devise embedded in the button on my jeans. The creaking of a leather chair made me realize I wasn't alone.

"There's no need to pretend, Lucky. I can tell by your breathing that you've awoken."

It was all I could do not to laugh behind my gag. Banks sounded like some B movie villain that skipped the theater and went straight to one of those lackluster cable channels or a streaming service. I had no idea if we were the only people in the room, so I didn't risk testing the ropes securing my hands. Whoever had pulled my arms around the back of the chair didn't do a very good job because my circulation wasn't impaired, and with blood freely flowing to my limbs, they hadn't incapacitated me very well.

I would have responded with a comment, but there was the issue of the gag in my mouth. I shrugged my shoulders instead but limited the movement so not to give my advantage away. The chair creaked again, then I heard footfalls as he walked toward me. Banks jerked my blindfold over my head and pulled the gag free of my mouth, pushing it down to rest around my neck. It took a few seconds for my eyes to adjust to the dimly lit room. As I suspected, we were in a beautifully appointed study. There was no one other than Banks in front of me, and I couldn't detect any movement behind me. I took a chance and wiggled my fingers and rotated my wrists as discreetly as I could. I wouldn't hesitate to take a few blows to the face and upper body to allow my backup time to arrive, but I drew the line at letting the guy inject me with something, shoot me, or cut me with a knife. The ropes were tighter than I first thought but not debilitating.

"Have you nothing to say to me, Lucky?" Banks asked.

"Have you gained some weight since the last time I saw you?"

Banks narrowed his eyes but didn't take the bait. Chances were slim that Banks himself was going to rough me up or kill me, which meant I needed to know how many goons he had with him. I was only aware of one man in the van with me, but it was too much to hope that I only had to take down two men to regain my freedom.

"You're looking a little softer than usual too, but then again, your American lover weakens you."

I forced myself to look surprised by widening my eyes the slightest bit, but I didn't say anything. I only needed to bide my time and let things play out.

Banks's mouth curved into a sneer. "You didn't think you could fool me, did you, boy? You can't get anywhere near the guy without losing control. Why do you think I sent you to Cincinnati?"

"I thought you sent me there to fill in for Deverish after his accident."

"*Accident.* Yes, that's what we'll call it." Banks removed a remote from his pocket and pushed a button. A flat-screen television rose from a console behind his desk. "How would you like to witness Deverish's next *accident* live?"

I scrunched up my face in confusion. "What do you mean? You were behind his hit and run?"

"He outlived his usefulness. Now, Percy has become useless to me too."

Banks hit another button, and the television turned on to show live feed from a body camera. The person stood outside a hotel door as if waiting for a command. Banks picked up his phone from the desk and tapped a message. Within seconds, the person wearing the camera unlocked the hotel door with a keycard and let themselves inside the dark hotel room. The intruder raised his hand again and flipped on night vision goggles, so he could see to navigate.

To play my part, I began thrashing in my chair. "Call him off, Banks. Deverish has been nothing but loyal to you."

"Deverish has proven loyal to you, not me. I can't keep someone on my payroll I don't trust, and I can't afford to let him walk away."

"You sick fuck. What do you want from me?"

"It hurts to lose people you care about, doesn't it?" Banks asked. "Keep watching. I promise you it will happen so fast they *probably* won't feel it."

"I won't watch," I said, squeezing my eyes shut.

"Stavros," Banks yelled. A door behind me opened, and heavy thuds sounded as one of his thugs entered the study. "Lucky doesn't want to watch his friends get their brains splattered on the headboard, but I really want him to see it."

A large hand yanked my head up while a finger poked painfully in the soft tissue beneath my left eye. "Open your eyes, or I'll fucking replace my finger with something much sharper and cut one of them out of your head." He either had a knife on him or had access to one close by.

I opened my eyes to comply and had to bite my tongue to keep from laughing when the assailant on the live feed entered the bedroom only to find the bed empty except for a pile of electronics and various vibrators in the center. The man picked up a note lying on top of a hot pink laptop that could only belong to Percy. Through the night-vision goggles, I read: FUCK YOU, BANKS! In case you don't know how, we left you some helpful devices. It wasn't like we were going to risk taking them with us in case they were bugged. XOXO, P.

"You've got to love Percy's flair," I said.

Banks turned on me with narrowed eyes. "You think I won't find them?"

"I think you'll try."

"Stavros," Banks said in a deadly tone.

The big man released my hair and walked around to stand in front of me. He was the same man who drove me here, which meant it was just the three of us, or Banks was waiting to spring the others on me. I did a quick survey to check for weapons and saw a knife sheathed on his belt. Stavros cracked his big knuckles then delivered a hard blow to my solar plexus. Even though I'd been prepared, I felt it reverberating throughout my body. Rather than cower, I gave him a look that said: is that the best you got? Stavros wouldn't be able to resist the challenge, and Banks would get off on seeing me take a beating. I just hoped my cavalry would arrive before things went too far.

The second blow snapped my head back when his meaty fist connected with my right eye. The fucker was wearing a ring, and the skin beneath the outer corner of my eyebrow busted open, and blood trickled down the side of my face.

"Not so pretty looking now," Banks said, sneering as he leaned against his desk.

"You thought I was pret—" The air whooshed out of me when Stavros punched me again in the stomach then followed it up with three more quick jabs, not letting me recover between the blows. One final solid punch and I felt my ribs on the right side of my body crack. I never tore my eyes away from Banks or allowed the smirk to fall from my face. He would not get the best of me, even if he put a bullet in my brain.

"Did you think that daughter of a whore was powerful enough

to beat me at my own games? Once again, you've chose to ally your-self with the wrong person, and it will cost you everything."

Yes, I did think it, but I chose to keep my mouth shut. It was bet-ter to let Banks ramble on like most villains were prone to do. If he were bragging about his masterful plan, he wouldn't command his thug to hit me. I could work on freeing my hands from the ropes. On second thought, step one was going to be painful, and I probably couldn't pull it off without at least a grimace.

"Carmen Santiago is better at everything than you'll ever be, you child-raping pervert."

As predicted, Banks commanded Stavros to strike me. The big man was slowing down a little which changed up his reaction time and caused him to telegraph his moves. I braced myself for the impact and dislocated my left thumb at the same time his fist plowed into my mouth. I had a busted, bleeding mouth but my dangling thumb made it possible for me to slip my left hand free of my bindings. I ro-tated my right wrist and firmly gripped my left thumb. I just needed one more blow to masquerade the source of pain once more. Stavros landed the punch to the left side of my rib cage, and I snapped my thumb back into place, grunting and swearing. Stavros smiled, think-ing he was getting the best of me.

"Carmen is weak. She takes in the strays no one else wants, ex-pecting them to be loyal to her. What she failed to realize is that it was only a matter of time before one of those mutts would turn on her. It's their nature to do so, and she didn't respect it."

My blood ran cold. Did Banks have a mole inside Carmen's op-eration? Was Ryder in danger? I took a calming breath and realized he was either bluffing, or he only thought he had a mole in her organi-zation. Otherwise, he would've known Dev and Percy weren't in their hotel room. "Nice try," I said. "You're the one wasting energy, Banks. This all ends tonight, and you need to accept it."

"The only thing ending tonight is your life, Lucky."

Stavros went to town on me then, alternating between my face, stomach, and ribs. My left eye was swollen shut, blood blurred the vision in my right eye, and my mouth had multiple cuts—inside and out. My breathing became labored, but I didn't think the damage to my ribs was severe enough to have punctured my lung. There was no doubt my injuries would slow me down once I received my signal to move, but I wasn't out of the fight. Not by a long shot. My chances would improve greatly if I could get Banks to start talking again.

"Why me, asshole?" I asked. "Will you at least tell me how I ever ended up on your radar?"

"I was recruiting Hiram Chandio and stumbled across you in the process. A homosexual with his connections was a perfect candidate."

"Recruiting? Is that what you call it?"

"I guess it depends on your perspective."

"You were going to use those photos to *blackmail* Hiram in to working for you?" I asked.

"Yes, but then I decided I wanted you instead." His creepy tone of voice made me shiver.

"How did you know I'd go along with it?"

"You've seen the pictures, Lucky. You were in love with him, and you knew what would happen if I released the photos to the press. He wouldn't live as long as he did." *Did.* There it was: a roundabout confession. Sitting there and listening to him speak so casually about taking another person's life made me ill; knowing it was someone I once cared greatly for made me burn with rage. I couldn't let him goad me into showing my hand. He thought he'd preemptively snatched me off the street before our meeting and had no idea he played right into our hands instead. *Anytime now, Carmen.*

"What did you do to Hiram?"

"You haven't heard?" he asked, eyes widening in delight. "Hiram and his friends died in a tragic boating accident. It was all over the news. I can't believe you didn't know."

"Why would you kill him after all this time?"

"Haven't you figured it out yet? Who is the person Deverish,

Hiram, and the pissant museum nerd have in common?"

"You're in love with me? Why didn't you try the usual tactics like sending me flowers and chocolates?"

"I don't love you, Lucky. Love is for pussies. I wanted to own you and control you. I wanted to have all your loyalty. I finally realized I'll never have who I want, and I can't permit anyone else to have you either."

I desperately wanted to understand how I could possibly attract the attention of a lunatic, but that right there was the answer. There was no rationalizing an irrational mind. I would never understand why I became the object of his obsession. I could accept it as fact and move on or make myself crazy trying to figure him out. "You're a sick fucker."

"I wear many labels," Banks said with a casual shrug. "I shy away from none." He rose from the edge of his desk and walked toward me. Stavros stepped aside to make room for him. Banks grabbed the top of my shirt and ripped it open, scattering buttons everywhere. Of all the things I mentally prepared for, him touching my bare skin wasn't one of them. "We could've ruled the world together, Lucky. In and out of bed," he said wistfully.

"I heard you prefer unwilling bed partners," I jeered.

"I do." The look he gave me made my skin crawl. Signal or no signal, I had limitations on how far I'd go to get the information we needed.

The power shut off suddenly, throwing the room in darkness with only the crackling fire for light. *Signal received.* Banks and Stavros both jerked their attention from me. I used the distraction to free my right hand then held the rope in my fists so they wouldn't know it just yet.

"Find out where Edgar is," Banks barked, telling me there were just two goons and him. Piece of cake for Carmen and me to disable.

The study door kicked in with a thud. Stavros reached for his knife but didn't get a chance to grip it because I swiftly rose to my feet and swept his legs out from under him. I kicked his jaw with the heel of my foot hard enough to render him unconscious.

"Nice job, Lucky," Carmen said when she came through the door. I noticed she was carrying a Glock 22. "Edgar is down also."

"As in dead?" I asked. We planned to turn everyone over to the police, or at least that's what we'd discussed.

"Lucky doesn't like guns anymore. He's seen enough violence," Banks said.

"Edgar is unconscious and tied up. I did a much better job of securing him than this idiot did with you," she said, tipping her head to where Stavros sprawled on the floor. "I saved my bullets for dear old dad."

"You think you have the balls to shoot me, little girl?"

"I wasn't aware testicles were a requirement to own or use a handgun. Get on your knees, disgusting pig."

"You won't shoot me. You're too soft, like your mother. How does it feel to stand in the home she once lived in? Had I known you would turn out to be so beautiful, I would've made similar arrangements for you and earned back the money I wasted on your mother's education."

Carmen lowered the gun and fired a bullet into his knee. Banks screamed and fell to the ground, holding his hands over his knee.

"Don't tell me what I will and won't do," Carmen said, moving to stand closer to him but out of the range of his legs should he try to kick out with his good one.

"Carmen, you're better than this. What happened to turning him over to the authorities?" I asked, slowly approaching her.

"Men like him always get away with their crimes. They use their money, power, and connections to escape prosecution," she said. Her voice shook with emotion, but her gun remained steadily aimed at the man screaming and writhing on the floor. "There's only one way to end his reign of terror."

"Carmen, would your mother want you to have his blood on

your hands? Do you think it would bring her comfort to watch the guilt eat away at you?"

"I won't lose a moment's sleep over killing him. I've dreamed of this day for so long, Lucky. I used my rage to fuel me. I learned everything I could about him, then I set out to beat him at his own game. I wanted to be on his radar; I wanted him to seethe every time I recovered an artifact before one of his men did. I wanted to take away everything he'd built piece by piece, but it wasn't enough. They were hollow victories."

I reached her side but made no move to disarm her. "Every time you kill someone, a piece of your soul dies too. I've taken down some of the deadliest terrorists in the world, and even though I did humanity a favor, it stained my soul. I don't want that for you, Carmen. Give me the gun. If you need this bastard to die, let me kill him."

"I'm not weak, Lucky. I can do this," Carmen said vehemently.

"You're one of the strongest people I know. Sometimes strength means walking away."

"No, Lucky."

"He's right, Carmen."

I whipped around at the familiar voice in the doorway. *"Hiram?"*

"No!" Banks shouted from the door. "You're dead. I killed you."

Hiram lifted his arm and shot Banks between the eyes. "No, I killed *you*."

Carmen let out a sob of relief. I carefully removed the gun from her hand, stuffed it in the waistband of my jeans, and pulled her into my arms. "It's over now," I told her. "He can't hurt anyone else." I looked over her head and saw that Hiram was watching us.

"Good to see you again, Lucien."

"Are you real? Am I dreaming this?"

Carmen stepped out of my embrace and looked up at me. "Please don't be mad at me. I was able to intercept Banks's plans and warn Hiram. There was no one on the boat when it exploded."

"You let me think he was dead? Why? To ensure I'd help you?" I stepped back from her.

"It was my decision, Lucien," Hiram said. "If you want to be mad at anyone, be mad at me. She wanted to tell you from the start." I looked at Carmen for confirmation, and she nodded. "You don't have the right to be mad at anyone anyway. Right now, we have a mess to clean up. Later, we'll discuss why you didn't tell me about Banks blackmailing you when it first happened."

"Clean up?" I asked, looking around the room. Stavros was still out cold, and Carmen had another man tied up someplace in the house.

"You two get out of here. Lucky needs medical attention. I'll fulfill the rest of the mission."

I suspected Hiram's definition of clean up meant leaving no witnesses behind, but I wasn't in the position to argue with him. Shock and adrenaline were quickly wearing off, and my injuries were catching up to me. "Not feeling too good," I admitted to Carmen.

"You don't look too good either. Ryder is going to kill me when he hears about your injuries," Carmen said.

"Yep," I agreed. "You'll have to give him your dogs to make up for it."

"He can get his own dogs," Carmen said. "I'm parked too far away for you to walk, but Harry is close by. He'll come pick us up."

"Good. Can we stop for fish-n-chips?"

"Maybe later, Lucky."

Carmen wrapped her arm around my waist and guided me to the door. What little I could see through one eye started to spin. We stopped when we reached Hiram; he opened his arms and hugged me gently.

"I'm mad as hell at you, but we can talk about it later," he whispered in my ear.

"Mad at me?" I asked, soaking in his warmth. "I'm mad at you too. You let me think you were dead. Both of you did. I never got to tell you I was sorry." My words sounded sluggish like I had too much to drink.

Hiram chuckled. "Fine, we can both do some apologizing. Get checked out first."

"Bring fish-n-chips with you." My head felt funny, the room started to spin, and their voices sounded far off. I must've sustained more brain damage than I'd realized.

Hiram tightened his hold on me briefly then released me. Then, seeing me swaying, he said, "I'll help you get him down to the car."

Somewhere between the study and the front door, I gave in to the encroaching darkness.

Chapter Twenty-Nine

Ryder

LEARNING HIRAM WAS STILL ALIVE FROM CARMEN WAS ONE THING, but seeing him sleeping in the chair by Lucien's hospital bed while holding his hand was something else. I'd foolishly googled him in my weaker moments after Lucien left for London and had regretted it immediately. Hiram Chandio was one of the most beautiful men I'd ever seen, and he also happened to be Lucien's first love. Lucien had said it was merely infatuation and lust, and they would've drifted apart. During a different conversation, Lucien had said Hiram's unwillingness to live in the open was the reason he knew they wouldn't make it. Here sat Hiram beside the man I loved, looking like he belonged there.

I didn't want Hiram dead; I just didn't want him sitting in the chair I thought should be reserved for me, holding the hand of the man who was supposed to be mine. I'd boarded the first available flight after Carmen told me about Lucien's injuries, but that didn't put me in London until almost eighteen hours after he arrived at the hospital. I looked away from the two men's joined hands and got my first look at Lucien. His beautiful face was marred with bruises and distorted by swelling. Both eyes had been blackened, but one was so swollen it would be impossible for him to open it. His lips were puffy and had busted open in at least three places. I wanted to go to him, but shock and uncertainty about my role in his life kept me frozen at the foot of his bed, but my stunned gasp was loud enough to startle Hiram awake. His eyes widened when he saw me and guilt washed over his handsome face. He started to rise and untwine his fingers from Lucien's, but the love of my life moaned and gripped Hiram's hand tighter.

"Stay," Lucien pleaded with Hiram.

The desperation in his voice brought instant tears to my eyes. I started backing out of the room because it was obvious Lucien had made his choice: Hiram. I'd just turned to leave when I heard Lucien whisper my name.

"Ry. Don't leave me. Stay."

I turned back around, and this time Hiram's face only showed compassion.

"He's been asking for you for the last few hours," Hiram whispered. "He's really uncomfortable, and his concussion limits the types of pain medication and dosages he can have. Lucien was thrashing around, and we were worried he'd cause himself more injuries."

"We?"

"Yeah," Hiram said, motioning for me to come closer. "Carmen pulled the last shift, and I relieved her so she could get some rest. He thinks we're all you, and it's helped keep him calm when he's resting. It's a completely different story when he's awake though. I'm so glad you finally made it."

"I got here as fast as I could," I said, walking toward the bed. "The first flight had mechanical issues, and passengers got bumped. It just felt like the universe was trying to prevent me from getting here."

Hiram and I swapped places, and he gently untangled himself from Lucien's long, graceful fingers. I always thought he had the hands of an artist or a musician, but those dexterous digits came in handy in his line of work too. Lucien started to get restless, and I quickly took his hand in mine. It was like coming home after being gone for decades.

"There you are," Lucky whispered then sighed in his sleep. "I've been looking everywhere for you."

"He knew we were poor substitutes." Hiram's smile was kind when I looked from Lucien back to him. "I'm so happy he has you, Ryder. I wish I could stick around until he wakes up because I have a lot of questions for him."

"You're going?" Five minutes ago, I was tempted to launch him through a window. His smirk said he knew it.

"Hiram Chandio *is* dead for all intents and purposes. I won't be swimming up to the shore in the Maldives like a miracle and reclaiming my life. Carmen has offered me an opportunity to live free of the burdens I've been saddled with since birth. I only want to live happily and in peace."

"I understand," I told him.

"Tell Lucky I'll be in touch soon. Take good care of him," Hiram said.

"You can count on it," I said, lifting Lucien's hand to my mouth for a kiss.

"So long, Ryder. Until we meet again."

"That sounds like a great line for my book," I whispered, wishing I could write it down.

"Book?" Hiram asked.

"Oh, I'm just being silly. Lucien wanted a love story, so I'm giving him one."

"In more ways than one," Hiram said with a raised brow. Then he glanced at the bed to where Lucien was starting to stir. "I'll be in touch. It was nice meeting you."

"Same," I said, not looking away from Lucien. I wanted my face to be the first thing he saw if he could open his eyes.

It turned out he could open one all the way and the other a slit. It was enough for him to recognize me standing by his bed. "Love," he said softly, reaching for me with his other hand.

I leaned over so he could hook his arm around me and give me a one-armed hug. "Was getting the shit beat out of you part of the plan?" I admonished lightly. "You shaved ten years off my life."

"I'm sorry I scared you, but it's over now. I'm free, and we can start our life together."

"That's right," I said. "First, we need to get you healthy again. Then, we can discuss where we're going to begin our new lives." I brushed my fingertips over Lucien's forehead, and his eyes drifted shut again.

"I love you so much, Lucky," I whispered then kissed his forehead.

"I want to go home," Lucien said crankily. "I've been cooped up in here for weeks."

"Babe, you only left the hospital two days ago. You're not healthy enough to travel yet. Besides, we're not exactly roughing it," I said, gesturing to Carmen's luxurious, London guest suite.

"You could at least fuck me. How long has it been?"

"I gave you a handjob this morning after breakfast," I reminded him.

"That was a long time ago. What have you done for me lately?"

I set my borrowed laptop aside and looked at him. "Did you ever stop to think that asking me to jerk you off and blow you because you're bored might feel a little insulting to me?"

"It's the only part of me that doesn't hurt. Will you at least read me some of Reed and Leo's latest adventure?"

"I haven't accomplished much today, but I can read what I've managed so far."

"I know you're writing one of those erotic scenes."

"Were you peeking?"

"Don't need to," Lucien said. "Your squirming gives you away. Oh, ho ho, look at you blushing. I must insist you read it to me now."

"Fine." I picked my laptop back up and scrolled to the beginning of the chapter.

"Reed, just hand me the stones, and you'll never have to see me again."

Reed quirked a brow and gripped his cock and balls through his dark wash denim.

"Dark wash, huh?" Lucien asked. "Why is it always dark wash? Whatever happened to faded jeans with holes in them? I think Reed needs to wear those instead. Leo can finger his holes and tease his bare skin."

"Are you finished critiquing?"

"Yes."

I deleted the dark wash denim and replaced it with faded jeans with rips in the thighs.

"Yes, rips. That's sexy. Maybe Reed's cock will fall out if he's not wearing underwear," Lucien suggested. "Okay, I'll be quiet now."

I read the line over again with the revised jeans and pinned Lucky with a look that dared him to open his mouth again.

"These stones here?" Reed asked, giving his junk a good bounce. "They're the only ones I have on me, but you're welcome to search me."

"Take him up on it, Leo. Give him a proper cavity search."

"That's it," I said, shutting my laptop again. "Story time is over. I'm going to make lunch."

"What are you making?"

"Chicken noodle soup. That's what recuperating people eat."

"Not the stuff from a can," Lucien whined. "I'm going to starve to death. I need carbs and grease to feel better."

I was about to torment Lucien a little more, but someone knocking on our door saved him.

"Special delivery," Percy said, lifting a grease-soaked bag in the doorway. "Did someone order fish-n-chips?"

"Me!" Lucien said, raising his hand. "Please pick me."

I stepped aside, allowing Percy to saunter in wearing black leggings, charcoal gray suede knee boots, and a dove gray cable knit sweater that hung to midthigh. It was the tamest outfit I'd ever seen him wear. "Where's Dev?"

"Down in the training facility. Dev's so glad to have his stupid cast off. The walking boot isn't high couture, but at least he's mobile. *Sooo mobile.*" He added a throaty purr. I left him to get settled while I retrieved plates and utensils.

"How are you feeling today, Lucky?" Percy asked.

"Jealous of Deverish right now. I want to be in the training center playing with Carmen's toys."

"One more week of rest, and you'll be good as new," Percy assured him. "You'll be training with the team before you know it."

"Training with the team?" I asked, tipping my head to the side. "What team?"

"Oh," Percy said softly. "You haven't told Ryder yet."

"No, he hasn't," I said, setting the plates on the coffee table a little too hard.

"I haven't discussed it with Ryder yet because I'm not sure the job will be right for us."

"What's going on?" I asked, dropping down on the sofa beside him.

"Carmen told me she is planning to make some big changes and would like me to join her team."

"When?"

"When is she making the changes?" Lucien asked.

"No. When did you discuss this with Carmen?"

"Before the operation," Lucien replied calmly.

"Why am I just now hearing about it?"

Lucien squeezed my hand. "I told her I couldn't make that kind

232

of decision without talking to you first. It's been the last thing on my mind since I woke up in the hospital."

"We have so much to consider," I told him, thinking of the latest job offer I'd received from the museum. They assumed I was playing hard to get and offered me Daniel's position. I couldn't be too upset with Lucky, because I hadn't shared my news with him either. It hadn't seemed like the right time.

"I agree, but we don't need to decide anything today."

"I want dogs," I told Lucien. "Two German shepherds."

"You can have your dogs." He looped his arm around my shoulders and pulled me to him. "What say we eat our greasy fish, throw Percy out, and you can tell me more about Leo playing with Reed's stones."

"I want story time too," Percy said, perking up.

"No," Lucien and I both said at the same time.

"Is my book that bad?" I asked Lucien. I didn't have plans to publish it, but he sounded adamant that no one else should read Leo and Reed's adventures. It stung a little bit.

"Love, it's not that," Lucien said. "It's a great book, but you are writing it for me." Lucien winked at me and added, "Maybe we'll let Percy read a snippet if he tells us what he and Dev did for a living before working for Banks."

"No can do," Percy said emphatically.

"Okay," I said with a shrug. "You must not want to read it that badly then." Not that I expected anyone other than Lucien to read the book. "Why don't we try working on a happy ending for ourselves, Lucky?"

"Now you're talking. Percy, get out," Lucien said. "Dev isn't the only one who's *sooo mobile* these days."

"Baby, you can't go jostling your brain, or you'll take longer to heal. Today is your first day without a headache."

"Do you know what keeps headaches away?" Lucien countered.

Percy stood up. "I must be going now."

"You didn't eat yet."

"Lucien can have my share. I'll just pop by Q's office to say hello then wait for Deverish at home." Dev's flat was only a few blocks away from Carmen's London headquarters. Percy had mentioned something about much-needed renovations since he was living there too. Dev's orderly neutral world was about to explode with color.

"How's Q liking his job working for Carmen?" I asked, ignoring Lucien's hand slipping down the back of my pants. "Do you think the two of them will ever give in to the tension between them?"

"It's only a matter of time," Percy said, heading for the door. "Don't rattle his brain too much, Ry."

"Don't listen to him," Lucien said when we were alone again. "Leave no *stones* unturned."

"How about a nice blow job?"

"Maybe to start with," he said, shoving his sweatpants to his knees. "I need to feel you inside me. It's been too long."

"You heard what the doctor said about no sudden movements. You need to keep still."

"I'll hold my knees against my chest and lie very still while you make sweet, slow love to me. Aren't you excited to be inside me without condoms for the first time?" Lucien grinned because he saw the way my eyes glazed over from the images his words conjured. We both got tested while Lucien was recuperating in the hospital. I was dying to be inside him with no barriers between us.

"Fine, but first you must promise you'll tell me to stop if something feels off."

"I promise."

"Let me go grab the lube." I started to get up, but Lucien grabbed my belt loop to stop me. He reached under the decorative pillow and pulled out a bottle of lube. "Wow, Carmen does think of everything," I teased.

"She doesn't get credit for this masterful plan," Lucien said, pulling me to him for a kiss.

It felt like years since we'd made love, but I was careful not to move too quick or jostle him too much when I removed his clothes then mine. I lay Lucien on the sofa before me like a feast then started to nibble a trail from his Adam's apple to his groin, detouring many times to lick and suck my favorite places.

Lucien's dick was erect and proud, already leaking from anticipation. I nuzzled my nose in his trimmed hair, breathing him in. I loved his masculine scent and took my time kissing a path across his pelvis then licking the crease of his leg until I neared his balls. I looked up his sexy body and caught his hot, dark gaze. I raised a brow and firmly cupped his sac in my hands. "Is the treasure I seek hidden beneath these stones?"

"Suck them, love. You know how I love it."

I sucked one ball in my mouth then the other. "Like that?"

Lucien moaned and threaded his fingers in my hair. "Again."

I lifted his heavy balls and licked across his taint until I reached his pucker then flicked it with my tongue. "Maybe you want me to suck on this too?"

"Fuck yes. Don't forget the cavity search."

I sucked, rimmed, and fucked Lucien's ass with my tongue until he started to shake, then I worked him open with two lubed fingers. "I think I've found the holy grail of treasure," I said, pushing against his prostate.

"Uh huh," Lucien whimpered. Beads of sweat dotted his forehead and upper lip. "Give me your cock."

"So soon?" I teased.

"It's been days," Lucien moaned. "Give me my fix."

"I'm an addiction now, am I?" I asked, smearing lube on my dick.

"Don't. Want. A. Cure." I loved the effect I had on him.

I entered Lucien carefully then pressed my body fully against his, which prevented him from moving too much. I slid my hands inside his hair, stabilizing his head while I made love to his mouth and his body as gently as I could.

"Feels so good, baby," I whispered against his lips. "Just you and me now."

"You and me," he repeated, his breath hitching as his climax drew nearer. "Fill me up, love."

Lucien's clench tightened seconds before he covered our stomachs with cum, slickening the slide of my body against his. He grabbed my ass, holding me tightly against him as I spilled deep inside him, careful not to thrust too hard.

"Are you okay?" I asked, pushing Lucien's wet hair off his forehead.

"Perfect."

"Are you sure?"

"You doubt me?" Lucien quirked a brow. "Again?"

He was talking about the situation with Hiram in the hospital. I'd come clean to Lucien about my fears, and he promised me one day I would stop doubting us. "Are we going to talk about your ex-lover when my dick is still buried inside you?"

"No, we're going to clean up, and you're going to get back to work on your first best seller while I take a nap. When I wake up, I want to hear all about Reed's stones."

"Best seller? Whatever." Lucien was out of his mind. I'd be lucky to finish the damn book. Reed and Leo made me nuts. I wanted to throttle them one minute and hug them the next.

"Care to make a wager?"

"What's the prize?"

"If Leo and Reed become a best seller, then you have to marry me."

"Did you just propose to me while my dick is softening inside your ass?" I questioned.

"I'm living in the moment here, love."

"Okay, I'll play along. What do I get if Reed and Leo are a miserable flop?"

"You get to marry me," Lucien replied.

"All roads lead to marriage to you?"

"Now, he gets it," Lucien said smugly. "You're the one who said my heart is your home."

"I did say that."

"So, let's make it permanent."

"You haven't met my family; I haven't met yours. We don't know where we're going to live or work or... None of it matters."

"Nope. We'll figure it all out."

"Okay, so when are we getting married?"

"Not until after you publish your book. Weren't you listening to the first part of my proposal?"

"That wasn't a proposal; it was a dare."

"Fine. Ryder Jameson, I fucking dare you to marry me."

My heart pounded, and tears pooled in my eyes. Every dream I'd ever had was coming true. "Fine. I will."

Chapter Thirty

Lucien

Eight months later…

I couldn't tear my eyes off Rider's tongue swirling around and around. I heard him chuckling because he knew what he did to me. I heard a loud bang and turned around to see some poor schmuck pull his bike away from the back of the parked compact car he'd plowed into.

"Look what you did," I said to Ryder. "The poor chap was so distracted by you performing fellatio on your ice cream cone he ran into a car."

"He should've been looking where he was going," Ryder said, continuing forward when the guy rode off down the street.

"Love, don't look now but I think our favorite bookstore is displaying *No Stones Left Unturned*."

"What?" Ryder asked and whipped around so fast he nearly dropped his ice cream cone. Of course, Duke and Duchess, our adopted two-year-old sibling German shepherds, hoped he would. "Oh my God! People might read it."

"Isn't that the point of publishing a book?" I asked. "Besides, you published it under the pen name Sebastian Somersby, so no one will know it's your book unless you tell them." His near meltdown was causing quite a stir on the quiet street in Hyde Park—the historic Cincinnati neighborhood, not the famous part of London.

After the media fervor over Charles Banks's sordid life and death by murder-suicide fizzled out, Ryder and I had some serious choices to make. Carmen had offered me a position in her London office overseeing the training of recruits while she worked to expand her role working with law enforcement agencies all over the world to prevent and recover stolen artifacts. Ryder was offered the position of director of the board at the museum. While he was flattered, it was easy for him to turn it down because his passion was in conserving art, not pushing pencils around and being a dick to one and all. Turning Carmen down wasn't as easy for me. While I loved the position she offered, I knew the location would be an issue.

Ryder belonged in Cincinnati with his family, regardless if he worked for the museum, and I belonged wherever he was. A curious thing happened once we arrived back in the Queen City after our caper. Agents Kiphart and Marshall visited me at Ryder's flat one day. Not only did Carmen nail Daniel Perez's gonads to the wall, she did it in a way that implied I was also partly responsible for bringing him down. The bureau wanted to know if I was interested in consulting with them on outstanding cases. I would work in the Cincinnati field office, and I'd only have to travel on occasion.

I jumped at the chance because I thought it was an intriguing opportunity, and I knew it would help me get in Celeste's good graces. I'd meant what I said to Ryder; I wanted to come clean to his parents so we wouldn't build our life on lies. Celeste was angry at first, but she came around when she saw how committed I was to making Ryder happy. Iris was every bit as feisty as I believed her to be, and we became cigar-smoking, bourbon-drinking best friends in an instant. Edmond was more concerned about my background than the ladies were and dismissed my transgression once he found out who my father was. As it turned out, he'd heard about my father's reputation and was looking forward to meeting him.

He got his chance when my parents flew in for a visit after we purchased our home in April. Mother fell in love with the photos I sent her of our stately Victorian home on Observatory Avenue. God, we loved our magnificent house with its big yard for the dogs to play. As I'd told Ryder, our parents were almost interchangeable except for Celeste's warmth. She'd become Ryder's biggest champion when he decided to publish his book; the same book that was causing him to panic.

I pulled my phone out of my pocket and pulled up the tab I kept open on my phone. "Guess what else happened?"

Ryder spun around and looked at me with huge eyes. "What?"

"Someone's book made the New York Time's best seller list."

"Shut up!" he said then grabbed my phone. "I don't believe it. Never in my wildest dreams did I think this was possible."

"Told you so," I said smugly. "Do you know what else this means?"

Ryder looked up from the phone and smiled. "How does eloping to Las Vegas sound?"

"I was thinking more like a beach wedding in Miami. We know a lady."

"Yes, it would mean more if our families and friends witnessed our marriage."

"You call Carmen and ask," I said. "She likes you better."

"True. I'll get on it."

"You need to finish the sequel for Leo and Reed."

"I'm feeling more motivated to finish the book now," he said, picking up the pace a bit.

"I'm motivated to help you plot the sex scenes. Just because Leo and Reed are a happy couple doesn't mean they can't tear it up in the bedroom."

"Maybe Leo can burn dinner and Reed can angry-fuck him over the kitchen table," Ryder said.

"Why is Leo always the one fucking up?" I asked.

"It comes naturally to him." Ryder smiled wickedly. "Did I tell you Horatio, a man from Leo's past, shows up in this book."

"Not that again," I moaned. I'd only spoken to Hiram once after leaving the hospital. It was cleansing, and we both got the closure denied to us years ago. Ryder still liked to bust my balls about it though.

"Reed isn't worried about Horatio; he knows where Leo's heart lies."

"It's about damn time. Reed is quite a knucklehead," I teased.

"Takes one to know one."

When we got back home, Ryder hustled to his study while I got busy making plans. My guy was drawn to adventure and romance, and I was going to give it to him.

Epilogue

Ryder

One week later…

"HONEY, I'M HOME," I YELLED WHEN I ENTERED THE HOUSE after walking the dogs. I saw Lucien's car parked in the driveway and knew he had returned from his trip to the FBI field office in San Francisco. "Lucky?" I unhooked the leashes from Duchess's and Duke's collars, and they trotted into the kitchen for a drink.

I tossed my keys onto the table we kept by the door and saw a large manila envelope that had Sebastian Somersby written on it in large black letters. The envelope was battered and stained like it had been bouncing around in the mail for a long time. Who the hell knew my real address? When I inspected the envelope closer, I saw the postage stamps were tiny images of my fictional characters taken from my book cover.

"What's he up to?" I asked while opening the envelope. I pulled out a battered map with crude drawings, a dotted line, and an X to mark the spot. At the top was written: Mi Corazón. I covered my mouth to stifle my joyous laughter because I didn't want Lucien to think I was laughing at his drawings, even if they looked like our eight-year-old neighbor, Mary, drew them.

The fork and spoon represented our kitchen, the paint palette for my restoration studio, books for my office, and a bed with a heart above it and an X below it that marked it as the location I would find my treasure. My first thought was to head straight to the bedroom, but I stopped at the locations in order.

In our kitchen, I found a pastry box with a decorated chocolate cake inside. The elegant writing said: *Boundless treasures await you if you dare.* I stopped by my studio and saw a bouquet of my favorite Tropicana roses. I plucked up the card nestled between the blooms and smiled at Lucien's messy writing, making it obvious he hadn't decorated the cake. He'd written: *An adventure I can always guarantee.* Tears had already started falling by the time I reached my office to find the next hint. A bottle of chilled champagne and two crystal flutes sat in the middle of my desk along with a heart-shaped note. Through my teary vision, I read: *There will never be another who loves you more than me.* I grabbed the champagne and flutes and headed up to our bedroom where my treasure waited for me. There was a note taped on the closed door that said: *Only thrill-seekers may enter.*

I pushed open the door, and Lucien sat in the center of our bed, naked as the day he was born. "Hi," he said. "Miss me?"

"Always," I answered. I set the champagne and flutes on the dresser and stripped my clothes off as fast as I could. "Now I get to claim my treasure. I should take a shower first though. The August sun is brutal today."

"You have a bit more work to do before you find the real treasure."

"No, I'm looking at him," I told Lucien. "What's going on?"

"Did you really think that silly dare was the best kind of proposal I could come up with?"

"I didn't think it was silly; I thought it suited us perfectly."

"Nah," Lucien said. "My guy wants to romance some stones and seek treasure."

"Are you trying to tell me you've tucked an engagement ring under your sac?" I asked with a raised brow.

"Why don't you come here and see?" I took a step forward, and he held up his hand. "Not so fast, big fella." Lucien pulled a small remote from behind his back and hit a button. Dozens of laser beams shot across the room from every angle.

"Is this like Carmen's perimeter fencing?"

"Of course not."

Even though I knew I could charge straight toward the bed, I took my time carefully ducking beneath some light beams while stepping over others. When I finally reached the bed, I tackled Lucien to the mattress and reached between his legs. I was disappointed my treasure wasn't there, but I hadn't given up.

"Time for a cavity search," I said eagerly.

"Or we could look under the pillow," Lucien countered.

I reached beneath the pillow and pulled out a ring box. Lucien took it from me and opened it. I gasped when I saw what was inside. It wasn't the type of ring I expected to find; it was a platinum ring engraved with a jeweled coat of arms featuring a dragon that looked just like the one inked on his chest.

"Dudley!"

"That's no name for a magnificent beast."

"Is this your family coat of arms?"

"This is *our* coat of arms. I had it designed a few months ago and was waiting for the right time to present it to you. Ryder Jameson, will you marry me?"

So many memories flashed in my mind, not all of them were wonderful, but they each led us to the happiest moment in my life. I leaned forward and wiped the tears from his eyes just as he did for me. Emotions rose swift and hard, making it impossible for me to speak.

Lucien slid the ring on my left hand and said, "I know, love."

The End!

Acknowledgments

First, I need to thank my husband and children for their constant support and encouragement. It's not easy living with a writer who often disappears into a fictional world for long periods of time. They do so many things to help me out so that I can realize my dream. I love you guys more than words can ever express.

To my creative dream team, thanks seem hardly enough for all that you do. Miranda Vescio of V8 Editing and Proofreading, thank you for your tireless work, feedback, and many laughs while editing. Jay Aheer of Simply Defined art is an incredible artist, and I love how she brings my words to life. Stacey Blake of Champagne Formats is also an amazing artist who does incredible interior formatting, illustrating, and designing for e-books and paperbacks. Let's not forget Judy Zweifel of Judy's' Proofreading. She does an amazing job of finding the tiniest details that make a book shine.

To my lovely PA, Michelle Slagan. I'm not sure how I ever did this without you. I love you to the moon and back!

Lastly, I am so grateful for my beta readers and the honest feedback they provide me. Thank you for all that you do, Racheal, Kim, Dana, Jodie, Michael, Michelle, Brittany, and Laurel.

About
AIMEE NICOLE WALKER

Ever since she was a little girl, Aimee Nicole Walker entertained herself with stories that popped into her head. Now she gets paid to tell those stories to other people. She wears many titles—wife, mom, and animal lover are just a few of them. Her absolute favorite title is champion of the happily ever after. Love inspires everything she does, music keeps her sane, and coffee is the magic elixir that fuels her day.

I'd love to hear from you.

You can reach me at:

Twitter—twitter.com/AimeeNWalker

Facebook—www.facebook.com/aimeenicole.walker

Instagram—instagram.com/aimeenicolewalker

Blog—AimeeNicoleWalker.blogspot.com

www.ingramcontent.com/pod-product-compliance
Lightning Source LLC
Chambersburg PA
CBHW020749250626
47155CB00003B/996